BILLIONAIRE EVER AFTER

BLUE COLLAR BILLIONAIRES, BOOK 3

JESSICA LEMMON

Lemmon
ink

BILLIONAIRE EVER AFTER

PROLOGUE

Last spring

Talia

I n a posh hotel's bar, decorated like a high-end jungle in vibrant greens and creams, I finish my drink and pretend I'm on the hunt for the king of that jungle. Which is a great deal more exciting than what's actually going on.

The Heart-to-Teen fundraiser's "festivities" seem as if they'll never end. First, there was a cocktail hour, then there were speeches while we ate off gold cutlery and sipped from crystal goblets, and now is the time for men in suits to press the flesh and conduct business.

The fundraiser is a fine one, but I'm not here to ensure I have a write-off for charitable giving for the tax year. I'm here for the king, or in this case, Archer Owen.

Since I've been researching Archer Owen like a private investigator, I know plenty about him. His brothers were adopted, perhaps explaining the family interest in a fundraiser focused on adoption. He's opened bars and night-clubs, but mostly nightclubs, to lines wrapped around the block, regardless of what city he's in. Exclusivity is his jam, and I'm here to convince him to loan some of his expertise to me. Well, not me, per se, but my boss. Ed Lambert owes me a raise, and after I talk Archer into working with us, Ed won't be capable of denying me one.

Attending the fundraiser is a bit of a sneaky way to Archer, I admit. I live in Miami, Florida, and this hotel is in Venice, Florida. He was practically in my backyard and it seemed like a sign from the universe. I randomly overheard a conversation at my sister's restaurant. A couple chatting about how the Heart-to-Teen fundraiser was happening at the home office this year and how the "Ohio Owens" were invited. I had heard of Archer Owen and his high-end clubs in my fair city. My interest was piqued.

Attending the fundraiser cost me a sizable donation, aka, a chunk of my precious savings. Heart-to-Teen places teenagers, who I hear are the hardest to home, with foster and adoptive families. It's nice to know my money wasn't wasted. Especially once I land the raise along with the title bump I've been chasing.

Other than asking a pair of ladies who were dating the other two Owen brothers about Archer, I've yet to corner him and convince him of anything. My patience is waning. I tip my glass to my lips, only to realize I've already emptied it. That went fast.

Then the object of my infatuation materializes over my shoulder.

"If that was bourbon, I'm going to have to ask you to marry me." His voice is deep. Low and rocky. *Commanding.*

Full-body chills race the length of my skin, and I know without turning around it's him.

"Vodka soda, no ice." Empty glass in hand, I turn to face him, excited to finally see him close up. I'm not disappointed.

He assesses me coolly, his lamplight-green eyes languidly traveling over my person. Not in a lecherous way. More like he's logging details into a mental database. Nothing prepared me for being face-to-face with Archer. Not the photos I saw online, not the glances I've thrown in his direction at this fundraiser. I'm unprepared for how insultingly handsome he is now that he's right in front of me.

"Shame," he responds before ordering a bourbon from the bartender. "And whatever she was having." He tosses down a few large bills like he can't be bothered to find out how much our drinks cost. His eyes never stray from my face, even while he folds the cash into a money clip—an honest-to-God money clip—and tucks it into his front pocket.

I watch him back, incapable of looking away. I expected Archer Owen to be smarmy. Presumptuous. A touch disingenuous. His playground is nightclubs. Doesn't that scream cheesy? Not that I'd expected him to arrive with an entourage but...why wouldn't he? It wasn't hard to picture a scantily clad girl hanging off each of his arms, or security guys with earpieces flanking him. Instead, I'm presented with a cool, crisp billionaire who trotted out a marriage proposal before he learned my name.

Interesting.

One tanned hand hugs his rocks glass, and he lifts it, waiting for a toast. I lift my own glass, tapping it against his. Our eyes lock while we each take a sip. He licks his lips, swallows, and turns his head toward the sound of raucous laughter coming from the other side of the room. I am suddenly distracted by his neck. I can't recall admiring a throat before. By the time I snap my gaze north, I encounter inquisitive eyes. Definitely not a cheesy nightclub guy. This man has layers.

"You're taking my refusal well." I tear my own eyes away from him—color-changing hazel often mistaken for green in certain light—to study the thinning crowd. I have a few precious minutes to ask what I came here to ask him. He's kept my attention. Can I keep his? Playing it cool is a risky strategy, but it's the one I'm going with. "Is proposing marriage to strangers at the bar typical for you?"

"There's nothing typical about me, Wildflower." His mouth flinches, but he doesn't give me a smile. Of the photos I found online, I didn't find a single one of him smiling. I'm surprised by how much I was hoping for one, and pulling a smile out of him instantly becomes my next goal.

Focus, Talia.

Right. I'm here for a reason. And it's not to admire Archer Owen's tanned throat or trick him into smiling for me. Though I am curious how a grin would reshape that impeccably groomed beard of his.

Also, wildflower? The nickname came out of nowhere. He didn't explain. I'm not going to take the bait and ask. Where's the fun in that?

Earlier tonight, when I met Vivian Vandemark—better known as Nate Owen's fiancée and Archer Owen's future sister-in-law—she warned me of Archer's "prickly" disposition. I'm not picking up "prickly" from him. His boldness is aggressive, captivating. This excites me, but not because I find him achingly attractive. Well, not *only* because I find him achingly attractive. I'm excited because my instincts were correct. He's the perfect candidate for my offer.

"First time?" Flirty, forward banter is quickly becoming his signature.

"At a fundraiser, or nearly being proposed to at a bar?" I quip in return.

"Either. Both." He rolls one shoulder like he couldn't care less about the answer. His gaze is locked on mine, refusing to leave.

"First time on both counts." A smile pulls my mouth. I can't help it. This is the most fun I've had in the last... gosh...*years*.

He lifts his glass for another toast. This one includes words. "To stuffy fundraisers that lead to better things."

Since I've come here to court him specifically for "better things" in my life, I *tink* our glasses together and sip my vodka. Aware I'm running out of time, I move past the pleasantries and go for the jugular. My eyes return to his neck, distracted by that thick column once again.

With a shake of my head, I leap in with both feet. "I happen to have a proposal for *you*, Mr. Owen."

"Is that so." His flat tone suggests he's not surprised. I wonder if Vivian ratted me out and told him why I've come here. I hope not. I prefer to do my own reconnaissance.

"I'm in need of an expert. I hear you're the best."

"Did you?" Rather than sit on the stool next to mine, he leans one elbow on the bar, facing me. I catch a whiff of pine and leather, a hint of eucalyptus, and resist with everything I am not to admire his bitable neck. "And here I've tried to be so discreet."

Sarcasm. He's good at that too.

I'd forgotten how great it feels to be the object of someone's attention. To soak in the shared sexual chemistry saturating the air. It's evident in his casual lean and captivating stare. It's in the way I hold my glass curled to my chest, my chin tilted slightly upward. Too bad I can't take advantage of the heat sizzling between us and take him to bed. Otherwise, I'd lay my tongue on that throat the second I had him alone.

Damn.

I snap out of the fantasy beginning to form, which takes some doing as I don't often fantasize about random men. Ever, actually.

I make a concerted effort to steer our conversation into more professional territory. "Would you like to sit?"

"Thought you'd never ask." Still no smile, but his lips twitch slightly.

So close, I think, even as I remind myself I'm not here to flirt.

He settles onto the stool sideways, so I twist in my seat to face him. Sliding one pinstriped pant leg over the other, I notice he notices and wonder if he's wishing he could see my legs. He should be so lucky. I have fantastic legs.

I offer my hand. "Talia Richards."

"Archer Owen." He clasps my palm. "But I assume you already know who I am."

"Nightlife Kingpin," I say, watching closely for his reaction. During my research, I encountered a recent article that included the nickname. It's not very inventive, sort of insulting, or funny, depending on your perspective. His face scrunches, the reaction brief. A nanosecond later he's back to his cool, calm, collected self. Despite my commitment to be the same, my curiosity prompts me to ask, "Why did you call me Wildflower?"

His eyes flare with interest for the beat of a butterfly's wing before the vivid light banks. He takes a pull from his drink and nods to the room beyond the bar. "Take a look around. What do you see?"

"Rich people." Sadly, I'm not one of them. I never wanted to be, and honestly have no idea what I'd do if I had as much money as Owen. Doesn't it stress him out that he might lose it someday?

"Stodgy, flashy. *Cultivated.*" He states each word carefully. "You stand out. You go where you please, not confining yourself to where you've been planted." He nods, his conclusion complete. "Wildflower."

I emit a low laugh. "You're saying I don't belong."

"I'm saying you're impossible not to notice," he rumbles.

I swallow thickly, my fingers toying with the silk necktie dangling loosely from my neck. I dressed for him tonight. I didn't want to be another woman in a sparkly dress, easy to forget. In the event I made him an offer and he shot me down, I wanted him to go home thinking about me, about how I stood out. That would leave room for a yes later. So far, my tactic is working.

"What if I told you I have an offer impossible for you to refuse?"

He dips his chin, studying me below thick eyebrows and a fan of dark eyelashes Maybelline would die to patent. "Don't be so sure. I've refused many, many women."

"Not any with an offer as lucrative as mine, *Kingpin*." I nearly earn a smile, but he's more practiced than I am at controlling his mouth muscles. "Next January, a Lotus Leaf spa is opening in Miami. I've noticed you attract celebrity clientele to your nightclub grand openings. I'm sure that's not accidental."

Those calculating eyes narrow. "It's not."

"I want you to teach me how to do it."

"Sorry." He sits back, prefacing his no by putting literal distance between us. I can sense he's walling up. He's slipping away. "I don't give away my secrets."

"I'd be paying you for them. Generously. Ed Lambert's pockets are deep. Lotus Leaf isn't a charity." I smile while twirling a lock of hair around my finger. "You can keep your *precious* secrets if they're so important to you. Just don't be surprised if I ferret them out. I'm very perceptive."

His eyes twinkle in challenge, his full attention back on me. He leans in a bit closer as a thrill of delight races down my spine.

Got 'im. If I can't have sex, I might as well indulge in a little competition.

"Refill, miss?" the bartender asks as I drain my second drink.

I turn my attention to the billionaire next to me finishing his own drink. "Yes. And one for him too. This round's on me."

CHAPTER ONE

Now

Archer

You might think January in Chicago would be a shit time to open a nightclub.

All due respect, but you would be wrong.

My latest "den of sin," as my brother Nate likes to joke, is packed with gyrating bodies. Sequins and short shorts, sweat-soaked T-shirts and smudged makeup. Throbbing bass thumps low in my belly as I navigate through fog-filled air, in the direction of the exit.

January isn't just cold, but *fucking cold* here in Chi-town. Everyone in the surrounding neighborhoods has cabin fever. Two weeks after New Year's Eve, and the elite are already bored. Loud laughter rises over the music, invigorating me like bubbles in a hot tub. These are the sounds I have steeped myself in for years. I love this business. I can't help myself.

Unlike the well-dressed crowd who have come here to

lose themselves in alcohol, music, and whatever relationships they make come closing time, I'm not lost. I've kept an eagle's eye on the bar staff, as well as the till. It's imperative every person in this place is served a drink in a timely fashion. I also kept watch over the club's security team, who are here to make sure those imbibing the drinks don't stir up trouble.

My attention is drawn to a dark corner, where a blond woman stands, her fair skin and hair aglow in the meager light. She's staring. Sipping from her cocktail straw with glossy, pursed lips. Her dress is scandalously short, like most dresses I've seen tonight. She bites her lip, trying to look coy, but there's no way she can pull it off. What she wants is written all over her face. One night of hot, sweaty fun wouldn't be a bad way to spend the evening, but that's not why I'm here.

"I'm out," I shout over the noise to Reginald Mowry, my Chicago regional manager.

"Yes, sir, Mr. Owen." He shakes my hand, dipping his chin to confirm he has tonight under control. I trust him. He used to bartend at one of my other Chicago locations. He's been in my employ for too many years to count. I could have left tonight in his capable hands rather than fly in from Clear Ridge, Ohio, and, given how tired I am at only one a.m., maybe I should have.

I step onto the street, my ears ringing as they adjust to the quiet. I love what I do. Love the process from start to finish. But I admit, it's getting old. I've been thinking of shaking things up for months now. Seven months, to be exact. Since last spring, when a certain brunette wearing silver rings on nearly every finger and a loose necktie dangling over a slouchy white shirt, distracted me from within an inch of my life.

Women don't distract me the way they used to. That's by design. But somehow, Talia Richards, with her confidence and that snarky "rich people" assessment snagged my utter and complete attention. In my defense, who wouldn't have been enthralled by a beautiful woman with confidence to spare? But she shouldn't *still* have my attention. I should have been able to walk away from her the way I did the blonde inside.

I wind around the line of people waiting to gain access into my club. Some are bouncing on their toes in an effort to keep warm, especially those dressed in very little. I consider it a compliment when people stand for hours in the frozen tundra to gain access to a new club I built. But then, I'm not surprised. I'm the best at what I do.

Which is interesting, since Talia asked me to do something different.

See? There she is again. *Distracting me.*

Last spring she challenged me to apply those same principles to the swanky spa she is opening as an employee of Ed Lambert, otherwise known as the founder of Lotus Leaf. The offer of a new and shiny project appealed. I'd been craving a challenge, and nightclub openings were becoming rote. That night, over bourbon, I gave Talia the yes she'd come for, and then I threw my expertise at an establishment that served wheatgrass juice instead of alcohol. Where muted pan flute was piped over Bose speakers rather than garbled lyrics nearly indiscernible when paired with too much bass. Yes, I had been craving a challenge. I also liked Talia a whole hell of a lot.

In the end, she'd been right. Turning her down had proved impossible.

I've seen her exactly twice since I've taken the job. The first time I showed up for a meeting at Lotus Leaf headquarters where she worked closely with some dickweed named Brandon. I don't like Brandon. He's spoiled and boorish. One of those preppy types you want to punch in the face just for fun. Rather than deal with him, I've gone around him to correspond with Talia instead.

The second time I saw her was last month. I was in Miami, a week before Christmas, and stopped by the office to gift her a bottle of bourbon tied with a red bow. It couldn't be helped. Like the night at the fundraiser, I hadn't been able to keep my distance. One look at her waist-length brown wavy hair that long-ago night, her unique attire, and the rocks glass in her grip, and I was intrigued as hell. Happening to be close by checking out a potential future nightspot, there was no way I was going to miss the opportunity to surprise her.

But she's more than intriguing and drop-dead gorgeous. She also knows what she's doing. She's hungry, which I appreciate. I like ambition. I understand it. Since Talia looks damn fine doing what she does so well, I decided no video conference calls. And since the boundaries are blurry when it comes to texting, we don't dabble in that form of communication, either. I've kept to email out of respect for her position, and because I need to focus on the work and not on Talia's smart, delectable mouth. What I wouldn't give to experience her lips on mine.

Christ. There I go again.

I whistle for a cab, my breath fogging the air in front of my face. It's colder than shit out here. I tug my wool coat tight as I climb into the cab. I give the cabbie the name of my hotel and the street and settle in for the ride, my gaze on the window rather than the city beyond.

So, yeah. Talia and I email each other. Though we still found a way to flirt over that antiquated form of communication. I started my first correspondence to her with "Hey, Wildflower." I ended it with a cheeky "Sincerely, Kingpin." She followed suit, using our nicknames in her response. I enjoyed it way too much to stop.

The woman in the club with the perfected pout and the thick, fake eyelashes might catch my dick's attention, but there wasn't anything there to intrigue my brain. Don't get me wrong, she could have been interesting. Hell, she could have been a brain surgeon, I don't know. High-end clubs attract all types, and if I've learned one thing about the clientele, it's you can't assume to know who they are by looking at them.

Aside from privileged twenty-somethings, who are there to hook up and get trashed, the remaining crowd is a mystery. Hell, I've met investment bankers, celebrity golfers, literal brain surgeons—men and women who had come out not to get trashed and hook up, but to let go of the grueling, stressful week behind them. No matter how interesting or successful the women who go to my clubs are, I learned a long time ago not to date them.

If I embark on a personal relationship, I'm careful to keep it separate from work, which includes any interactions with my family. To the Owens, work *is* personal. We practically bleed the shade of blue in our Owen family crest. Plus, any time in the past when I've bothered to bring a girl home, her presence was met with disapproval from my father.

Nothing new there. He doesn't approve of much when it comes to me.

Contrarily, Dad reserves his seal of approval for my brothers, Nate and Benji. I suppose if I really wanted to whine about it, I could blame the fact that they're adopted. He chose them, after all. For a while, I resented how he wasn't as hard on them as he was me. Later I realized it didn't bother me when he took a light touch with them. What bothered me was how they'd received his coveted approval while I, well, *didn't*.

Nightclubs and bars aren't William Owen's idea of respectable businesses. It's one of the many topics on which we disagree. I've been defying him since I drove my first stake in the ground in this company. I wonder if defying him is more of a bad habit than anything.

The more I worked on the spa's grand opening with Talia, the more my wheels cranked. Could there be more to life than thumping bass, fog machines, and the smell of sweat mingled with alcohol? I'm not sure, but I intend to find out. If I end up winning my father's approval in the process, that's a nice bonus, but I'm not seeking it.

I know what you're thinking. Something like, *Wellness centers, Owen, really? Spas are the epitome of health and vibrant living—the opposite of what you do now.* Hear me out. Who's to say professionals at the end of a long week at work don't want to unwind with a massage or a full-body mud mask? Why couldn't the entire experience at the spa have a nightlife feel? I mean, am I the Nightlife Kingpin or not?

I can pull this off, but in order to do it and do it well, I need Talia. I plan on asking her to do a side job for me. She can continue working for Lotus Leaf, and moonlight for me. I recognize this as potentially dangerous. For her, because I know Ed. He's a greedy bastard, and he won't want to share her. For me, because this project will mean seeing more of her, which means I'm going to have a difficult time not sweeping her into my arms and finally tasting those lips.

Damn. How many times is that now?

The cab deposits me at the hotel's entrance. I pay him and climb out into the cold as snowflakes begin to swirl and blow. I think of sunny Florida as I shuffle into the lobby, and then mindlessly check my phone as I step onto the elevator alone. I'm heading home tomorrow morning, technically *this morning*. I have an early flight, but missing sleep is one of my hobbies. Besides, I can nap on the jet. My email finally loads as I'm swiping my keycard to enter my room—shitty Wi-Fi. I pause, caught halfway between the hall and the threshold as I read the message.

Dear Kingpin,

The grand opening was a "smashing success"—Ed's words. An actor, a Grammy award winner, and three football players for the Miami Dolphins all made appearances. I'm impressed. Not by them, but your ability to lure them here. Is "lure" the wrong word? Anyway. You should have seen it. Ed's announcing design manager and bonuses tomorrow at a brunch at the office. I'll be polishing my crown tonight in preparation. If you were here, I'd finally crack the seal on the bottle of bourbon you gifted me...

Sincerely,

Wildflower

I'm smiling as I shut the door, and not only because she made sure to remind me the Miami Dolphins guys were "football players." I reread her email, trip over the part where she asked if "lure" was the right word, and smile wider, which isn't typical for me. Benji is the smiley Owen. He's right chipper, which can be pretty damned irritating. Nate is the easy one, a big teddy bear with a thrice broken nose. Me, I'm the stoic one. The business-minded one. The one who *doesn't* smile like a dope when a woman he works with emails him.

"Get a grip," I tell my reflection.

I toss my phone onto the dresser and empty my pockets of my money clip and earplugs that I probably should have worn tonight. I wiggle my finger in my ear, greeted by a shrill ringing I'll have for another twelve hours or so. Thirty-six years old is a far cry from being an old man, but nights like tonight remind me that thirty-six is equally far from an age where I considered nightclubs my "scene." Building them is one thing. Frequenting them is a whole other.

I step into the bathroom and peel off my clothes. As I crank on the shower I realize Talia's email has somewhat reinvigorated me. Not even somewhat. As I'm absently soaping my chest, my mind vanishes from the room I'm in and travels to Miami, to the Lotus Leaf grand opening. To what she wore tonight. Not a bright pink minidress, I'll bet. More than likely a sassy pantsuit, tall heels, a handful of silver rings. I can picture her inviting wide mouth, those long, loose brunette waves flowing over her shoulders like water.

Fuck.

She does it for me. That's all there is to it.

How perfectly inconvenient.

CHAPTER TWO

Talia

I love an early afternoon brunch. Especially *Sunday* brunch. My favorite meal is huevos rancheros with spicy black beans, enjoyed with a mimosa while perched on the patio at my sister's restaurant—with her, if I'm lucky enough to reserve a Sunday brunch when she's not on the clock.

Calista is the head chef at Mango's, a swanky yet approachable restaurant I absolutely adore. The food is epic, the view of the water is phenomenal, and the company of my sister is better than meeting the pope in person.

Sadly, this Sunday's brunch will offer no huevos rancheros, mimosas, or stunning view of the ocean. I'm at work, bleary-eyed after an exhausting grand opening last night. I smiled my face off for hours upon hours and ended up getting very little sleep. As tired as I was, I stared at the ceiling for a long, long time wondering what Archer was doing. All after I sent him a late-night email that screamed anything but professionalism.

I know. Ridiculous.

A teetering tower of wholegrain muffins on a massive tray is sitting alongside a smorgasbord of fresh, tropical fruits. Pineapples, mangoes, grapes, kiwi—you name it. There's a juice bar with a barista of sorts, ready to turn those gorgeous fruits and veggies into the latest trendy health concoction. My coworker orders a carrot, mango something-or-other. I flash her a smile and move down the line. Thank God Ed allows coffee in the office. I grab a mug and meander over to the carafes, my yawn reminding me I should have started with coffee at home rather than wait until now.

As I raise my hand to pump the caffeinated beverage into my mug, the elevators ding open, drawing my attention. I freeze, my jaw dropped, my mind having trouble believing my eyes. The man of my dreams is standing in Lotus Leaf's lobby. Or, rather, the man who invaded my thoughts and kept sleep away last night.

Archer Owen is as tall, fit, and delicious as I remember him. He's wearing a pair of charcoal-gray pants with a white button-down shirt tucked into them. It's open at the collar, revealing his neck (yum), which leads to a neat, dark, perfectly trimmed beard. His thick, equally dark hair is a smidge longer than when I saw him last month.

I stare, my empty mug dangling from my fingers, and watch as the billionaire scans the bustling office area for me. He finds me a second later, sparkling green eyes surrounded by a million lashes taking me in. My chest leaps. I like being sought out by him way too much. I set my mug down and stride over to him, knowing I look like I'm excited to see him, but unable to contain my excitement long enough to play it cool. Playing it cool takes preparation. I was not prepared for him.

"You're here," I observe needlessly and a tad breathlessly. "Why aren't you in Chicago?"

No smile, but merriment plays around his fantastic lips. I regret never having kissed him, and wonder if him being here uninvited, and after the project is over, means I might soon have the chance. Unless he's here to see my boss, Ed. A disappointing possibility.

"No crown?" He pulls a small square of fabric, likely for cleaning his sunglasses, from his pocket. "I was going to help you with the polishing."

"Not yet. You're early."

"Well, you said brunch. That's a wide window."

"You could have asked," I say with a grin.

"And ruin the surprise?" He tucks the cloth back into his pocket. "Forget it."

He flew from Chicago to Miami to see me. Because I sent him an email in the middle of the night. He looks half as tired as I am, the circles under his eyes giving away his lack of Zs.

"It's a nice surprise," I can't help mentioning. I flip my hair over my shoulder and he follows the movement, his head tilting, his gaze trickling down only to ascend again. It's probably for the best that he hasn't been in Miami more than twice since he took on our project. I might've compromised my job by doing something truly scandalous. Like wrapping my legs around his waist and asking him to kiss me like he means it.

Ahem. Anyway.

Several dozen people behind me erupt into applause. Lotus Leaf's employees are crammed in the small area between our desks and the food tables, cheering on Ed Lambert, President's arrival to a short stage. The microphone is hot, the speaker system offering feedback when he wishes us good morning.

"Looks like your timing is perfect," I tell Archer as I turn to face my boss.

Ed is dressed in suspenders and brown suit pants, a short-sleeved button-down shirt stretching over his broad belly, his belt spanning the generous circumference. His nephew, Brandon, steps out of his office, buttoning a tailored navy blue suit jacket. Paired with a red-and-navy-striped tie, his patriotic attire lends him a political air. He has gelled blond hair, a nice smile, and for about eight months I thought he was going to be my future.

I never should have moved in with him.

My sister, Calista, also my roommate then and now, had fallen in love with a line cook back in the day. In what has become her usual, she'd been infatuated with a man who wasn't worth her time. She moved out of our flat with little notice, and I couldn't afford the place alone. I mentioned to Brandon I was going to put out feelers for a new roommate, and he invited me to stay with him.

I wasn't in love with him. I just assumed we'd continue on with the motions, living together for years to come, neither of us questioning what worked. He and I split up a year ago, a few weeks before I made it my mission to hire Archer Owen and finagled my way into a fundraiser I had no business attending.

Brandon slides his cool blue gaze over to me before he notices Archer and does a double-take. Then his eyes harden, seemingly displeased by my unexpected guest. When I sneak a peek at Archer, he blinks slowly, lazily. As unaffected by Brandon's glare as a lion napping in the sun would be to a fly buzzing by his ear.

They've met before. Twice. Both times I had the idea they didn't like each other. I was on Archer's side on that one. I don't like Brandon much, either. And not for the reasons one might expect. I'm less a woman scorned in a romantic sense. It's more personal. He doesn't know what the hell he's doing. He hasn't worked for Lotus Leaf as long as I have, and yet we are both team leaders. Nothing anyone could say would convince me he's not paid way more than I am for the same position. Never say die, misogyny!

It was Ed's brilliant idea to put Brandon and me in charge of Lotus Leaf's aesthetics and design department. I have no idea if forcing us to work in such close proximity was for sheer entertainment purposes for Ed, or if he was instead ignorant to the fact Brandon and I had dated at all. That could be the case. Brandon and I made it a point to keep our relationship under wraps at work. There were no stolen elevator kisses or meet-me-in-the-supply-closet sex. Ours was not a passionate relationship.

Brandon steps around the stage and joins the crowd, hands folded in front of him like he's waiting to be knighted. Presumptuous asshat. He boasts two business degrees, which, in case you're keeping count, is two more than I have. He brags nonstop about his accomplishments, something I didn't notice until I lived with him. He's exhausting. He has told me more than once that he's a natural in our department, even though I've been making most of the decisions on this project. I picked what night to have the grand opening. I arranged for Archer to help us with PR. I hand-selected the contents for the lavish gift bags. It was my idea to give away gift certificates to five different radio stations. He had no problem taking the credit whenever Ed praised our efforts, that was for damn sure. Me, I wasn't spoon-fed my position or given a hefty raise for no reason. I started out at Lotus Leaf as a receptionist, dreaming of the day I would be in upper management.

Four years. *Four freaking years.* I shake my head in wonderment at my own persistence as well as my unwavering patience. I've been drooling over the pay bump for every one of the four years I've worked here. I've managed to climb in tiny increments, but chipping away at success is taking forever. Why not achieve it in one fell swoop? I pulled off a grand opening, complete with celebrity guests and lines around the block. That has to count for something.

Ed's been flapping his gums about a management shakeup, and a few people on my team have commented they think I'm a shoo-in for design manager. I mean, I did manage to have *five* celebrities at our grand opening and a slew of paparazzi outside the doors last night. With Archer's guidance, but still.

"Did anyone see this morning's paper?" Ed asks now, holding today's *Miami Herald* high. The applause and whistles start up again. The "Out and About" section features a photo of Amanda Mitts, a gorgeous Grammy-award-winning twentysomething actress and one of the celebs who attended our event last night. "The grand opening of our latest Lotus Leaf spa was a smashing success, thanks to the entire team working diligently on every aspect of this project."

I grunt under my breath. While I won't begrudge my coworkers credit where credit is due, both Ed and I know the grand opening was its own behemoth, and one our team tackled personally.

"Whether your contribution was big or small," he continues, "you should feel very proud of your hard work. Extra kudos go to our design and aesthetics department."

Well, I'll be damned. I shrug my mouth at Archer, who brings his hands together to applaud my team's efforts.

"We wouldn't be standing here if it wasn't for our dynamic duo, Brandon Lambert and Talia Richards!" Ed adds, prompting my frown. Brandon twists his neck and gives me a tight nod. We applaud each other half-heartedly.

Prisha, my head designer, elbows me, her hands carrying a tray of cups filled with green juice. "Take one, boss. We're going to toast," she whispers. I do as I'm told. Archer follows suit, palming a cup in one large hand. Nice hands. Really nice hands. I spare him a nervous smile before turning back to Ed.

"On to the announcements you've all been waiting for! Let's start with naming the new woman in charge of our financial department. Please give a round of applause to our own Krista Moody, your new Vice President of Financial Services."

The crowd does its best to cheer on Krista while juggling paper cups filled with green juice.

"This last choice was a tough one. Who is capable of carrying the weight of the design and marketing departments, selecting their own management team, and continuing to plan grand openings even more spectacular than the one yesterday?"

Archer's palm warms my back as my heart leaps into my throat—only half caused by him touching me. The years I've worked at Lotus Leaf have been packed with overtime, successes, and no small amount of kudos from Ed himself. Where he's stingy with raises, he excels in compliments. I'm so obviously the best choice for the managerial position, I almost feel bad for Brandon.

Almost.

Ed winks at me and then his mouth opens to say words that don't match the ones in my head. "Congratulations to Brandon Edward Lambert, my namesake and nephew, who will usher in a new decade of Lotus Leaf!"

Murmuring around me infiltrates my buzzing brain. Ed invites Brandon to take the floor and Brandon begins his speech, one that sounds suspiciously prepared. He mentions my name and how he "couldn't have done it without Talia."

No shit.

While Brandon gives his speech, Ed makes his way to the food table and picks up a muffin. I ungraciously hope he chokes on a walnut. I don't want him to die, but, well, is wishing for a close call bad for my karma? He points at Archer with the muffin. "I look forward to working together in the future, Mr. Owen. Your connections have proven lucrative."

"You gave my raise to Brandon," I state without preamble, my blood pressure on the rise. "I always knew you were a misogynist. I had no idea you were into nepotism, as well."

Ed's smile disappears. "It was never *your* raise, Ms. Richards. Most of the people in this room weren't awarded a new title. I don't hear them complaining."

"Most of the people in this room don't have the experience I have. Most of the people in this room couldn't have secured the talent needed to land Lotus Leaf on the eleven o'clock news, or in the *Herald*. You've been overlooking me for years."

"I see you just fine, Talia." He rakes a gaze over me like he's examining day-old fish at the dock. "You do what you have to do to get ahead, and that's your choice. But your behavior won't win you favor in my eyes."

"Sorry?" I breathe, surely misunderstanding the barely veiled accusation.

"Brandon." He points at his nephew, who is still blathering into the microphone, and then to the man beside me. "Archer. Who's next?" He makes a show of looking around the office for contestants. "I imagine you'd approach me if I was willing to sleep with you as well, but I'm a married man. I'd never indulge in such a pathetic cry for attention."

My face goes cold with shock. The entire time I've worked here, I've wondered what Ed and his ilk truly thought of me. I have put on a pained smile whenever he announced me as his "pretty" designer. I've bitten my tongue when he failed to introduce me while lavishing praise upon Brandon during important meetings with colleagues.

I'm officially done playing nice.

My arm lifts of its own accord, delivering a cup of green juice to the top of Ed's balding, gray head. Then I swipe Archer's juice and dump it onto Ed's head as well. My boss, mouth ajar, blinks green foam from his eyes as more juice streaks his cheeks in thick trails.

By the time I look around, I notice my coworkers have turned their attention to the action unfolding behind them. Some are watching with stunned expressions, others with amused smiles that say *he deserved that*. Brandon's speech trails to a halt. Ed continues blinking, looking for all the world like the Swamp Thing with lake algae dripping off his jowls.

Turning on one heel, I wade into the sea of desks, aiming for mine in the back corner. Balloons are tied to my chair, a copy of the *Herald* on my desk with gold-star stickers decorating the photo of Amanda posing in front of Lotus Leaf's sign. Congratulatory greeting cards stand open on my desk.

I yank out an oversized backpack from the bottom drawer and snatch up the cards, a framed photo of my sister, Papa, and me at her culinary school graduation, and my planner. I grab the laptop too, deciding to wipe it and return it if and when I feel like it.

I nearly crash into Archer, who followed me. Funny, in that brief trip to the back of the office, I forgot all about him. How, I don't know. Now faced with him, his bold and beautiful scowl has my full attention.

"The bourbon," I remind myself. I dig the bottle, still wearing a red Christmas bow around its neck, from the other bottom drawer of my desk. I hid it behind a row of files. Anytime I caught a glimpse of red, I thought of Archer. I hold the bottle up for him to see, almost pulling a smile from his stubborn lips. "Care to join me?"

"Lead the way." As if I didn't just juice my boss, Archer calmly takes the bourbon and gestures with one arm in the direction of the elevator.

"Real mature, Talia." Brandon, mopping his uncle's brow with a handful of napkins, says as I pass by. His scolding tone is a better fit for a misbehaving toddler.

I open my mouth to say what, I don't know. Probably more things I'll regret later but will feel good in the moment.

Before the first syllable is out, Archer positions himself between Brandon, Ed, and me.

"You're done, Owen," Brandon tells him. "Consider our ties cut."

"And if you ever come within fifty feet of Talia Richards," Archer says in a calm, yet growly tone, "consider your ass kicked." He takes one step in Brandon's direction, his left hand still wrapped around the fifth of bourbon. His threatening stance is a warning my ex-roommate ignores.

"You don't have to piss on your territory," Brandon returns with a slippery smile. "I've already been there and hit that."

The punch comes out of nowhere. Archer lifts his right arm and delivers a short, precise *pop* to Brandon's jaw. Brandon stumbles backward and falls into the food table. Muffins topple onto his splayed form as the pitcher of green juice dyes his blond hair a decidedly less attractive color.

"Oh my God." I blink dumbly at Brandon, akimbo and dressed in baked goods and wheatgrass like a spread in a weird fetish health calendar. He sits up, his face reddening to a dangerous color, but it's Ed who speaks.

"You're fired, Richards," he tells me. "Good luck finding work in this industry again."

"She works with me now." Archer takes a menacing step closer to Ed, who backs up and nearly trips over one of Brandon's legs.

"She does?" Brandon asks.

I do? I think but don't say.

Ed chooses not to reply at all.

Archer nudges me in the direction of the elevator. "Let's go."

27

Brandon lumbers to standing but wisely chooses to keep his mouth shut. I do *not* choose to keep my mouth shut. I'm not quite ready to board the elevator for the last time. Not until I've said what I've been dying to say for months.

"You're the one who slept your way into the position I worked for, Brandon. You rode my coattails, not the other way around. The only reason you have this promotion is because you're related to him." I point at Ed. "Don't forget that."

I spin on my heel, encountering Prisha, her eyes wide with adoration and confusion. I am reminded I am not an island. I have a team. I have friends. I have a responsibility to the people who have worked alongside me. And now they have to deal with Brandon and his ineptitude.

"I'm so sorry, Preesh," I tell her, meaning it.

"Are you kidding? That was *awesome.*" Her smile broadens when she looks over my shoulder at Archer. "Can I work for you too?"

CHAPTER THREE

Archer

I followed her home and, as instructed, parked in the guest spot next to hers marked 3B. She invited me in, explaining how she shares an apartment with her chef sister, how it's not that big so I should prepare to be unimpressed. She then bypassed the elevator and we climbed three flights of stairs to her front door. I figured she had more steam to blow off, maybe since I stole her thunder by popping Brandon in the mouth instead of letting her do it.

That would have been something to see.

Her apartment is small, tidy. Minimalist, but not by design. More because she and her sister don't have much, or because the "much" they had was lost somewhere between abandoning their previous lives and combining their current ones. I don't know the story there.

The sofa appears to be newer, but the slouch in the cushions suggests it's well-loved. It's in front of an entertainment stand made for an old fat-back TV, a small flatscreen sitting in the big, square opening.

The kitchen barely fits the table and two chairs, let alone us in it. Everything in here is within arm's length of everything else. Stove, sink, fridge.

"God, I'm so stupid," Talia mutters as she piles ice into a dishtowel. She drops additional ice cubes into two short glasses and then slaps the freezer door shut. "I was rash and hot-headed and *stupid*. And now I have no job."

"Wildflower, you're not stupid. And you have a job," I tell her. "You work for me now, remember?"

The glare she flashes me says she thinks I'm placating her, or this could be her way of refusing my offer. I guess that's fair. We didn't talk about it. Hell, she has no idea what "it" is yet. She's perfect for the position, and, bonus, her time has suddenly been freed up.

She knots the dishtowel and gingerly places the ice on the knuckles of the hand with which I decked Ed's nephew. Then she pours a splash of bourbon in each of our glasses and points to the tiny square kitchen table next to an equally tiny window overlooking a parking lot. "Have a seat."

I oblige her, lowering my ass onto an uncomfortable metal chair and abandoning the ice pack on the table.

"I just left my team to Brandon, that worthless, clueless, dickless..." She shakes her head, trailing off into a feminine grumble I find cute, even though I shouldn't. "What was I thinking when I dated him?"

Great question, and one I've wondered myself. She never mentioned them dating, but the way he watched her suggested they were familiar. As in *familiar* familiar. At first I thought he liked her and she never returned his affections, but as of right now, I know that's not the case. I agree with her but opt not to rub it in. "We all make mistakes."

She sips the bourbon. Licks her lips. Stares out the window down at the not-picturesque parking lot below. "Maybe Ed will give me my job back."

"Not the mistake I was talking about." I tip my own glass to my lips. It's none of my business. Talia has a life, bills, responsibilities. I have no right to advise her, especially since she didn't ask. I know this, but in the end, I'm not able to keep my trap shut about Lambert. "Didn't peg you for the blond-Captain-America type. *Yikes.*"

That earns me a weak smile. "I cannot believe you hit him."

"Neither can I," I admit, replaying the scene in my head. I flex my hand. I'm not a complete stranger to physical altercations. I've helped my security team haul drunk guys out of my clubs over the years, but punching someone in the face isn't my go-to. Usually a stern conversation can deescalate the situation. I didn't think Brandon would respond well to conversation while he was peacocking about his newfound title. Plus, hitting him was fun. He seemed like a guy who deserved to be punched.

"You're sort of awesome." Talia, wearing a pale pink camisole beneath a matching jacket, looks the part of the businesswoman above the waist. Then there is the pair of leather pants skimming her long legs. Every time I've seen her, she's worn pants. I'd love to see what those legs look like beneath the material. Are they toned and muscular? Curvy and thick? Either option is fine by me.

She chews on one fingernail painted with black polish. Her rings are out in full force, one on nearly every finger save the index on her right hand and the two middle on her left. From her head of wavy dark hair to the tips of her sexy open-toed shoes, it's painfully obvious she belongs in my world more than Ed Lambert's.

"Is that why you flew here from Chicago? To punch out my ex?"

"I came to see you be crowned. Punching your ex was a bonus." Rather than leave it at that cheeky remark, I decide to tell her the truth. "You offered bourbon if I came. That read like an invitation to me." I bottom out my drink, and she does the same while wearing an innocent smile that is anything but. "Do you like it?"

"It's better than I thought. Not sure if it's worthy of a marriage proposal." Her hazel eyes twinkle in the copious sunlight. Even chilly, Florida is a beautiful state in the winter. More beautiful with Talia in it, but if I have my way, she'll be taking a leave of absence. I have plans for her, and they don't involve her staying here. As if she reads my mind, she prompts, "What would working for you entail?"

She's back to her no-nonsense self, which I've learned is her go-to. Talia Richards is a woman who wasn't handed everything at birth. Not my story, either, but it wound up looking that way. My blue-collar roots were intact when I was born, but my self-made billionaire father lent a hand at the start of my success. It was his seed money with which I built my Kingpin Empire he despises. Oh, the irony.

My guess is Talia hasn't had it easy but would sooner die than tell the sad tale of how she's had it hard. Or, more likely, she doesn't perceive the hard stuff as hard, but as just...*life*. She's survived, thrived, and is dealing with another blow in the form of being overlooked for the raise she's more than earned. All because Edward Lambert is a piece of shit, and Brandon is an opportunistic, entitled prick. I flex my fist.

"Why'd you want the pay bump and the title change?" I ask.

She laughs an incredulous laugh. "Because I deserve it."

"Not what I meant."

She stands, refills her glass, and leans on the countertop, one leg bent at the knee, her round ass utter perfection. Studying the apartment she shares with her sister, she goes quiet for a moment.

"I wanted a raise for the usual reasons. I want my own place," she answers. "I want to be in charge. Not of people, but of myself. I want to set goals and meet them. *Exceed* them." She drops her head, her shoulders rolling forward. It's a defeatist position I don't like seeing on a woman as tough as Talia. "I'm thirty-four years old and have nothing to show for it. Every inch I manage to move forward, I'm knocked back three *feet*. I'm no stranger to starting over, but I'm damn tired of it. I worked for Lotus Leaf for almost four years. I never should have accepted Brandon's offer to move in with him, but I never imagined it'd cost me my career."

I frown. I had no idea she'd lived with him. Hearing how he had Talia in his bed nightly for a stint makes me hate him more than when I punched him in the face. I didn't think that was possible.

Deep breath. This isn't about me.

"You don't want a raise or a title change." I lean back in my chair and regard her earnestly. "You want freedom. Choices. You can have those with me."

"Sure, why not put another man in charge of my paycheck?" She drinks her bourbon in one swallow and gestures between us with the glass. "I'm sure this will end well too."

I'm on my feet and standing in front of her before she realizes I'm there. Her head tips, her eyes sparking with both challenge and interest. I like that look on her way too much.

"You're in charge of you if you work with me, Talia. I don't babysit. I don't require performance reviews. It's a contract. Limited time. And you're writing up your terms, not me. I've seen the effects of your labor. You're an asset. Ed can't see that because his head is in his ass. Or maybe it's in Brandon's ass. Hell, maybe he alternates."

A startled giggle softens her face, smoothing out the worry lines from her forehead. That's what I like to see. Tough Talia is attractive as hell, but the smile she's wearing goes straight to my dick. I have the foreign desire to beg her to touch me. Awareness between us crackles to life like a live wire dropped into a filled bathtub, just like the first time I saw her—the second and third time too. I have an inkling she feels that awareness too but resists. Why does she do that?

Then I answer myself.

She ignores what's between us for the reasons she stated. She's tired of making forward progress only to be knocked back by greedy bastards like Ed and Brandon Lambert. Men like them can't handle a woman taking what she wants and needs in life.

For that reason, I don't lean in and kiss her to satisfy the craving hollowing out my gut. Even as her eyes flare with interest and her gaze darts to my neck. Assuming she's not meeting my eyes to deescalate what's between us, I step back to give her space. I won't take anything from her she's not willing to give me.

"Think on it today. Will your sister be home soon?"

She shakes her head. "Late. Midnight, probably. If she doesn't go out with her friends and have after work drinks, which she usually does." Her eyes stray to my glass. "Stay for one more."

"I'd love to, but I have a rental car to drive and the sleep I had was shitty *before* I climbed on the jet this morning to come here. Sleep deprivation, I can handle, but sleep deprivation and tipsy, you're gonna be bailing me out of jail."

She grins, amused. Despite my earlier promise to myself, I fight to keep from scooping her into my arms and kissing her senseless. I bet she tastes like heaven.

"Where are you staying?"

"Haven't booked a room yet. I came straight to you."

Her face changes, softening like it did when she smiled. Vulnerability leaks in. Just enough to stop me from turning around and walking out of her apartment. I study her for a long while. Long enough that when she fists the front of my shirt, I'm too stunned to react.

Her open mouth hits my throat, plush lips sliding over my skin. They close on a kiss before opening again. Her tongue darts out and travels up the side of my neck, past my beard, and over my cheek. When her fantastic mouth reaches my ear, I'm shaken from my stupor. My hands come up to grip her arms, but instead of setting her away, I pull her closer until her jacket brushes the front of my shirt.

She nips my earlobe and whispers, "Stay with me a little longer."

She lowers to her heels and sends me a demure smile. My chest heaves as I suck in oxygen I apparently needed very badly. I'm looking into her warm, kind eyes, wondering if this is one of those tests life gives you. One where you should say no even though every fiber of your very horny being is screaming YES.

Her eyes are crystal clear, knowing. She's not drunk. She's just Talia. And she's asking me to stay while wearing skintight black leather pants that make her look like a badass, paired with a pink camisole and jacket that make her look like a confection.

What happens next takes me more by surprise than her offer. A smile splits my face. A big one.

She lets out a throaty chuckle. "You look like you really, really want to say yes."

Guilty. I slide my fingers into her dark, luscious hair—a first—and tilt my head. "Hell, Wildflower. How can I say no?"

Her fist tightens on the front of my shirt again as her eyes zoom in on my lips.

I lean in a scant inch, giving her a chance to take charge or back off. Her call. She satisfies us both by kissing me again, this time on the mouth. I don't hold back. Not this time.

Not anymore.

CHAPTER FOUR

Talia

He tastes divine.

I mean it. After months of wondering (and believe me, I've wondered), I'm finally learning the exact feel of kissing his mouth. His lips are firm, yet soft. His beard tickles me but isn't scratchy. I have the errant thought he must use some sort of conditioner when his hand cradles the back of my head. It's not like he's holding me in place, but more supporting me in case I faint. Not gonna lie, overexposure to Archer Owen is a possibility.

His mouth knows just what it's doing as it moves along mine. He applies pressure to my mouth, opens, and teases his tongue along my bottom lip. Then he pulls his delicious tongue back into his mouth, leaving my lips damp and, frankly, my panties too.

It's been a while.

A long while since I went to bed with someone, and, sadly, that someone was Brandon. He was uninspired, selfish, and boorish on a good day. I've essentially blocked further details from my memory. Making the decision to sleep with a coworker isn't my proudest life moment. I knew better. Shame nudges its way forward in my chest, stunting my time with the man kissing me now.

"Second thoughts?" Archer murmurs against my mouth, dragging his soft beard over my open lips. "You seem distracted."

He pulls his chin back, waiting for my answer. Like he really wants to know. His hand is nestled in my hair; his smile is slight. A zing of excitement zips through me at the sight of his smile. I suspected he had a brilliant one but worried I'd never see it.

"I've never seen you smile until today." I've been rewarded with the hint of a smirk or a sideways slant of his mouth, but nothing more. Now he's standing in my kitchen drinking bourbon after having socked Brandon in the nose. His smile is a prize I never dreamed of winning. I didn't know it was available to me.

Can you believe I had the gall to ask him to stay?

"I'm skilled at keeping myself in check, generally speaking. You make it hard."

"What else do I make hard?" I wiggle where I stand, thrilled to have him close. And alone. I flatten my hand on his shirt, stroking one firm pectoral and then the other, delighted by the shadow of a male nipple denting the fabric. I peek through my lashes and watch his expression go from warm and easy to hot and bothered. It's an unforgettable sight.

His mouth covers mine, parting to accommodate my seeking tongue. I waste no time tangling with his. He tastes of sweet bourbon and pure masculinity, and every inch of my jittery, impatient body responds.

"I'll tell you what you make hard." He bends and lifts me, depositing me onto the tiny kitchen counter. I'd slide off the edge if he wasn't standing between the V of my legs and holding me there with his torso. I'm drowning in his sharp green stare with no desire to be saved. His hands bracket my hips, palms down. He nuzzles my nose with his while he speaks. "I can't think straight when you're two thousand miles away, did you know that? I see your email, my brain quits working. I read the word Kingpin and picture your cute smile. I can't concentrate on anything but you when you're not around, let alone when I'm standing in your apartment, my mouth on yours while I wonder what's beneath this outfit. I'm a brainless bastard with you, Talia. That's not good for the bottom line."

I melt toward him, my arms resting on his shoulders, my fingers linking behind his neck. I expected dirty talk, not flattery. Although if I'm weakening his brainpower whenever I'm near, I'm not sure if flattery is the right word. I've long suspected sexual chemistry was lurking beneath our banter— yes, even over email—but I had no intention of starting anything with him. Now that he's standing in front of me, I can't think of a reason why I shouldn't have him. I want him. We're both adults. We have the house to ourselves. What's there to lose? I warn myself not to answer.

"Are you going to be okay?" I whisper, unsure if I can handle more of his signature brand of wooing, but tempting him all the same.

"Are you?" he asks against my mouth, his own tipping into an amused bow. His palms on my ass, he yanks me to the edge of the counter. I gasp as my center encounters something hard and unyielding...and it's growing in size. "Sure you want me in your bed? I'm impossible to forget."

God, I bet. I'm so enjoying his hoisted, cocky eyebrow, but I won't let him believe I'm the only one with something to gain.

"Silly boy," I murmur, noting the exact moment he registers the word *boy* and resists. His eyebrows curve downward and his mouth pulls at the edges. "You're the one who's going to have trouble handling me. And who says we're going to bed?"

I slide my hand between our bodies and reach for his belt. As I unbuckle, his mouth lands on mine, moving languidly, exploring carefully. When I have his zipper open, I wrap my hand around his cock and stroke. He's both smooth and long, hard and thick. I try not to compare but I don't remember having felt one so exquisite. I end the kiss to look my fill, admiring the smooth plump head capping his rigid length.

My God, he's glorious everywhere.

He shakily unbuttons my jacket, his breaths coming faster while he works. He palms my breast over the silky camisole, thumbing my nipple in the same rhythm as I'm stroking him. His eyelids are at half-mast, nostrils flared. Archer Owen wears pleasure like the finest, most luxurious silk.

He lowers his head and covers my breast with his mouth, dampening the material of my shirt. My other hand in his hair, I watch as he bites down. I cry out in pleasure, my head tipping back where it bumps the cabinet.

I settle for resting my head against the cabinet door, cognizant of avoiding the handle while he wrestles my jacket off my arms. I move to unhook my bra, and my hair becomes tangled in the cabinet handle—because of course it does. The sharp pain elicits a surprised yip, followed by a wince as I reach for the tangle of hair wrapped around the metal pull.

The heat in his lust-filled eyes tempers. He blinks, regards me with a half-smile, and then reaches for the knot. Gently, his wide fingers untangle my hair, his breath in my ear as he murmurs, "How the hell'd you do that?" Once I'm freed, he rubs the back of my head with his fingertips to soothe the pain. "Sure you don't need more room to groove than this countertop, Wildflower?"

"I want you in every room," I tell him plainly. "I wanted to try here first."

He dips his head into a regal nod. "That, I can do."

I lean in to taste his incredible neck, as obsessed with the column of flesh as I was the first time I saw it. My hand, still in his pants and wrapped firmly around his length, picks up speed. He pushes my camisole up and over my breasts, taking my bra with it. His thumbs and forefingers pluck my nipples, urging them into turgid peaks as my belly drops. I sink my teeth into his throat when he tips his head to the side to give me clearance.

"I wanted to do that the night of the fundraiser and every night since," I admit.

"So you thought about me," he concludes, leaning forward and tracing the shell of my ear with his tongue.

"Yes."

"Did you touch yourself when you thought about me?" His open palm cups my sex. He mutters an expletive when he encounters heat. "Tell me about it."

"No." My next breath is shallow. My eyes shut as pleasure shimmers through me like the sun baking a desert floor. He switches focus, taking my nipple on his tongue. I moan my approval since words aren't forming at the moment. He suckles gently, plucking the other nipple. I release him to claw at his hair with both hands, crossing my ankles at his back and tucking him close. I tilt my hips, rubbing my soft against his hard. The bloom of what I expect will be a spectacular orgasm begins. He notices.

"She has something for me."

"For *me*," I argue. "You're next."

I feel his smile, his teeth scraping my sensitized nipple before sucking it deep into his mouth. His hands on my ass, he shifts his hips and thrusts against my skintight pants. The friction through the barrier is enough to take me there.

I come hard, launching my arm out to brace myself. Magnets from the refrigerator clatter to the floor. This week's grocery list flutters into the gap separating fridge from counter, gone forever. I have the brief thought that my sister isn't going to like that, and then there's no thought at all. Only the sensation of his mouth moving away, his thick fingers working the button on my pants and drawing the zipper down.

He fruitlessly wrestles with the material, shimmying back and forth, side to side, and not getting far at all. "Damn, do I need a pair of scissors?"

I laugh. Funny and, well, possibly true.

"Let me."

He helps me hop off the countertop. My knees are shaky from my release, but I'm determined to maneuver out of my tight leather pants without falling down. I'm giving him quite the show with all this wiggling and bending. I kick off my high heels and balance on one foot and then the other as I turn each pant leg inside out in the process. To my immediate right, his boxer briefs are tented impressively through the open fly of his dark trousers. The second I drop my pants on the linoleum, he cups my bottom, bare thanks to the thong.

His hands trace my ass cheeks, squeezing, kneading. Then his palms slide up my back while removing my camisole and bra. Those useless articles of clothing join my pants on the floor. He dips his finger past the strap of the thong and slides it up and down, up and down, his rough knuckle teasing my tender skin. I try not to hyperventilate. An impossibility when he reaches around and cups my sex, finding me damp and ready for more.

"Please," I choke out. "I'm begging."

"No need to beg. I want this as badly as you do." His rough voice fills my ear before he bites the lobe gently, and then soothes it with a kiss. I lose his heat when he kneels to roll my thong off my legs. I hear the sound of more clothes being removed, and when I turn, I'm rewarded with a mostly naked Archer Owen. His shirt is untucked but still buttoned —a pity. His hand is wrapped around his hard length, sliding up and down the stalk of flesh in the most distracting way imaginable. "Turn around for me."

A sudden intake of breath gives away my excitement. I cover for it by snarking, "You don't want to look at me?"

"I'll be looking. Trust me." Cupping my jaw, he drags me forward for a long, wet kiss. His other hand braces my hip and pulls me close. Rather than spin me around right away, he lingers there, more kissing, more touching. More rubbing my naked body against the uncovered part of him. He releases my lips and twirls his finger in the air, motioning for me to turn. I lean over the countertop as my heart thrashes against my ribcage. His warm chest covers my back, his cock slipping between my folds. His mouth against my ear, he murmurs, "Don't move."

He leaves briefly to roll on a condom and then he's back. He slides between my legs, the feeling no less erotic than before he was sheathed. His hands bracketing my hips, he rolls forward and enters me with one smooth thrust. I climb to my toes to accommodate him. He pumps slow and shallow as I adjust to his size.

I whimper my way toward my second orgasm in record time. While I attempt to regulate my breathing, he gathers my hair off my back and rolls it in his fist. He gives it a gentle tug, keeping me in place while his other hand grips my hip. I push back to meet his each and every thrust, all the while coiling tighter and tighter. I feel everything at once and want more.

His breathing is labored, interspersed with gruff grunts. My own breaths are shallow, my release hanging by the thinnest of threads. He notices, drives into me harder, and tugs my hair with enough force to send me over.

I cry out, cupping my hand over my mouth so the neighbors don't hear, if it isn't already too late. He loosens his hold on my hair. It falls over my face, tickling my nose. I rest my cheek flat on the cool counter while Archer, fingertips digging into the flesh of my hips, slams deep. Sensitive from my earlier release, every thrust dazzles me with sparks of light behind my closed eyelids. He doubles his efforts, arriving at his own destination a few strokes later. A deep groan works through his chest, the front of his thighs touching the backs of mine as a post-orgasmic shiver works its way up my spine.

He slides my hair aside, his lips landing on the back of my neck for a sweet kiss after down-and-dirty sex. He kisses vertebrae by vertebrae until he reaches my smiling lips. He's folded over me again, his chest warm against my bare back. He's buried inside me, his shirt sticking to my back thanks to a thin sheen of sweat. His voice is rough and rocky when he says, "You like me, Wildflower."

It's so absurd, I burst out laughing, but I have to agree. "Yeah, Kingpin. I do."

CHAPTER FIVE

Talia

I managed to remove his shirt for round two, but we moved to the couch. I didn't rush right into more sex but instead took my time admiring every square inch of him. It was worth the wait.

Now I'm lying on my back, completely nude, out of breath. My eyelids are struggling to stay open after our workout. He heads for my tiny kitchen in naught but a pair of boxer briefs. It takes nearly every remaining drop of energy I have left, but I manage to prop up on one elbow so I can watch as he pours us each a fresh bourbon.

His chest is thick and wide, not waxed bare like Brandon's. I never thought about my preference until now. Archer is the kind of man who can wear a sleek suit, be properly manscaped and trimmed where it counts, but would never dream of waxing his chest hair. It's proudly decorating his firm, round pectorals, in defiance of any trend suggesting otherwise. It's not too thick. Just enough to tickle my breasts when he was sliding into me moments ago. I hum in the back of my throat, curling a pillow against my middle and fantasizing-slash-remembering it all over again.

He glances beneath the cabinets, his lips twitching into a not-quite smile. "You want a snack?"

"Sure. Are you making it?"

"You're going to need your strength tonight, so yeah." He moves out of sight, and I hear the refrigerator door open. Happy zings zip up and down my body in a parade of sexual satisfaction. The promise of more of him is too much to resist. I want to ask how long he's staying, but I also don't want to ruin tonight with talk of the future.

"What are the Post-It notes for?" he calls out.

"Those are Calista's. She marks the food she's saving for testing recipes in case I'm tempted to eat it after mind-blowing, sweaty sex with a billionaire nightclub kingpin."

He gives me an aren't-you-just-so-funny look through the gap between counter and overhead cabinets before vanishing again. "So we can have cottage cheese, eggs"—a rustling sound—"or cookie dough."

"Sounds about right. I haven't gone to the grocery in a week."

He steps into view again, tube of cookie dough in hand, our glasses pinched between the fingers of his other hand.

"What are you going to do with that?" I ask when he sets the glasses aside and sits next to me. He unwraps the already opened cookie dough tube, a spoon strategically tucked into one palm. He's planned ahead. He dips into the cookie dough and offers me a bite. I pinch the dough off the spoon and eat it. It's the most amazing thing I've eaten in my life. I suspect that's the sexual satisfaction talking.

"I assume these teeth marks are yours." He shows me the roll of dough, on which there are no teeth marks, thank you very much. I shove him with my foot. "Don't tease me."

"'Vegan,'" he reads off the label. "'Safe to eat raw,'" he continues reading. Eyebrows raised, he pops a bite into his mouth, no spoon, and decides, "This is good."

"It's my only vice."

"You sure?" He leans forward and pops more cookie dough into my mouth before I can answer.

I'm not sure. A Sunday spent with Archer Owen could easily replace cookie dough as my new vice. I shift on the couch so he can sit more on the cushion rather than perch on the edge. I grab the soft afghan blanket draped over the back of the couch, but he takes the other end of it.

"I'm cold," I argue.

"I like you naked," he argues back.

"But I'm cold."

He gives in, turns his attention to the cookie dough, and observes, "You won't make it in Ohio. It's about twelve degrees there right now."

I shudder and curl deeper into the blanket. His low chuckle warms me further. I pick apart his comment. "What do you mean I *won't* make it in Ohio?"

He shrugs. "When you come to work with me."

"I'm not going to Ohio."

"You'll have to if you work with me," he states, eating another dough ball. "I bought a building in Clear Ridge, used to be a dental office. Gutted it, changing it into a day spa. Well, a *night* spa. It'd help if you toured the project you're working on."

"You're opening a wellness center?"

"Surprised?" He lifts his eyebrows, waiting for my response.

"A bit," I tell him, though I'm not sure I could be more surprised today if I tried.

I didn't expect anything that's happened today. I didn't expect him to walk into Lotus Leaf's office this morning, witness me being overlooked for a raise, hit Brandon, follow me home, and have spectacular sex with me twice (so far).

"Are you tired of nightclubs?" I ask, curious.

"I want to do something new. Shake it up. Keep whoever crowned me the Nightlife Kingpin on their toes."

"No one paints you with one brush?"

"Not if I can help it."

When I met him at the fundraiser, he was definitely a version of the man he is today, but I would have told you to jump off a cliff if you'd suggested he'd ever sit in his underwear and eat cookie dough out of the tube. "What is a *night spa?*"

"It's not like a Lotus Leaf spa, that's for damn sure. My spa will be a destination spot for dates, girls' nights out. Nightlife, for sure, but with massages and manicures instead of dancing and debauchery."

I smile. So clever.

"I broke ground for a large wading pool. Indoors, of course." He reaches behind him and pinches my toe. "Since it's cold for half the year."

My brain whirs to life. "You're building a nightclub but it's a spa."

"Yep," he says before eating another bite of cookie dough. He offers me the roll, but I wave him off. He folds the wrapper and sets it on the table while I push myself to sitting.

I'm suddenly rejuvenated. Holding the blanket to my naked chest, I reach for my backpack on the floor by the couch. Unearthing my laptop, I fire up a blank document and start typing every disjointed thought in my head. I'm fascinated by this idea.

"Will there be alcohol?"

"Yes, but only classy alcohol. Like bourbon."

His tone doesn't change, but I can tell he's teasing. My fingers on the keyboard, I continue logging details. "What are the hours of operation?"

"Like a club, but slightly earlier. I was thinking six p.m. to one a.m."

"Eleven thirty," I correct, typing some more. "Will there be music?"

"Yes, but no pan flute."

I chuckle as I type. His dry sense of humor is growing on me.

"Maybe I should reconsider the dancing. Women like to dance," he continues. "They don't like when guys hit on them while they're doing it. These boneheads at the clubs shimmy over to every woman on the floor, hoping one of them will rub up against him. I don't want that there."

My fingers pause as I digest what he said. It's a valid observation. Whenever I go out with my girlfriends, none of us want a sweaty, gyrating man in our space.

"Thought you could help with that part. The design. The aesthetics. I want a relaxing nightspot, minus the pretentiousness."

"And no pan flute."

"Definitely not."

Mid-sentence, the laptop is pulled off my lap and

replaced by him. He gives me a kiss. I'm about to protest I wasn't done with my notes, but before I can, he hands the laptop back and stands up. I continue pecking in my ideas while he moves to the fridge once again.

I lob questions at him for the next hour or so. I ask about the pool, the size of the facility (approximately), the date it'll open (approximately), how many team members he has assigned to this project, if they're in place. I'm so engrossed in the idea of a night spa I don't notice him pulling on his pants and sliding his arms into his shirt at first.

"Wait, are you leaving?"

"Not leaving. If your sister has an early night, I don't want her to find me in my skivvies."

I swipe the screen to check the time on the laptop. "She won't be home for a few hours. You're good."

He settles next to me on the sofa, takes a pull from his bourbon, and watches me. "Hours. What will we do..."

Flutters thrum to life at the sound of his voice. The deep resonance ticks off each one of my ribs and curls into a ball in my belly. Swallowing around the lump of lust in my throat, I hoarsely reply, "I have a few ideas."

I shut the lid on my laptop and he takes it, finishing his drink and handing me my glass. "Bottoms up."

Smiling around my glass, I offer a cheeky, "We did that already."

"Careful, woman. You'll awaken the sleeping dragon." He doesn't smile, but there's no mistaking his signature dry humor. He lets me drain my glass before taking it from me as well. I throw the blanket from my body, no longer cold now that I'm covered from chest to legs in Archer.

He kisses my throat, ducks his head, and circles one

nipple with his tongue. My eyes roll back into my head when he moves down the length of my body.

"How sure"—he kisses my belly button—"are you that your sister won't be home for hours?"

"Pretty sure." I arch my back, my hands clawing his head as he places a damp kiss on my hipbone.

"Sure enough for this to happen on this couch in full view of the front door?" He slides his tongue to my other hipbone and places a kiss very, very close to where I want his face buried.

I flutter my lashes, considering. "Um..."

"This could take a while," he murmurs against my pussy. His tongue comes out for a casual lick. "A long, *long* while."

"Oh, God." I sit up, taking in his position between my legs. His shirt is open, the heat of his chest warming my thighs. He's the most beautiful specimen, and what he's offering to do to me... I shudder without meaning to. "M-maybe we should go to the bedroom. Just in case."

"Thought you'd see it my way." He helps me to my feet. I double-check the deadbolt but disengage the chain so I don't have to let Calista in when she returns home. I'll be busy.

He follows me down the short hallway to my bedroom, his hands cupping my rear. When we enter my room, he's already pulling off his clothes.

I sit on my double bed, which isn't big by any stretch of the imagination, but it's huge compared to the tiny countertop and cramped sofa. He rolls his shoulders like he's ready to welcome whatever additional space he can get. Then he puts a knee between my legs, palms my lower back, and lifts and scoots me a foot up the bed.

I yip, impressed by how easily he relocated me, but not

really surprised. He's practically bionic in my mind. He repeats the move and scooches me up another foot. I reach for my hair that became trapped beneath my back on the way.

Moonlight sifts through the slatted plastic blinds, striping his body, and curving over the delectable hills and grooves making up his mouthwatering physique. He gives me his weight, sinking me deeper into the mattress. Elbows on either side of me, he nestles his fingers into my hair, touching my scalp. His lips tip as he watches me from beneath a thick swath of eyelashes.

I shift beneath him, wanting him, impatient for him. Wrapping my hands around his wrists, I urge him down, but he doesn't budge.

Instead he sighs and announces, "Bad news, beautiful."

"Oh?" My heart hammers an SOS. Did he change his mind?

"I brought two condoms. We used 'em. Do you or your sister have a stash? If not, I have to make a run."

Oh. That is bad news.

"I'm not sure if I'm upset you didn't buy a giant box before you came to my office today, or relieved you didn't think I'd be this easy."

He grins, his teeth flashing bright in the dark room. My first Archer Owen grin. *Swoon!* "You have given me *zero* signs you were going to be easy."

I resisted him for months. Much easier to do when he wasn't standing in front of me. Or lying on top of me.

"And I sure as shit didn't expect to be an accessory in the drive-by juicing you gave Ed. Neither did I expect to have to teach Brandon Lambert an unforgettable lesson."

I lapse into a vision of Brandon crashing into the table. "That was pretty epic."

"We're a good team." Archer narrows his eyes for a second, like his thoughts are elsewhere, and then he says, "Before you were unfairly fired, I planned on asking you to help with my night spa. I figured you could work remotely, and via as many video chats as I could talk you into. I planned on flying you up on the weekends so you could have a feel in-person too. But now"—he shakes his head—"seeing how you have plenty of free time, I'm thinking you should come to Ohio with me, and stay 'til we open."

"Stay? In *Ohio*?" I blink, my mind moving through the details of relocating to the Midwest for a handful of months.

"Yeah."

With his body warming mine, it's hard to think of a single reason to refuse him. Being near him for an extended period would likely mean more horizontal naked time. And, let's face it, vertical naked time.

"You can stay in my townhouse."

"Excuse me?" Sleeping with him on a random Sunday is one thing, but *moving in with him* is a whole other situation I'm sure I'm not ready for. I moved in with Brandon on a whim too, and look how that turned out.

"My *other* townhouse," he corrects like he read my mind. "Next door to mine. It's big. The family who used to live there had kids, dogs. They were louder than hell. The second the for-sale sign went up, I called the realtor and bought it. I was going to resell it. When I'm at home, I prefer peace and quiet, so I left it empty. You don't have kids or dogs, and are fairly quiet unless I'm having sex with you against a countertop—"

I slap my hand over his mouth. He licks my palm, and I jerk my hand away. "Gross! What are you, fifteen?"

"All guys are fifteen on the inside." His easy smile is less blinding than before, but no less captivating. He's relaxed. Happy. I feel happy and relaxed too, and after the day I've had, that is a stone-cold *miracle*. "So what'll it be? Am I making a condom run? Are you coming home with me tomorrow? Will you be moving into my spare townhouse?"

I shake my head at his audacity. Also, at the idea he has a "spare" townhouse. I can barely afford the apartment I rent, and I split payments with my sister. I can't fathom purchasing a home and leaving it empty simply for peace and quiet.

"Well?" he prompts.

"Do you need answers right now?" I squeak, my nerves jangling. On one hand, I need a job, and he's offering. On the other, moving away isn't a decision easily made while cocooned in his warmth. I'm tempted to say yes just to earn more of his smiles, kisses, etcetera. He's potent.

"I can wait on the last two, but the condom issue needs your immediate attention."

Before I can address said "condom issue," I hear keys jiggle in the knob, the front door open and close, and a pair of voices.

"My sister is home," I tell Archer.

And she's not alone.

CHAPTER SIX

Talia

The muffled voices progress down the hallway, one of them laughing—Calista—the other whispering. I don't recognize the male voice.

"Who'd she bring home?" I ask myself, rolling out from under Archer. On my way to the bedroom door, I snag his shirt off the floor, pull it on, and do up enough buttons not to be exposed. A light knock comes as I'm reaching for the knob. I open the door and peer out of the crack at my sister. Her smile is wonky, her cheeks rosy.

"You're home early," I inform her, grateful to Archer for suggesting we come in here for privacy.

"I didn't go out for drinks. I had a few at the bar at work instead. Webber drove me home," she adds, deflecting a lecture about driving under the influence.

"Who's Webber?" I look past her to her closed bedroom door, where Webber is probably taking off his pants. At least I hope that's what he's doing in there rather than raiding her jewelry box.

"He's the floor manager. Julio knows him."

Julio's the owner of Mango's. He's also a chef and Calista's mentor. I thought for a long while Julio might be the guy Calista brought home for *sexy times*, but according to her, all they do is fight. Over the menu, over technique. She told me he reminds her daily if she was in a five-star restaurant, she would have been fired by now or put on oyster-shucking duty, I assume because it's an undesirable task.

"How *well* does Julio know him?" I ask when I hear rustling in her room.

Music starts playing, the bass thumping through the wall. She turns and looks over her shoulder before promising, "I'll keep it down. Don't worry."

I do worry. She's my younger sister, and her track record with men is not great. I realize this is a bit pot/kettle, but she's more of a risk-taker than me. The last time I took a risk, I ended up playing house with the man who, as you know, took my raise out from under me.

"What's going on?" Her eyes sharpen on my attire. The oversize white button-down shirt I'm wearing is very obviously not mine. "Who do you have in there?" She pushes on the door but I stand firm. I'm taller and weigh more than she does so she doesn't get far. She mouths "Brandon," and I can't help answering aloud.

"Ew. No. Not Brandon. Never Brandon."

The door is pulled from my grasp a second later as a wall of male heat blankets me from behind. "I second the *never* part." Archer reaches around me to extend a hand to my sister. "Archer Owen."

"Archer. *Owen*," she says meaningfully. She knows everything about him that I know...except what has transpired in the last eight to ten hours. She attended the fundraiser with me last year, so she's seen him before. No idea if she remembered what he looked like, but her slack-jawed expression suggests she didn't recall as many details as she's absorbing right now. Her wide eyes suggest she's stunned by his good looks, and really, how could she not be?

"Nice to finally meet you," she says after shaking his hand.

"If he's trouble, let me know." He tips his chin toward the bedroom door. "I'm in rare form today." He sends me a meaningful glance. "I'm going to grab my bag from the car. Fingers crossed I find what we need in there."

He literally crosses his fingers and then slips past Calista. Shirtless, as I've commandeered that article of his clothing, he walks out of our apartment wearing only pants and shoes.

"Holy shit, Tal, he's gorgeous," Lis tells me after he shuts the front door behind him. "What's he hoping to find?"

"Condoms. We used the two he had."

"*Why didn't you tell me he was coming here?*" she loud-whispers.

"I didn't know! He showed up at the office unannounced and...then a few other things happened."

"What *things*?" Her dark eyes narrow. She looks a lot like me. Dark brown hair, warm complexion with bronze undertones. Her eyes are brown instead of my hazel, and she's about five inches shorter than me, having inherited our mother's stature: curvy, with a cute button nose.

"It's a long story, Lis."

She folds her arms, the picture of stubbornness. I sigh,

knowing a standoff could last hours with her, and give her the bottom line. "I quit. Or, I was fired. Or both. I don't know. I dumped green juice on Ed's head after he gave my raise to Brandon. And then Brandon started mouthing off about how he'd 'hit that,' meaning sex with me, and Archer punched him in the face."

"What!" She blinks a few times in quick succession, then she smiles, and her eyebrows rise when she adds, "I would have *loved* to see him hit Brandon."

"It was awesome. Almost worth losing my job over."

Her temper ignites. "Those dirty bastards. How could they do that to you? The grand opening *couldn't* have gone half as well without you. Brandon can't tell his elbow from his blowhole. I can*not* believe no one had your back over there after how hard you've worked building that company!"

I smile. Not only at her "blowhole" comment, which was damn funny, but at how she rushes to my defense, assuming I was in the right. I was, but it's still nice to hear.

"Same old story, right?" I heave a sigh. "Overlooked by men. Undermined by the people in charge." I glance at her bedroom door and lower my voice. "Forced to sleep with the floor manager when you want the guy who owns the place."

"I do not want Julio!" Her cheeks turn pinker. She's pretty when she lies. She flaps one hand in front of her face to change the subject. "Anyway, this isn't about me. I need details. Put on your clothes."

"I just gave you details," I tell her as she twists the doorknob on her bedroom door and calls Webber's name. "Plus, Archer and I are a little busy."

"Uh-uh." She wags a finger at me. "This is important. I need to hear *every detail* of what happened today, and then

59

we are going to sue that rat bastard for harassment. We'll take your job back, Tal, don't worry."

"I don't think I want my job back." It's a conclusion I've been coming to slowly over the course of today. The idea of seeing either of those men—let alone begging for my menial position back—fills me with dread.

"Well, you at least deserve compensation for having to deal with their crap."

Her bedroom door pops open, and there stands Webber in all his plain, khakied glory. He glances at me, eyebrows winging upward before taking in Calista. His blue polo shirt with the restaurant's logo embroidered over his heart is untucked and hanging over the front of his pants. Yeah, our boy was hoping for a lot more than he's going to get tonight.

"Sorry, Webber. We're going to have to postpone." Calista's voice is soft and oddly enough, she sounds sincere. I'm genuinely surprised she's asking him to leave. She rarely (ever?) brings guys home, and Webber is the first since we've moved into this apartment. She could wait until morning to find out the scoop on my day. She doesn't have to send blond-haired, medium-framed Webber packing. Unless the point of bringing him home was a big F-you to Julio.

Intriguing.

"Is everything okay?" Webber's gaze flits to me, his expression looking very not-okay. I'm grateful I had the foresight to hide my lower half behind the door. Archer's shirt sits high on my legs, and I'd rather not flash Webber my bare thighs since we're not remotely acquainted.

"Yes," I say at the same time Calista says, "No."

She glares at me and then addresses Webber once again.

"My sister had some trouble at work and she needs me. Raincheck?"

He exhales, his shoulders slumping. He doesn't bother hiding his vast disappointment when he leans close to her and mutters, "I thought we were going to—"

"Another time," she chirps, dragging him by the arm out of her bedroom. In my head, I make up another story about how he's been pining for my sister who only has eyes for Julio. Webber finally girded his loins and asked her out, believing until this second he'd won her over. Now she's kicking him out before they get to the good stuff.

Love unrequited. What a tragedy.

Calista walks with Webber, who is tucking in his shirt as he shuffles across the living room. Archer, shirtless, muscled, and carrying a black carry-on-sized suitcase, opens the front door and dips his head to Webber, a silent hello. Or maybe condolences. It's hard to say in this case. He sidles by Calista and leaves them to their awkward goodbyes and then pushes his way into my bedroom.

"She's making him leave," I explain needlessly as I close the door.

He drops his suitcase on the bed and unzips the outside pockets, doing a quick search for you-know-what. "She can do better."

He flips open the top next, checking a netted section, and then pulls out a brown leather toiletries bag. He unearths a beard trimmer, deodorant, and a few other personal items before he strikes gold. Literally. Scissored between two fingers is a shiny gold foil packet.

"One more shot tonight, Wildflower."

I take the condom, breaking the news as gently as I can.

"She's making him go because she wants the lowdown on what happened today. She's not going to leave us alone until I talk to her."

A swift knock comes next, followed by my sister's raised voice. "Don't get naked yet. I need answers! You too, Archer Owen. Put on your clothes and strut your fine ass out here."

I groan and regard the ceiling as Archer repacks his toiletries. He cups my waist and leans down, covering my lips with a soft kiss. I repeat my sister's sentiment to Webber, only when I say it to Archer, I mean it.

"Raincheck?" I offer him the condom.

"Tuck that into your nightstand. After you satisfy your sister with answers, I'll take care of satisfying you."

THE NEXT MORNING, my eyes flutter open at the usual time. 7:25 a.m. The morning sunrise is filtering in through the partially open blinds. I never closed them. After we joined my sister at the kitchen table for an interrogation that would have impressed the KGB, we went to bed. Lis, to her room sans Webber, who she'd kicked out for reasons I couldn't make her admit, and Archer and I to my bedroom. He talked me into one final round of sex, which didn't require *any* talking, and by the time I collapsed under the weight of my second (or was it third?) orgasm that round, I passed out cold.

Lying on my right side, hands in prayer pose under my right cheek, I watch him sleep. He's facing me, his long, dark eyelashes shadowing his cheeks. His mouth is at rest, neither smiling nor pulled into a taut line.

He has a handsome face, with the tiniest, shallow scar high on his right cheekbone. I never noticed it before, and maybe it's because the sunshine is hitting it just the right way that I notice it now. His breathing is deep and peaceful, one arm wedged beneath the pillow under his head, the other resting on the bed. I admire his long, strong fingers. The way his skin is tanned like mine, but a different tone than my own. Unable to stop myself, I touch his forearm, stroking the dark hair there. He's nothing short of yummy while fast asleep on my pale blue floral bedding.

I guess I shouldn't be surprised he's a deep sleeper and not an early riser. One would assume a guy who opens the hottest nightclubs in the Midwest and on the East Coast wouldn't be a member of the five-a.m. club. Or maybe he's normally driven to rise at an early hour but yesterday's activities—and I don't only mean the sex—tuckered him out. I have the idea he needed a release as badly as I did.

After dating Brandon, who treated me like a new piece of furniture in his condominium, being needed is foreign and not as unpleasant as I would have guessed. Dangerous thoughts to have the morning after the best sex I've ever had.

I roll off the bed and pull on a pair of leggings and a shirt. Archer's eyelids don't so much as flinch. Closing my bedroom door behind me, I slip into the hallway and follow the heavenly smell of coffee to the kitchen.

My sister is at the table, writing in her stained and battered recipe journal. "Well-loved," she calls it. A plate of food is next to her left elbow. I grab a mug and pour my coffee before going to the fridge to add a splash of whole milk.

"Spinach and bacon crepes with hollandaise sauce," she announces. She slices into the stack of rolled crepes with a fork, making sure to stab a fat mushroom. She then dunks it into the hollandaise before offering it to me.

I take the offered bite, expecting perfection. I'm not disappointed. "Wow," I say as flavors burst on my tongue. "That's amazing."

"Too much thyme?"

I swallow, swirl my tongue around my cheek, and seriously consider her question. "Maybe a touch more pepper, but other than that, it's perfect."

She jots down my suggestion and drops her pen. "I'm making apple-cinnamon crepes next." She hops up and moves around the kitchen, where bowls and pans litter every surface from counter to stove. A typical picture in our kitchen.

"He wants me to come with him to Ohio." I sit and fork another delectable bite into my mouth. We talked about Archer asking me to advise him on his new spa last night, but I didn't mention me moving. "Temporarily. Until the spa opens."

"Really." She cracks an egg on the side of a bowl and sends me a bemused look.

"Am I crazy?" I wrinkle my nose, unsure.

"With my track record, you're asking me? I bailed on you to move in with Ryan." She makes a face. We both know how that turned out. Not well. "You moving in with Archer doesn't sound as crazy as it should."

"I wouldn't be living with him. He offered me the townhouse next door. It's a separate space. And he's providing it free of charge. I'll still pay rent here, though. I won't leave you in a lurch."

"I can handle rent for a month without your help, Talia."

She cracks another egg into the batter and whisks. Neither of us intended on leaning so hard on each other. But after Brandon and I incinerated, Lis and I realized that the best roommate to have was one without a penis. They're too much responsibility. And yes, I'm talking about the penises.

Eyes on my empty fork, I ask, "What if I told you I'd be there for two or three months?"

The whisk halts for a second before starting up again.

"I don't want you to worry about making the bills after I irresponsibly quit my job. Plus, Archer said I can name my price for the contract."

"You weren't being irresponsible. You were standing up for yourself." She *tsks*. "What's the going rate for consulting, anyway?"

"If I charged what he charged, astronomical. I'm not sure I'm worth it, though."

Heavy steps approach from the hallway. Archer appears, his hair rumpled from sleep, no shirt, his pants hanging low on his hips. He nods at me and then my sister. "Ladies."

Oh, his voice in the morning is very, very nice. Low and throaty. I hum against the rim of my coffee mug and hope no one notices.

"Mind if I grab a shower? I didn't want to take up the bathroom if one of you needed to be somewhere."

And he's thoughtful, folks. His gaze heats when it hits mine. Tingles work their way from my arms to my chest, where they bloom into a solar flare.

"Help yourself. When you're done, crepes," Calista informs him cheerily.

"I, uh, I'll be taking off soon, so that won't be necessary. I will take a cup of coffee, though."

"Your loss," my sister says. "My crepes are legendary."

"Mushroom and bacon with hollandaise sauce." I scoop up another bite for myself, fervently ignoring the urge to ask where he's going. A hotel? Or is he flying back to Ohio with or without me? It seems like something I should know about the man I had sex with three times in one night.

"I won't be long." He disappears down the hallway.

"Well?" My sister points in his direction with her dripping whisk. She adds a pat of butter to the hot skillet on the stove, ladles in the crepe batter, and then lifts the pan to swirl it so it covers the surface.

"Well what?"

"Are you going to join him?"

Distracted by the smell of warm butter, I ask, "In Ohio?"

"In the *shower*. You can wash his back." When I hesitate, she shrugs. "If you don't, I will."

I can't help it. I burst out laughing.

CHAPTER SEVEN

Talia

I didn't join Archer in the shower that Monday morning, but I was able to talk him into having crepes. Calista made herself scarce, claiming she needed to take her own shower, and telling him it was nice to meet him just in case she missed saying goodbye.

I appreciated her thoughtfulness.

Over warm apple-cinnamon crepes topped with fresh vanilla bean whipped cream, I asked Archer his plans for the week. He told me he was flying back that day, after all, though he offered to save me a seat on the jet if I wanted to join him. At my hesitation, he mentioned that if I came back with him, I could take a look at the facility and see what I thought. I could also check out my would-be temporary town-house before flying back home to pack and rejoining him the next week on a more permanent basis.

"That way you can make an informed decision," he said.

To which I replied, "I've already decided. I'll do it."

He also let me know he'd overheard me talking to Lis earlier when he said, "Charge me whatever you want, Wildflower. I can afford 'astronomical.'"

He grabbed his suitcase and kissed me goodbye at the door. Just a brief peck, not the lingering, body-pressing, heated exchange I was expecting.

Then, he left.

I've spent the week practicing writing up a contract. After doing an online search and learning everything I could about consulting fees and contract wording (I couldn't very well copy Archer's, now, could I?), I finally cobbled together a respectable document. He not only agreed to the amount I asked for, he added in a section for bonus compensation if I meet his timeline parameters or do an "exceptional" job as determined by his team. It was all very official.

In between contract negotiations, I tidied the apartment for my extended leave and packed my mismatched luggage for my trip. I also transferred any personal documents, including the contract, from the laptop onto my cloud drive and returned said laptop to Ed Lambert, Chief Executive Butthead of Lotus Leaf. Thankfully, I encountered Krista while I was there, and she gave me my final paycheck. Regretfully, no bonus. On the bright side, I bumped into Prisha, and she offered to turn in my company laptop to Ed so I wouldn't have to. I also successfully avoided Brandon. Before I left, I promised Prisha we'd get together at a later date over cocktails, though I knew it'd be a while, so I was vague. I wasn't ready to share the news of my recent relocation plans with her.

A week after the day I spent losing my job and gaining a different one, I'm at yet another Sunday brunch. This one with my father and sister. We are seated outside under a jaunty yellow-striped umbrella at the Bread Basket, a charming seaside brunch destination. Calista insisted we eat here instead of Mango's, which made me wonder if there has been a development with Julio, or Webber, for that matter, and she hasn't told me yet. Alas, we're with Papa today, and my flight to Ohio is a few hours from now, so I'll have to grill her at a later time. Not having brunch at Mango's also means no mouthwatering huevos rancheros. I settled for Belgian waffles with thick-cut black pepper bacon, because *come on*. Lis ordered eggs benedict with crabmeat, and Papa is digging into something called a chorizo scramble, but by the looks of it, should have been named The Heart Clogger.

"How are the jobs?" Papa asks us collectively as he forks up another bite of greasy sausage and eggs. His thick, dark mustache twitches as he chews.

"Fine," Lis answers like a twelve-year-old who's just come home from school. "My crepes are on the menu this week."

I gasp. She didn't tell me. How'd she manage to land an item on the menu Julio guards like the Hope Diamond? "The mushroom or the apple? And why aren't we at Mango's enjoying them?" I frown at my Belgian waffle, suddenly dissatisfied.

"Both are on the menu." She shrugs, oddly humble as she focuses on her plate. "If we ate at Mango's, I'd be staring at every plate as it comes out of the kitchen to check if my crepes were on it. And if they *were*, I'd be tempted to check each plate to make sure they were served exactly as I specified."

"Ah." I relax in my seat, understanding. So she's not

hiding an affair with her hot boss from me. "You didn't want to be stressed out."

"Would you be able to have a relaxing meal at your former workplace?"

"Former?" I feel Papa's censure from across the round table. Lis flinches, catching her gaffe far too late. Granted, we scheduled this brunch so I could tell him I was flying to Ohio today, but I was going to broach the topic gingerly, peppering in the details of my firing intermixed with the opportunity to work with the Owen family. "You are unemployed?"

"No, Papa. Nothing like that." I chew on a strip of bacon to buy myself time. *Blessed nitrates, help me out here.*

"She took a temporary job in Ohio with Archer Owen, who is a very talented builder. He needed a design expert, so he contacted Talia. Isn't that great?" Lis is smiling, her head swiveling from Papa to me. So much for gingerly peppering the details. That was more an Emeril Lagasse-style *BAM!*

"When does this new temporary job end? How much does it pay? What will you do after?" Papa asks, not caring about any other detail save for my monetary security. My father, while I love him and treasure him and adore him, is a bit...old-fashioned. He wants his girls taken care of and has always encouraged us to find steady work where we can advance. Needless to say, my job-hopping has been a source of worry for him and was once blamed for his hernia. I argue it's because he was moving a slab of concrete on the jobsite, but what do I know? Before I can answer his three other questions, he lobs one more at me. "What happened at Lotus Leaf?"

"Brandon stole her raise," Lis blurts. I glare at her. She drinks her orange juice, her eyes wide with apology.

"I always liked Brandon," Papa says affectionately.

Sadly, that's true. He met Brandon twice and was charmed by Brandon's, well, *charm*. I know it's fake charm, and so does nearly everyone else, but it was effective. When I moved in with Brandon, my father wanted so badly to believe I was finally in good hands, that Brandon would take care of me and Papa could stop worrying.

Mama wasn't that way. At all. She was assertive and strong, bold, and, like Lis, talkative. While Papa never encouraged either of us to go into business for ourselves like he had, Mama often brought up the topic of our independence as women. She didn't want us to solely rely on a man for our well-being. In my adult years, I have wondered if their marriage wasn't the healthiest. If she'd come to rely too much on Papa, or if Papa held her back in the name of protecting her. In the end, she passed away from cancer when all the protection in the world wouldn't have helped.

I dust my hands on my napkin, my appetite vanishing with the thought of her. I miss her. I would give anything to run this whole Archer situation by her to hear her opinion. As it stands, I'm stuck with my overprotective father.

"Well, Brandon is now in charge of my former Lotus Leaf team, and I am flying to Ohio to work on a project for a few months."

"Months?" His mouth drops open. The waiter pauses at our table, long enough for me to request a second espresso I don't need.

"Yes," I answer Papa after the waiter leaves.

"What will your sister do?" He gestures to Lis, who is frantically chewing so she can respond. I beat her to it.

"She'll work at the restaurant and enjoy the time alone."

"I can give you additional money if you need it," he tells Lis. His head swivels to me. "You too."

Lis and I both shake our heads.

"Stop worrying. You don't need the stress. You're already taking pills for hypertension," she tells him.

"You are?" I ask. I turn to my sister. "You didn't tell me that."

"I just found out." She puts up her hands to shield herself from my accusations.

"It's no big deal." He swats the air and scoops another bite of the nutritional equivalent of hypertension into his mouth. Figuring he'll ask again, I explain the rest, carefully gliding over the details. I tell him lodging is included, though I doubt a townhouse next door to Archer will be as rustic as I made it sound. I also tell him I was able to name my price for the job, and my employer was generous. I leave out my personal relationship with Archer since I'm not sure it will continue. When I considered working with him on this project, I imagined being next door would afford us all sorts of naked endeavors, but now I'm not so sure.

Alas, the only contact I've had with him since last Sunday was via text message, and that was when he gave me my private flight itinerary. My work email is null and void, and in hindsight, I never should have sent emails to Archer from that address. There wasn't anything too damning in them, but the cheeky nicknames would have raised a red flag to Ed if he'd looked. Thinking of him reading my personal correspondence turns my stomach.

Brunch ends with Papa hugging both Lis and me and reminding us (again) that he could give us money if we need it. I second Lis's earlier argument and tell him we don't need it. Papa's extra money comes from him taking on additional jobs, and he already works a ridiculous amount of hours. I'm kind of shocked we were able to be together on a Sunday given his and Lis's hectic schedules.

My sister drops me off at the hangar where the private jet is waiting. Which is a hilarious sentence. As I board alone, I marvel at how quickly my life has changed in a short period of time. I also think about how Archer was the catalyst for that change, though I did dump the first juice cup.

I land in a far less desirable climate than the one I left (seriously, it's freaking cold in Ohio in January). Outside of the jet, there's a car waiting to shuttle me to the townhouse. The door is opened for me. I slide in, waiting as the driver loads my luggage and wondering if I should tip him.

The driver, Robert, is friendly. He navigates a tidy neighborhood and chats while he drives. He points out some of the areas I should check out while I'm here, including his favorite restaurant, which has "the best hot wings in town." We arrive, and Robert parks in a marked space by the curb. I stare out the window, blinking as I take in the posh surroundings.

When Archer said townhouse, I pictured an apartment with a second floor, not the deluxe homes surrounding me. Each pair of townhouses on this street is set apart by a narrow walkway between them lined with slim trees—naked branches thanks to the season, but I imagine them with thick leaves and blooms in the spring. Robert hands me a key and then retrieves my bags from the trunk. He leads the way to the largest building on the corner.

We walk beneath a wide, arched entryway where there is one doorway on the left and one on the right. Robert tells me my townhouse is to the right, so I enter the breezeway and find a zigzag staircase leading to a front door. Beyond the staircase, the breezeway expands onto a patio leading to a long, narrow yard.

As I take the stairs I note the openness of the brick-and-mortar alcove as well as the echoey sounds of my shoes scuffing with each step. I unlock the front door and step into a massive furnished living room. Beyond that is a state-of-the-art, even more massive kitchen. Every furnishing and appliance appears to have been delivered yesterday. From the shining stovetop to the pristine lighting to the couches that look like they have never been sat upon.

"Holy wow."

I didn't realize I'd spoken aloud until Robert chuckles. My luggage in his hands, he shuffles by me. "I'll put these upstairs in the master bedroom for you, Ms. Richards."

"Thanks, Robert."

While he's doing my bidding, I give myself a tour of an interior designer's dreamhouse. The color palette is gray and blue, but an occasional pop of spring green keeps it from being drab. The contemporary style isn't overtly feminine. I have no clue why Archer kept this townhouse when he could have sold it for hundreds of thousands of dollars. As I take in the narrow backyard with a low brick wall surrounding it, I wonder if hundreds of thousands of dollars is an understatement. Are we in the *millions* of dollars range?

Robert, having returned, asks if I need anything else.

"No, thanks. I'll show myself around." Again, I have the nagging sensation that I should tip him. I reach into my purse praying five bucks is better than nothing, but he waves me off with a stern head shake.

"No, ma'am. Mr. Owen takes good care of me."

But of course he does. Well, I can also take care of people. I proffer the folded bill and try again. "I insist."

He gives me another firm head shake but a smile of gratitude accompanies it this time. He reminds me to "check out those hot wings" before he exits via the front door.

Alone in the luxury townhouse, I hang my purse and puffy coat on the back of a chair and run my fingertips along the kitchen island. It's pale gray and blue marble. I pull out my cellphone and snap a few photos of it, as well as the six-burner gas stove. Calista will faint dead away when she sees this palatial kitchen. The dining room is furnished with a table with seating for six, a heavy iron lighting fixture hanging overhead.

On this floor, a screened porch separates dining room from the backyard below. A low brick wall flanks the patch of cold, lifeless ground. I imagine in a few months the grass will turn envy green and straight-backed tulips with their pastel heads will line the wall like loyal soldiers. Now, though, nothing but bleak brown and gray. With a shiver, I step inside from the chilled air and open a door to find a furnished office, complete with an Apple desktop computer.

Again, holy *wow*.

I retrace Robert's steps and take the staircase to the top floor. I hang a right and encounter two smaller bedrooms side by side with a bathroom bisecting them. At the end of the hallway is a set of open double doors leading to the master bedroom, where my luggage sits by the bed. A regal set of French doors leads to an open-air balcony (who am I, Evita?) and a fireplace. A quick peek at the walk-in closet confirms it's roughly the size of my bedroom at home.

"Unbelievable." The balcony, with its stone wall and a

cozy-looking wicker couch tucked close to the house, is irresistible. Braving the cold, since I left the puffy coat I purchased two days ago downstairs, I step outside into the elements, arms tightly braced over my chest.

The clouds hang low and gray overhead, giving the afternoon an almost evening feel. I peer over the ledge, expecting to see the screened porch below, but I can't see it unless I lean waaaay out. Whoever designed this place thought of everything, even having an unobstructed view from the top floor.

"You like it?" a rumbly voice asks. I nearly leap out of my skin. Archer is standing on the balcony of his townhouse. It mirrors this one, right down to the stone fireplace and wicker couch.

"It's pretty incredible," I say, figuring he knows exactly how incredible it is. "I noticed an office space downstairs."

"Thought you'd need it." His hands are buried in the pockets of a dark wool coat, his mouth a firm line. Trying to get a read on him is impossible. A week ago he was smiling and flirting, dark intent shimmering beneath a cool façade. Now there's nothing but the cool façade...if it's a façade at all. I'm tempted to ask if he's gone professional on me after signing a contract, but I don't. That's probably for the best, considering what happened the last time I slept with a coworker. While I doubt Archer will screw me over, maybe limiting what we had to one night is for the best.

A purring ring comes from his balcony, and he pulls his cellphone from one of his pockets. "Let me know when you get settled. I'll show you the facility."

"I'm ready when you are," I answer. After the flight and the drive here, I'm too antsy to relax. I need to do something other than wend around this enormous townhouse by myself.

He nods once, takes the call, and walks back inside.

Back in my own bedroom, I unzip my suitcase and find my cosmetics bag. I brush my teeth and hair, and in five minutes I'm pulling on my coat, shouldering my purse, and pocketing my house key. When I open the front door to leave, Archer is standing on the threshold, still in his dark wool coat, still looking edible. This close up, my breathing goes shallow. I snap my attention to his lips, wondering if this week has been as long and sexless for him as it was for me.

If I were a different person, I might ignore the elephant in the room. He seems to be okay with that tactic, judging from his personality-free text and muted presence. But, that's not me. I'm not one to wait for the shoe to drop. I knock the shoe out of the other person's hand. It's not my style to ignore what's obviously happening in a situation. Even if he considers us a one-and-done, someone should say it out loud.

So, I guess it's going to be me who does it.

"It's okay if you don't want to have sex with me anymore." I add a shrug for emphasis, trying to appear nonchalant. I don't feel nonchalant, but he doesn't need to know that. I'm willing to be forward and have a hard discussion. I'm *not* willing to be vulnerable and allow my pride to be stamped out like a waning campfire. "We'll be working closely together for the next few months. No one understands better than me the wisdom behind keeping those two compartments separate. I respect it too. You don't have to worry about me misreading your actions while I'm here. If that's what you want."

There's not only the physical space separating us, but also the invisible wall keeping him distant in another way.

Sexual tension roared between us before. Now it's nothing more than banked heat.

"You think I don't want to have sex with you?" he asks, monotone. His eyebrows center over his nose, and his beard frowns along with his mouth. "I moved you into this townhouse because I wanted you close. I didn't want to make you feel like I'm watching your every move. You need time to settle into your new location and position. I'm trying not to pressure you."

Oh-kay. I open my mouth and then close it. His wasn't a statement of agreement or disagreement, was it? I bite my lip and grip my purse strap with both hands. "So...you want us to be on hold while I'm here?"

He cups the back of my neck with warm fingers. Chills skitter down my back when he spikes those fingers upwards into my hair. My heartrate ratchets up as I soak in his nearness, losing myself in the green of his eyes.

"The only hold I want with you, Talia, is *this one.*" His eyes burn into mine intently as he tightens his fist in my hair. Tipping my head back gently, he adds, "I haven't stopped thinking about your kitchen counter since I left Miami."

"Neither have I," I whisper, revealing way too many of my cards.

His lips curve. Not quite a smile, but his expression is a touch playful. He loosens his hold on my hair and slides the length of it over one shoulder, toying with the ends for a few mind-numbing seconds. "Are you available for dinner after I show you around?"

I laugh. "You think I'm unavailable for dinner?"

"This is the no-pressure part."

"Oh."

"You don't like it," he states.

"I didn't say that."

Palm on my hip, he backs me into the living room and kicks the door closed behind him with one booted foot. He leans in, his lips practically on mine while my heart patters like a drunken tap dancer. After he left Miami I tried not to think about him, tried to convince myself one night was enough. I was deluding myself. After the fundraiser when he agreed to work with Lotus Leaf, I thought of him daily. Sleeping with him, finally seeing his smile, made me more aware of how far away he was, not less.

"You exited a situation where your boss and your ex treated you like you were nothing." His voice is low and penetrating, his breath sliding into my mouth when he speaks. "You hollowed out a home for yourself there, a position you earned. Meanwhile, Ed is telling everyone he fired you when both you and I know you were well within your rights to quit. Less than twenty-four hours later, you decided to move to a state way too cold for your warm skin and work for me on a temporary basis. I signed a contract you drew up, after I amended it to make sure you were compensated fairly. Less than one week later, you boarded a plane and stepped foot into a house you've never seen before. Fifteen minutes after that, you haven't so much as unpacked a bag, and you're telling me you understand if I don't want to have sex with you?"

I don't know how to respond to his detailed and accurate recap, so I say nothing.

"Hear me, Wildflower." He cups my jaw and pulls his head back to meet my eyes unerringly. "I *want* to have sex with you. I've wanted to have sex with you for a week. I get hard every time I think of chocolate chip cookie dough."

"Does that happen often?" My lips twitch, and though he keeps his stoic expression, there's newfound warmth in his voice.

"Too damn often," he mutters, brushing my bottom lip with his thumb. His gaze follows the path, his eyes darkening in color. "I'm trying to be a gentleman. What I want is to flatten you against this wall and take what I've been craving for seven long, lonely days. I'm trying to let you gather your bearings, get a little bit of rest, and settle in. *Woman*"—he gives me a subtle shake—"you're making that hard for me to do."

This is the version of him I didn't know I wanted. The bossy version. The commanding version. The weak-for-me version. I lean forward, but he halts my forward movement with the hand cradling my jaw. We have a brief, intense standoff before he allows me to brush his mouth with mine.

I go fast.

He doesn't.

Intentionally slowing me down, he tilts his head and tongues my bottom lip. His hands slide down and around my back, and he pulls me close for a kiss that says *I missed you* so neither of us have to.

He pulls in a sharp inhalation through his nose and releases me, then watches my mouth for a suffocating beat. Fragmented thoughts swim in my head as I try to figure out why, exactly, it isn't a good idea to tear his clothes off and ask him to take me on the kitchen counter.

"Stop that," he warns.

I grin.

"Dinner?"

"Am I dressed okay?"

"Better than okay." He scans my dark jeans and sweater and boots, his gaze burning every inch of me like a flame. "We should leave before I make good use of the couch. Or the island." Before I can chime in with my wholehearted agreement, he takes my hand and leads me outside. He locks up with his own key while mumbling, "The dining room table looked sturdy."

"Easy, Kingpin," I tease as I take his hand. "I've been here like ten minutes."

He narrows his eyes in a silent scolding, sending a thrill of excitement through me. Our bantering has always been an aphrodisiac. At his car, an ice blue Mercedes S-class, he places a final kiss on my mouth before opening the passenger door for me.

I watch him round the car, his breath visible, his eyes snapping around at his surroundings. When he settles into the driver's seat, he brings cold air with him. I shiver, unsure if it's in reaction to the weather or his potent presence. When the engine purrs to life, he sends me one final, mysterious glance.

"Let the adventure begin," he says and then pulls away from the curb.

CHAPTER EIGHT

Talia

As we drive toward our destination, I watch out the window. We're downtown, where most of the buildings are older, but with modern upgrades. The trees planted along the sidewalk are looped with white lights, making me wonder if they were left over from the holidays or if they stay up year-round. I have the same thought as when Robert was shuttling me to the townhouse: Clear Ridge is too nice to be quaint, but too approachable to be considered snobby.

"Why do you live here?" I ask. "Wouldn't Miami be a better location for a nightclub kingpin?"

His eyes slide to me and then back to the road. What might appear as derision to someone else registers as consideration to me. I'm beginning to know his faces. Funny, I've only been around him a few times. Quality over quantity, I think, remembering how we've spent our time.

"Midwesterners need fun nights out more than you Florida folk know. You can go out whenever you like. Look around. We're not exactly taking afternoon strolls this time of year."

There's no snow on the ground, but the temperature has dropped significantly since the night sky drew down. I'm about to explain that Florida isn't all sunshine all the time, but he continues before I can. "I wasn't supposed to be in the nightclub business forever."

This sounds like a story. "No?"

He lets loose a soft grunt that might be a laugh. "No. My dad would have preferred it if I built more respectable establishments." He said those last two words in a rigid baritone, I'm guessing to impersonate his dad.

"Like a spa?"

"My spa will be categorized as nightlife. He won't like that either." Pride laces his voice like defying his father brings him joy. I understand his rebellious streak. My father would love if I settled down with a man—any man, it seems—and stayed in my safe, dull job, accepting whatever pittance I'm paid. I guess that's not entirely fair. He wants good things for me; he just doesn't believe I can have them without being taken care of by someone else.

Archer turns right, navigating us away from the parking garages of downtown and into an area with more space between the buildings, each with its own designated parking lot.

"What about your mom?" I wonder if she's as disapproving as his father.

He grins, as big as I've seen. It's a sight I missed terribly, so I stare, soaking it in. "She's amazing. You'll love her."

His smile disappears abruptly. I'm not sure if it's because he hinted I'd be meeting her and didn't mean to admit it, or if he misspoke because he didn't intend to introduce us.

"What about your brothers? What's Dad think of their chosen sectors of the company?" I ask, quickly changing the subject.

"They can do no wrong."

"Is that so?" I ask with a chuckle.

He pauses before amending, "That's what I used to think. They're adopted, so when I was younger, I suffered from not-enough-ness. My parents didn't choose me, but handpicked them."

It's such a revealing thing to say, I'm not sure how to respond. I know Owen Construction is involved in new builds and upcycles of all sorts. Archer's oldest brother, Nate, builds live-works. Benji is the white-collar desk jockey in charge of the money. Rumor has it he's a math wizard.

I saw them in person at the fundraiser. Each of the Owen brothers is attractive in his own unique way. Nate and his crooked nose and bulk, Benji and his suave sophistication, his smile hinting that his own thoughts are amusing him. That feels like too much to share, so, I respond with a generic, "I read they were adopted."

"Benji was first-in. He's the egghead. Number cruncher. And then came Nate, the rough-around-the-edges teen from Chicago. He builds live-work facilities, both here and in Chicago." He points out the window as we pass an enormous open-air shopping center. Even in this cold weather, people in puffy coats are walking from their cars to the brightly lit restaurants and stores.

"You Ohioans are impervious to cold." I rub my hands together to warm my fingers.

"I'll buy you some gloves." He rests one warm hand over both of mine, and again, I feel taken care of, looked after.

My mouth pulls at the corners as I replay Papa's reaction this morning. Wouldn't he love to see his oldest daughter being cared for by a billionaire.

"Bottom line," Archer continues, "Dad approves of Nate and Benji, but rarely approves of me. Nightclubs. Bars. My college girlfriends." He shrugs, though I imagine it hurts not to receive his father's approval. "I've stopped trying to please him."

Rather than point that out, I ask, "College girlfriends?"

"Only a few. I stopped bringing them home to meet the parents after a while. Learned my lesson to keep relationships light."

I learned a similar lesson at a tender, young age.

"What about you?" He slides me a glance. "Before Bonehead Brandon, who'd you bring home?"

"Uh, well." I hesitate. I don't want to lie, especially after he was honest about his past. So, here goes. "I was engaged after high school, actually."

"Really?" He doesn't hide his surprise.

"I wasn't pregnant if that's what you're thinking. I thought I was in love. *How you do* at eighteen. We were too young. And then Mama got sick and I—" The words stick in my throat. Whenever I remember Estevan, the grief of losing my mom feels new and fresh. It's a cut that never heals. "I called it off," I manage after clearing my throat. "It never would have worked out."

His hand squeezes mine, a show of support without saying a word.

"I've met your sister. Tell me about Papa Richards." It's a kind gesture to change the subject, and I let him.

"He worries about Calista and me, but he took to single parenthood like a champ. He'd prefer Lis and I were both settled down with husbands and babies, but only because he worries about us being alone."

"Sounds like a good man. What's he do for a living?"

"He worked for years as a foreman, but now he specializes in decorative concrete for the Miami elite." I automatically tense, awaiting Archer's censure. When I told Brandon what my dad did for a living, he said Papa was "a glorified laborer" and then added, "I hate working outside."

"An entrepreneur. It's a gift to make something as impersonal as concrete into art."

My chest warms at his approval. "I'm proud of him. He works too hard, but at least he's able to call the shots now."

"That comes with its own set of problems, but it's a hell of a lot better than asking for time off."

I hum in the back of my throat, remembering all the time off I *didn't* ask for when I worked at Lotus Leaf. I was too busy proving myself to Dumb and Dumber. Fat lot of good it did me. I mentally shake off my bruised pride.

"You ever think about branching out on your own? You're an artist too, you know. Design, aesthetics, having an eye for what looks good and feels good in an establishment... People with deep pockets pay well for that sort of work."

I'm flattered by the compliment. There is a lot of vision and creativity in the work I do, but I never thought about doing it for myself. Likely because Papa would freak out if I did. As he's said in the past, he wouldn't wish the long hours and stress he experiences day after day on Lis or me.

He's always advised us to "get a good-paying job and stay put."

"We're here." Archer turns into a parking lot.

The building is not what I expect. When he said dentist's office, I pictured a brick house and a little stoop with an over-hang. This structure is tall and square, with floor-to-ceiling windows lining the front. The glass is frosted halfway up to grant privacy to whoever's inside. The surrounding bushes and trees are weathering the chill nicely, their evergreen branches lush in winter.

"This is... Wow." I seem to be using that word a lot today. "Did it come this way?"

"Not exactly. We knocked out a few walls, installed the new glass. And added the pool around back." He reminds me to wear my coat since the interior of the building isn't being heated.

I grab my notebook and pen from my purse, ideas already kicking up dust, and I haven't seen the inside yet. A blank canvas. I've never had one. At Lotus Leaf, I was barely a decorator. They had specs, and I was charged with following them to the letter.

I replay Archer's question about branching out on my own. I don't know if I'm capable of pulling off entrepreneur-ship, but if I could...

The decadent idea shimmers like a mirage in the distance. For the first time in years, my entire being grasps for it. Working for myself would be risky, but the risk would come with a reward. *Freedom.* No more asking for days off. No more being overlooked for raises, no more performance reviews. I realize I'm probably simplifying something very complicated, but the second I'm inside, and before I take the first look around, I scribble down everything I'm thinking into my notebook.

Archer

Talia's enthusiasm is catching. I follow her through the building, hands in my coat pockets, a smile on my face. For the last week, I haven't felt like smiling. Not until I saw her standing on the balcony opposite mine. Then I took what felt like my first full breath in a week. And when I touched her—forget it. I could have breathed her instead of oxygen.

I held back. For the reasons I explained to her before we left. I wasn't sure how she'd feel about me—technically, her "boss"—coming on to her the second she walked through the door. Finding out she wanted me was good news, but we have time. And despite her eagerness to have me, I'm going to let her settle in. Get comfortable. See the possibilities.

She mutters the words "good bones," and I have to fight not to make a snarky comment. I don't want to pull her out of the zone. Plus, her excitement over this building that's not much more than "good bones" justifies my instincts when I purchased it. I knew the idea of a night spa was a solid one, but when it comes to setting it up, I wasn't as confident.

With Talia onboard, I can envision opening night spas all over the damn country. We could give Ed Lambert a run for his money. But I'm getting ahead of myself. First, I have to open this one.

The pool area isn't much more than a concrete hole in the ground, but she remarks about its "potential" anyway. One curved glass wall resembling a lanai looks out onto a gathering of trees. The house behind it belonged to the dentist who owned this place, so he had a very short commute to work each day. I bought the house too, intending to make it an offsite apartment for whoever manages the spa.

She falls quiet while standing in front of the curved glass, choosing to do most of her talking via pen to notebook. Her excitement is palpable as she scribbles furiously. She looks up as if she senses my staring.

"Well? Is there any hope?" I ask.

Her arms drop to her sides, the pen in one hand, notebook in the other. "You know this place is awesome. Shut up."

Chewing on the side of her lip, she seems to debate saying more.

"What?"

"Do you think people would pay me to do this?" She gestures around. "Design and aesthetics."

"I am." I shrug and walk closer to her. "Just because it comes easy to you doesn't mean it comes easy to everyone."

She nods, her smile cautious.

Caution is overrated. I know her well enough to know that she's independent and able to self-manage.

"I can help. I know a great lawyer who specializes in LLCs."

She hugs her notebook to her chest, her cheeks going tawny with embarrassment—or maybe I caught her off-guard. "I was just writing down a few ideas," she murmurs. "It helps me think."

"Let's hear 'em," I invite.

She flips back a few pages in her notebook, walking and

talking. I'm given a full tour from her point of view—how she sees it now, and how it could be in the future. I listen, rapt. She's magical. Damn sexy when she's in charge. Hell, yeah, people would pay for her expertise. She has an instinct for what goes where, mentioning the importance of "the flow." I've overseen a hell of a lot of nightclubs, so I'm not totally new to the game, but I don't know what I don't know. I appreciate her input. Already she's proving as valuable in this endeavor as I imagined.

I follow her down a corridor. I'm listening, swear to God, but I'm only a man. I can't keep my eyes off her perfect ass in those jeans. Her high-heeled, and highly impractical, boots are the stuff of wet dreams. Her hair is down, my second favorite look on her. Her hair wrapped in my fist with my lips on her throat takes first place with a miles-long lead.

We step into an oddly shaped space. The room is long and narrow, its windows tall and slender. There's a stone walkway outside, and mud from where the landscapers pried up overgrown bushes. It'll be a rose garden come spring. Mom's passion will lend a burst of much-needed color.

"Welcome to the meditation room," Talia tells me. "I suggest a fountain here"—she points to the blank wall—"and a grouping of flameless candles or diffusers here." She points to the windowsills. "Do you have plans for the outside?"

"Mom's roses."

Talia offers a warm smile. "Perfect. I was hoping you wouldn't say animal-shaped topiaries."

"Animal-shaped topiaries? No, I don't think so."

"Good choice. You could rent out the room by the hour if you wanted."

"Sounds kinky."

"For *meditation*," she enunciates, poking me in the chest as she heads for the front door. "Or you can teach meditation classes here and offer sessions included with their paid tuition."

This is exactly why I hired her. I knew she'd see options I couldn't. She's a genius.

"I'm overstepping." She waves her hand in front of her face. "Here you are asking me where the furniture should go, and I'm offering up business advice you don't need."

"I do need it. You're a visionary, Wildflower. Don't be ashamed of your gifts."

The curve of her lips proves irresistible. I lean in. She tastes as good as she tasted an hour ago back at the townhouse. Better, actually, but that makes sense. She's better each time I touch her. When we tear each other's clothes off after dinner tonight, the sex will be phenomenal.

Looking forward to that.

"Can I take you to dinner now?" I hope I don't sound like a horny teenager.

"You'd better," she agrees. I don't miss the feisty gleam in her eyes.

CHAPTER NINE

Archer

The second I'm inside my townhouse and take the key out of the lock, Talia is on me like a spider monkey.

My back hits the wall, knocking the breath from my lungs. I lift my arms to catch her, cradling one of her thighs as she loses traction and her other leg brushes the fly of my pants.

I'm rock hard in an instant.

I kick my front door shut and blindly feel for the dead-bolt, my mouth never leaving hers. She bites down on my bottom lip as I hoist her into my arms. Opening my eyes so I don't run us into a wall, I steer her past the living room and into my kitchen. She ends our kiss when I flip on the light. Her deep brown eyes are wild, her smile a spotlight.

I go in for more, but she presses her finger to my lips, stopping me. "I was promised wine."

My breaths come hard and fast, and I have to blink to reboot my offline brain.

"So you were." I squeeze her ass before setting her down. She straightens her sweater. I pop the door open on the wine cooler and pull out a nineteen-year-old Malbec.

We ate dinner at a French restaurant that is more of a cafe. The owner is an actual Frenchman named Pierre. I know, right? They serve the best crepes. I knew Talia would like them and figured it would give her something to talk to her sister about other than the fact she's obliterated my resolve inside of five measly hours.

I'm weak for Talia, a prospect as foreign to me as Pierre was pre-emigration. Weakness isn't an attribute I aspire to—especially when involved with a woman. I have had my share of experiences that were wham, bam, thank you ma'am, and while I'm not complaining, that sort of thing doesn't interest me any longer.

The arrangement used to work perfectly for me. I travel a lot, and my hours are shit. Putting up with my hectic schedule is a lot to ask of a girlfriend. Plus, my free time is spent mostly with my brothers or parents, and, as discussed, I avoid having dates for any and all functions with my family. I find it easier not to cross the streams, if you take my meaning. Having Talia here tempts me to do the unthinkable and cross those streams regardless of the consequences. No one has caught my attention since I bought her that first drink in Florida last spring.

I don't even want to consider what that might mean.

I pour two glasses of wine and hand one to my house-guest, who is finger-combing her long, wavy hair. I follow the sweep of hair down to her thick, curved hips, and back up to mesmerizing eyes. My hard-on pulses impatiently, which I find soothing. If my body is weak for this girl, that's excusable. I mean, look at her.

"To the second-best crepes I've ever tasted." She touches her wineglass to mine, and then we drink. The red is fruity, soft, and drinkable. She hums in the back of her throat, a sound I'd like to hear a hell of a lot more of tonight, before nodding her approval.

"Can I show you around?" I invite.

She purses her full lips. "Is this a trick to lure me into your bedroom?"

"Definitely." I take her hand. "But I won't make you stay there if you don't want to."

Talia

I admit, leaping on Archer the second we stepped inside wasn't the best way to play hard to get. Not that I'm playing hard to get...

Half of me warns to tread carefully. We're embarking on a business relationship and making this personal (again) is a not-so-great idea. The other half of me argues that we have a lot of fun together, so why not have more? Since I haven't decided whose side to take on the debate, I stalled by asking for wine.

He gives me the briefest of tours of the upstairs, which is the same layout as the townhouse I'm staying in, mirrored. Only instead of two guest bedrooms, one of them acts as his office.

"Steel gray and black is not a color scheme," I say as he

leads me away from the neutral rooms and toward the double-doored bedroom. "If anything it's a lack-of-color scheme."

We step into the master bedroom, a gargantuan space like the room I'm staying in. His bed is bigger, a California king, I'd guess. The comforter is navy blue with one fat white stripe running horizontally along the bottom. Crisp, clean white pillowcases appear to have been recently fluffed.

"Did your housekeeper come today, or are you extremely neat?" I ask, admiring the masculine walnut furniture.

"Yesterday," he admits easily. "I don't sleep in this bed. I crash on the couch when I'm here. If I sleep at all."

"Why?" I run my fingertips over the comforter and then test the springiness of the mattress with both hands. "Is this bed reserved for sex?"

I'm rewarded with a loose laugh, and I'm positive I don't hide my wide-eyed admiration of the rich, luscious sound. "You think I bring women here. That's cute."

"You brought me here." If I'm breaking one of my rules and one of his rules, do they cancel each other out?

"I don't have you yet," he rumbles, crossing his wide bedroom in two steps. I rest my hands on his forearms, tipping my head to admire the slope of his strong nose, his neatly groomed beard, and finally, those green eyes, heating to a distracting degree. I want him to kiss me. Even though I shouldn't.

"Archer…"

He presses his lips to mine, hovering there to test my response. I respond the only way I know how—I wrap my arms around his neck and shut my eyes. We make out soft and slow. Until my belly drops and my knees weaken and my mind spins and weaves a fantasy finally within reach. I hum as he pulls his mouth away from mine. My eyes refuse to open.

"Let's go outside and make a fire."

"Let's make one right here."

He smirks. "You're tired."

"I am not." I feign offense, but he's not wrong. I stifled a few yawns on the drive back. I fight one now.

"You have a glass of wine to finish. Let's do it outside." He nods toward the balcony.

"Are you crazy? It's like, zero degrees."

"It's *thirty* degrees. I have a heated blanket if you need it. Come on, Wildflower. Live a little."

"Will you promise to drive me to the hospital when I pass out from hypothermia?"

"Yes." He drops a fast kiss on my mouth. "Wait here."

He goes outside and begins doing manly things like rearranging furniture and stacking wood into the fireplace. Maybe the cold will wake me up. I want to be alert for the good stuff that will inevitably follow tonight.

Once the fire is lit, and an incredibly large, comfy-looking blanket with a cord is arranged on the outdoor sofa, he invites me out.

"Your cheeks are rosy." I touch his nose. "And your nose is chilly."

"I'll keep you warm." He presses his chilly nose to my cheek and I squeak in alarm.

We arrange ourselves in front of the fire. He sits with one leg crossed ankle-to-knee. I burrow into the heated blanket like I'm hibernating there for the winter. My teeth chatter audibly, which I assume is why he wraps his arm around me and tells me I'm "almost there."

Gradually, the blanket and fire do their jobs. He isn't superhuman, after all, and has joined me beneath the blanket. I'm now snuggled against the wall of his chest, which isn't as hard as I imagined, but quite comfy. Like he's contoured to the shape of my body.

He lifts our wineglasses, handing me mine before sipping from his. "Warm?"

"Perfect. I can't believe it." Even with the cold air nipping at my nose, I'm comfortable in enough other places to ignore it. I hide my face in his neck and inhale the luscious scent of eucalyptus.

"Feel free to fall asleep." His voice reverberates where my lips rest on his throat.

"Can't," I mumble, not wanting to admit how nice that sounds. "There is lots of acrobatic sex to be had. Plus, I have to transfer my handwritten notes to the computer while they're fresh in my mind."

"You can do that tomorrow. You need rest."

"Which one? The acrobatic sex or transferring my notes?"

"Yes." His free arm hugs me close, and I hum, content to cocoon in his warmth.

"This wine is thwarting my efforts to keep my eyes open."

"Good wine makes you sleepy." He sets his glass aside and then takes mine from my hand.

"I don't want to miss out on great sex. It's been a long week."

"Tell me about it." He chuckles. "What's your pleasure?"

"You go down on me for like, forty minutes or so..."

He growls low in his throat. "Just forty?"

"And then I'll go down on *you*." I poke his chest as he gathers me close. "And *then* we can have sex on your amazing bed until you're so exhausted you have no choice but to sleep on it."

A yawn attacks me out of nowhere. I didn't see it coming.

"Your body betrays your plans," he tells me.

"I'm not tired!" I argue as another yawn trembles my lips.

"Okay, you're not tired. But I went through the trouble of making this fire, so you have to sit out here with me for at least twenty more minutes."

"You have to keep me awake."

"I'll do my best."

I talk about my ideas for the pool area. I envision a row of loungers outfitted with fat pillows, a table between each stocked with rolled towels and glasses of water with cucumber slices in them. Lit candles in sconces on the wall in the corners. Seats built into the pool for those who want to soak, not swim.

Five minutes later, my nose is again buried in his neck, and my words are slurred from fatigue. After one more yawn, his arms hug me close. I give in and let sleep take me then and there.

CHAPTER TEN

Archer

A featherlight touch on my arm pulls me from deep sleep, but it's the scent of coffee that opens my eyes.

I blink awake, disoriented for a hot minute since I'm in a bed. Not on the couch or a hotel bed, which would be less disorienting, but my actual bed. The bed I never sleep in. Normally this room feels as impersonal as a hotel suite.

Last night, Talia fell asleep in my arms. I debated waking her and walking her back to her place, but when she sleepily murmured indiscernible words into my neck, I changed my mind. I undressed her, tugging off her boots and jeans and sweater. And bra, because it looked uncomfortable. I slipped her under my clean sheets, covered her up, and went downstairs to lock up. I corked the wine bottle, and then stood staring at the black TV screen, the prospect of mindless drivel a pale substitute for a warm, sleepy Talia.

Last night, I didn't want to sleep by myself.

I crawled into bed next to her. I don't know if it was her

rhythmic breathing or the way she smells—like cedar and vanilla, remind me to ask her what soap she uses—but I was out in no time.

Steam curls from the mug near my face. "Your morning java, Kingpin." Her voice is low and damn sexy in the morning.

I push myself onto one elbow and she pats my hair, probably trying to lay down the patch that stands up when I sleep on my side. I scrape back the strands and then accept the proffered mug.

"You sleep like the dead," she points out.

"You're one to talk," I mumble against the edge of the mug before taking a sip. Perfect. Damn. This is not a bad way to wake up. "You were comatose last night."

"I had a big day." She sits on the edge of the bed, and I scoot my legs aside to accommodate her. Her palm lands on my thigh and suddenly I don't care about coffee any longer. "It's seven thirty. I don't know what kind of hours you keep, but in case you slept in and weren't supposed to, I thought you might like a wake-up call."

I set my mug on the nightstand and scrub my face with both palms. "I get up whenever."

"*Whenever* is not a time." She smiles. She's in yesterday's clothes, and her hair is up in some sort of sloppy topknot.

"Fuck, you're cute in the morning."

She laughs and shakes her head. "And you aren't half as grouchy in the morning as one might expect."

"Why would I be grouchy?" I grab her wrist and tug. She obliges me by crawling up my body to place a kiss on the side of my mouth. "I have a supermodel in my bed. Bringing me coffee. Talking to me in a voice made of pure sin."

She laughs again, but I smother the sound with a kiss. I reverse our positions, rolling her to her back and blanketing her body with my own. "Let's finish what we didn't start last night."

She sighs. It sounds like a yes. I maneuver my hand under her sweater and encounter soft skin. I memorize each small noise she makes as I tickle my way to her belly and then her ribs and then her breasts, sadly hidden behind a bra again.

"You undressed me last night," she pants.

I pull down the cup of her bra and run my thumb over one smooth nipple. "You had on too many clothes. Kind of like now."

She moans a nonword and paws at my boxers—the only article of clothing I'm wearing. I unbutton her jeans as she gives me a raw, desperate kiss. It's frantic, wild.

God. *This woman.*

A second later, her mouth hits my chest, and she's kissing her way down my torso. I don't steer her. I don't need to. She knows where she's going. She rakes her teeth from my stomach to the hem of my boxers. With one hand she frees my pulsing, angry erection, and swallows it into her mouth with zero warning.

"Jesus. Fuck," I rasp. She's shocked me in the best way possible. I lift her hair away from her face. My ass clenches as I watch her cheeks hollow. Her nails scratch down my chest, and she sucks my cock with single-minded fervor. It's glorious. The best thing that's happened to me...maybe ever. "Like that, Wildflower. Just. Like. That."

My voice is a puny wheeze, but she doesn't need instruction anyway. In a short time, I'm reduced to a heavy-breathing, fragmented pile of sensations. By the time her mouth leaves my swollen member, I've knocked both pillows to the floor and I'm sliding into the gap between the bed and nightstand.

She climbs up my body, her sweater swiping my abandoned cock, and then lays a kiss on my mouth. When I reach for her, she hops off the bed and throws off her clothes. Literally. Her shirt goes flying across the room, her jeans, inside out, bounce against the closet door. Then she's on me, a naked woman with a mission.

I laugh.

She freezes over top of me. Blinks and then grins.

"What?"

"I love it when you laugh. You don't do it enough."

True story. I spear her hair with my fingers. "What can I say? Your mouth makes me happy."

"Is that so?" Her smile is smug. As well it should be.

I roll her to her back while clumsily but efficiently dragging my boxers off my legs. "Ecstatic."

"Archer Owen, there's no way you do *ecstatic*."

"How about orgasmic?"

She hums, her grin fading into a mischievous arc. "I know for a fact you do orgasmic very, very well."

"Don't you forget it, honey," I tell her, then I return the favor she gifted me, going down on her in a way I guarantee she won't forget.

TALIA SLIDES a soapy washcloth over my chest and down my torso, moving in circles like she's washing a car. With every other circle, she cradles my balls or massages my dick and then starts over again.

While sweat beads my brow and my mind travels to the ways I can have her in here, she talks about the night spa. And talks and talks. She's seemingly unaware I've gone rigid with need and want nothing more than to revisit her incredible mouth—with mine, and other parts of me.

I don't dare stop her while she's on a roll. If touching me and turning me into man-putty is helping her brainstorm, who am I to argue? She pauses to ask if she's overstepping by suggesting things outside of the aesthetics/design areas. The question temporarily pulls me out of my sexual stupor.

I stop the sensual massage, take the washcloth, and scrub her back. While I do, I explain as calmly as possible that I don't give a flying fuck what "area" she's advising me about, so long as she's doing it.

"Good input is good input, Wildflower." I soap her heart-shaped ass, enjoying the view as suds drip off her cheeks. She has the most beautiful skin. "You and I are collaborating. Don't draw lines around what you do the way Ed Lambert drew them around you."

She turns, her smile bright and grateful. She takes the washcloth and rinses it under the spray until the water runs clear. "I'm sorry I turned our shower into a board meeting."

I drape the washcloth over a bar in the glass-walled shower. The tiles are slate gray, and a tiled bench takes up the back half of the square. It's big, plenty of room to do a lot of fun things with her. But since we both finished each other off in bed and I have shit to do today, we'll have to wait.

Pity.

"Best board meeting I've ever had." I cradle her face and

kiss her nose. "I like how excited you are. It gives me permission to be excited too."

"You aren't usually excited?" She tilts her head in a show of concern.

"I am," I tell her honestly, "but I got in the habit of tempering my excitement in the past."

"Because of your dad," she guesses correctly.

"He likes to challenge the decisions I make. Rather than rejoice in my successes, he often criticizes them. I became accustomed to it and prepared accordingly."

"So you're never excited?"

"The last time I remember feeling vibrating, unyielding excitement was with Chance."

"Who's Chance?"

I shut off the water and squeegee droplets from her arms. "Your body is perfection."

"Focus." She turns my chin to her face. I kiss her. Slowly, intentionally.

"Focusing on your face doesn't keep me from thinking of how beautiful you are. Is there a single part on you that's not?"

"I could say the same to you." She pokes my stomach and I clench my abs. She rewards me with a husky laugh. She halts the sound immediately, like she didn't mean to make it. "Who's Chance?"

"Not who. What." I touch her nose. "Chance was the first club I opened." I push open the glass door and pull a towel for her and one for me off the shelf. "It's in Columbus. Nice place. Classy and ritzy and sufferingly generic. But I was in love with it."

She follows me into the bedroom where we talk as we

dress—she into her clothes from yesterday, while assuring me she's going to change the second she goes next door, and I into a gray pair of slacks and a button-down purple shirt Vivian and Nate bought me for Christmas. I debate on a matching tie before deciding *what the hell* and knot it around my neck.

I tell Talia how my style has both adapted and matured since my original attempt at selling nightlife. She follows me downstairs where I make us fresh coffee, still talking. She listens. Not with her eyes wandering off to the side like she's bored, not with her mouth opening to interrupt like she's impatiently awaiting her turn to speak. She listens like she's invested. Not necessarily because I'm paying her, but possibly because she's genuinely interested in what I have to say.

How...different.

Refreshing.

Addicting.

"I have several places to go today," I tell her before sipping my hot coffee, "including a visit to Owen headquarters. I have an overdue meeting with my assistant."

"Lynn," she says.

"You really were listening."

"I find you fascinating."

I could get used to this. I cup her butt as I lean in for a kiss. The kiss grows hot, our coffee mugs forgotten for a few distracting, moaning, panting minutes. Finally, she pushes both hands against my chest, stopping me short of saying to hell with my appointments and taking her on this counter.

Tempting. *Verrrry* tempting.

"What are you doing today?" I ask, handing her the mug. "You can take that next door and bring it back later."

"This sounds like a trick."

"It is."

That laugh again. Damn, I'm growing used to the sound, and it's way too soon to look forward to anything with her. Way, way too fucking soon.

"I'm going to figure out what to do next. Study the company roster you emailed me so I know who to contact about what. Do you want a report or a plan? What's my budget?"

"You do you, Wildflower. You don't have to clear anything with me on design. Talk to Jarod about budget. Unfortunately, that's a necessary evil. We have to make money, after all, or what in the hell are we doing with our lives?"

I reach for the square black dish sitting at the edge of the counter and hand her a key fob. "My car."

She's already shaking her head.

"You might need to go somewhere. Or explore."

"I can't drive your"—she makes a face like she's terrified—"Mercedes around town."

"Why not?"

She dangles the key fob between our faces. "Because it's a Mercedes!"

"That doesn't make any sense." I pocket my money clip and grab my coat off the back of a chair. "You should want to drive it *because* it's a Mercedes."

"I don't need—"

I press my finger to her lips and then give her one more

brief (too brief) kiss. I'm kept from further kissing when my phone dings.

"My real estate agent is here," I tell Talia. "She's driving me around today to help me find a building for another idea I have. I'll take a car home."

Okay, one more kiss—I can't help myself—and another gulp of coffee, and then I leave Talia Richards alone in my kitchen.

She promises to lock up, and reluctantly, when I give her my sternest frown, she promises she'll think about taking the car.

CHAPTER ELEVEN

Talia

I resisted borrowing Archer's car for a week. It was a busy week for him, so on the nights I've seen him (two) we had sex (two times per night) and then we hung out the next day until he went to work. He spends a lot of time shuttling between Columbus and Clear Ridge, and even stayed overnight at a hotel one of those evenings.

He didn't call, but he texted me a few times. Usually a "Good night, Wildflower" or similar sentiment. I was tempted to ask if this-or-that was okay but then remembered the conversation we had in his shower. He told me to do my thing. So, I did my thing and checked with Jarod on budget.

I've spent time researching how to establish an LLC. The idea hooked onto some ambitious part of me and I can't shake it. Neither my father's warnings about stability nor Archer's comment about how entrepreneurship comes with its own set of troubles scares me. The idea of my own business where I do what I want when I want tempts me like the largest, shiniest jewel in a treasure chest.

I've been working for other people since I was sixteen years old. I worked as a hostess in the restaurant my mom managed, and I worked as a receptionist one summer at the company that employed my dad at the time. I worked retail. I manned the phone lines at a vitamin company. I was a "customer service concierge" at an aquarium.

Lotus Leaf was supposed to be my forever job. Not because I loved it, but because I didn't want to start over again. Working with Archer isn't technically starting over. I'm doing what I did for Ed but with more freedom, and, face it, the company I'm keeping nowadays is leaps and bounds better. I spend most of my hours during the day planning and then communicating my ideas to Archer's dream team. I spend most evenings searching online for styles and ideas for the perfect design for his debut as a night-spa kingpin.

By Sunday I'm desperately in need of a day off. I set my own hours, but I haven't convinced myself to *take* a day off. I feel as if I need to earn my right to be here—in this deluxe townhouse and working on the most innovative, exciting project I've ever collaborated on. By noon, I'm on my third cup of coffee and have three different websites open. I'm comparing prices for the loungers for the wading pool. Archer wasn't kidding about the budget. Jarod is as immovable as the Rock of Gibraltar. He gave me the numbers and warned me not to veer from the budget by a single dollar. He then explained margins of error and something-something. I tuned him out. I can stay within budget, and I'm sure his comment about not going over by one dollar was hyperbole. I mean, I can toss in an extra dollar personally.

My cell phone rings, pulling my attention from my online price comparison. I'm not sure if I should ignore a work call or take it. I'm crap at establishing new boundaries. Luckily, it's Calista calling, so I answer right away.

"Lis!" I've called her twice this week, and both times she was at a work thing and promised to call me later. She didn't right away, but I'll forgive her. I'm sure she's incredibly busy arguing with Julio over which beans to use for the three-bean chili.

"I'm sorry I haven't called. I picked up two extra shifts this week. Webber quit—don't ask," she tells me before I can ask. "I'm heading to work for a double today. I haven't had a second to myself in two weeks," she shouts over the wind. I hear music from the car stereo. I picture her chatting on speakerphone, wearing her white chef's coat, the gloriously warm Florida sunshine bathing her arms in golden, buttery light.

Mmm.

"Describe how sunny it is there," I say, my tone wistful. "In graphic detail." Outside my home office windows, wind rattles the bare tree limbs. I shudder.

My heartless sister laughs at my plight. "Ohio not treating you well, sis?"

"It's gray here. Like, all the time. I need warmth!"

"It's winter here too, in case you forgot. Fifty-eight degrees today."

"Tropical," I sigh, earning another of her wonderful laughs. "I miss you. What's new?"

She tells me about her latest creations in our home kitchen, and I picture each dish, bursting with color, beautifully plated. My stomach growls. I had groceries delivered, but I'm due a meal out. Archer's been working too much to invite me out to dinner again, which is a shame. There are a lot of cool places around here. He promised me we'd go out next week when he's not so slammed.

"What about you?" she asks. "Anything new going on other than the kitchen you are definitely wasting?"

"I'm not wasting it! I've been cooking for myself all week."

"What did you cook, Tal?"

I'm quiet.

"*Tal.*"

"Mostly sandwiches, but I did turn on the stove to heat some soup."

She groans like it hurts her heart to hear I'm misusing the fancy stovetop for something as pedestrian as boxed soup. Hey, we can't all be Giada De Laurentiis. I flip the light off as I step out of my office. My back is tight from hunching over the desk. I need to escape my luxurious four-walled cell.

Making a snap decision to take myself to lunch, I drop the key fob into my purse and collect my coat.

"What are you doing today?" she asks.

"I'm on my way out. I haven't been exploring since I arrived, and I'm climbing the walls."

"Good for you. You're your own boss! Take advantage of it."

"I'm quickly learning being my own boss means everything rests on my shoulders."

"Well, don't turn into Papa on me. He doesn't know when to stop."

"How is he?" I ask, my heart squeezing. Ever since I

found out he was on medication, I've been worried. "I should call him."

I'm sort of avoiding him. I don't want to hear his opinions on my life choices and I definitely don't want him to offer to send me money again. Archer's dad and my dad are two totally different people, but they both manage to insert themselves into our lives uninvited.

"He's fine," she says casually enough that I believe her. "I'm taking dinner to him tonight after my shift. I'll probably sleep over, considering I'll be dead on my feet by then. But, sometimes that's nice, you know? I like to curl up in the blanket Mama crocheted and watch TV. It's hard to miss her, but it's nice to remember her."

At the front door, I pause, feeling tender and emotional at the mention of Mama. Losing her was hard on all of us. Papa hasn't been the same since she died. I remember her crocheting, her fingers deftly moving to loop the yarn into complicated stripes or geometric shapes. I look down at my own hands and smile sadly. I use my hands to peck on a keyboard most of the time.

"Okay, I'm here." Lis interrupts my melancholy. "I have to pick up shrimp and scallops before the dinner rush, and I can't let them sit in the car longer than strictly necessary. Enjoy your day out. *Loveyoumeanitbye!*"

"*Loveyoumeanitbye!*" I echo the sentiment and disconnect. Shaking off the sad proves harder to do when I step into a world of cold and gray rather than gold and green. The air is frigid, but hey, I'm out of the house. I bleep the key fob for Archer's car and settle into the chilled leather. I tap the push button to start the engine, take a moment to adjust the seat and turn on the heater—and the seat warmer. In almost no time my butt is toasty and I'm ready to see the world...or at least Clear Ridge.

After visiting a few neighboring spas and salons with spa treatments on the menu, I have a better idea of his competition. My mind is filled with overlapping ideas, and my notebook too. After I left each establishment, I scribbled every thought I'd had inside.

Now I'm in Grand Marin, the open-air live-work shopping area with luxury loft apartments, the one Archer pointed out as Nate's doing. Evidently, his fiancée, Vivian, runs this tiny town within a town. I'm impressed. Like Clear Ridge itself, Grand Marin feels both wealthy and elite, yet manages to be undeniably welcoming.

I step out of the car and lock it with the fob, angling toward the furniture store on the corner. It's massive and, I'm sure, incredibly expensive. I plan on talking them into giving me as close to their wholesale price as possible if I find what I need. Halfway up the sidewalk, a woman stops in front of me and cocks her head.

"Talia Richards," she says with unmasked confidence. It's been a while since I met Vivian Vandemark, but I remember her curious smile like it was yesterday.

"Vivian. How are you?"

"I'm well." She doesn't close in for a hug, but she does touch my arm with one gloved hand in greeting. "What are you doing in Ohio?"

I blink, trying to decide if she's fishing for facts she already knows or if she *doesn't* know what I'm doing here. I've been living next door to Archer for a week. He's with Nate today. Surely he told his brothers I'm here? I'm not a secret...at least I don't think I am. I debate telling Vivian the truth for two seconds before I decide Archer isn't hiding me and tell her anyway.

"Archer hired me to help with a new facility he's opening. I'm about to head in there"—I point at the furniture store —"and check out their options for patios and pools."

"*Really.*" Her brown eyes spark with interest.

"Loungers, in particular," I add, being purposefully obtuse.

"Not what I'm *really*-ing, honey." She loops one arm around mine, leads me in the opposite direction, and asks where I parked. When I point out Archer's Mercedes, she walks us directly to it and settles into the passenger seat. Once I start the car, she speaks. "They don't sell patio or pool furniture back there, but I know a place up the road that does. I'll come with you," she says with a smile, as if she hasn't already ensconced herself into my day. "Then we can grab lunch and a drink, and you can explain how the second-most emotionally reserved man I've met came to hiring you to work for him. Have you eaten yet?"

"Not yet." I like everything about her. She's forward, she's no-nonsense, and what's behind that "second-most" comment? I also like knowing a different version of Archer than she does. It's not the first time I've heard her describe him like he's a safe that can't be breached. Little does she know, I have the combination.

Half an hour later, we give up on the furniture store she suggested. They're high-end with a friendly, knowledgeable staff who agreed to work with me on price (after I slipped the Owen name into conversation), but they don't have what I'm looking for.

"I'm picky," I explain to Vivian when I feel her questioning stare on the side of my face.

"About furniture or everything? I want to choose the right lunch spot for us."

"My sister's a chef, so I'm pickier about food than anything. She spoils me."

"I must meet her," Vivian says as if it's an inevitability.

Eyes on her phone, she lists nearby options and menu highlights of local eateries as the weather worsens. The rain started when we walked into the furniture store, and by the time I navigate into traffic on the main road, it turns into sleet. Rain I can drive in, so I don't fret. Sleety snow is cold rain, right? I totally have this. I manually adjust the heat to warm the interior of the car while Vivian mentions how Nate hates olives but shakes up a dirty martini whenever she wants one at home.

"You two seem like a good match." The automatic windshield wipers increase in speed as ice falls from the sky and ticks the glass audibly.

"He's the best." She doesn't say he's responsible for the earth orbiting the sun, but she doesn't have to. Her love for him fills the inside of the car like rose-scented perfume.

"Have you set a date for the wedding yet?"

"May eighth. Nate asked Archer and Benji to be his groomsmen but refuses to pick which one of them is his best man. He told them to flip a coin."

I smile. There's something really sweet about not being able to choose which of his brothers should be his best man. Picturing Archer in a tux is a nice vision, and one I hold on to while she describes the venue and the reception. I automatically slide myself into the picture as Archer's plus-one, but that's a stretch, isn't it? Working for him is temporary, plus I'm going home to Florida when the job is done. I have no work lined up after the spa, and if I do pursue working for myself, it could be years before I can count on a steady annual income.

Gah. That was a depressing thought.

Rather than drag Vivian down with my worries, I say, "Where are you—" but before I can finish with *going for the honeymoon?*, the car is spinning.

I squeeze the steering wheel with both hands, watching with alarm as we slide sideways like the road is a nonstick skillet and the tires were recently oiled. We face oncoming traffic for a terrifying moment before I yank the wheel to avoid several swerving cars. Horns blare as the Mercedes careens in its own preferred direction—thankfully turning us so we're facing the right way once again. Instinctively, even though I know better, I step on the brakes and send us sliding.

"No brakes!" Vivian shouts. "Let up." I do as I'm told and steer us toward the entrance of a shopping center. Once we're off the road and bracketed by concrete curbs, she instructs, "Now! Brakes!"

I tap them gently but firmly. We skid to a stop, the side of one tire colliding with a concrete divider. There is a terrible screeching noise, and my left wrist slams into the door. Tingles shoot up my arm and down into each of my fingers simultaneously.

I cry out, cradling my wrist and taking my hand off the steering wheel to do it. My foot is glued to the brake, my entire body shaking from the adrenaline coursing through my veins. I'm in too much shock to register if I'm in pain.

"Are you okay?" Vivian reaches over to put the car into park before touching my right arm.

I nod, and that feels like an out-of-body experience. "I think so."

"Can you pull over? Or do you want me to do it?" She points at an empty area in the parking lot.

"Yeah, I'm good." I put both hands on the wheel and discover that my left wrist definitely *isn't* good. A pathetic sound exits my lips. I protect my left arm by curling it against my chest, and use my right to gingerly—ever so gingerly—steer us out of the entrance of the parking lot and to an empty parking space. Belatedly, I check on my passenger. "Are you all right?"

"I'm totally fine. Don't worry about me. I'll call Nate." She gives me a reassuring smile that doesn't look as shaky as I feel. I have the idea Vivian has survived worse things in life than a fender bender.

Archer

Nate and I drove to Owen HQ together, so we drive back the same way. He's talking about his latest project in between inquiring about mine. As always, the conversation is easy. Hands on the steering wheel of his really fucking nice Tesla, he mentions how the weather is shit today. Rather than comment I might buy myself one of these cars, I curl my fists on my legs and tell him what I haven't told anyone yet.

"I hired Talia Richards."

He takes his eyes from the road for a second to send me a disbelieving glance. "Talia Richards, the spa designer?"

"Yeah. She used to work for Ed Lambert, some blowhard who overlooked her for a raise in favor of giving it to his nephew. He fired her after she poured green juice on his head, so I offered her a job."

Nate laughs, a big, jovial sound filling the cab of the car. "I like her already."

"She's here." I study my brother's profile. His eyebrows climb his forehead. "I'm letting her stay in the townhouse next to mine so she can be onsite for the design."

"Is she staying there, or with you?" He half-smiles.

"Bit of both."

"You like her."

"More than I should," I admit. When I'm away, I miss her. When I'm busy, I miss her. When I'm with her, I dread the day when I won't see her again. In short, I'm fucked.

"You must. You don't tell me about the women you date."

"I don't know if you can call it dating." I watch out the windshield as ice bounces off the car. We're almost to Grand Marin, where we'll have lunch with Vivian if she's available. I thought about calling Talia, but I'm not sure she wants to brave this icy crap. I'll bring her takeout instead. Feed it to her in bed.

"Well, whatever it is, is it working?"

"I don't know," I answer, my frown genuine.

She's going back to Florida. I know better than to get attached. We've done this before. After I met her at the fundraiser, I was without her for months. I focused on work and tried to keep my thoughts professional. An impossibility now that I know how she feels beneath me; now that I have heard her high, tight sighs whenever I drive into her.

Damn. I blink hard, snapping myself out of the memory. Maybe I'll skip lunch and go home to her instead. Nate's phone rings, and he touches the screen on the dash to answer.

"Hey, Viv."

"Nate." Her voice shakes. "I was in a car accident. I'm fine."

My older brother's spine goes stiff in his seat. Equally alarmed, I sit up straighter in mine. Her assessment that she's "fine" hasn't set either of us at ease.

"Where are you?" he demands, checking the mirrors for openings to steer out of traffic and go to where she is as quickly and safely as possible.

"I'm in Archer's car in Penny and Dime's parking lot."

My car? My stomach gives a violent toss. There's only one reason Viv would be in my car.

"Is Talia okay?" I ask stiffly, my fists balled tighter than before.

"She's fine. Her wrist is hurt, but we're in one piece."

"Put me on speaker," I growl.

"Okay. You're live."

"You okay?"

"Yes, Kingpin. But your car—"

"I don't give a fuck about the car. We're on our way," I say. Nate slides across two lanes of traffic, earning loud honks for his efforts. Unfazed, he makes an illegal U-turn. The tires wobble, but we don't slide.

"Be careful," Talia says. "Okay?"

"Nate's driving. See you in five."

"It's slick, Nate," Viv warns, fear outlining her voice.

"I know, honey." He carefully navigates through both low visibility and slow-moving cars. "Hang tight."

It takes *eight* minutes to get where we're going. Despite Vivian's and Talia's assurances that they're both okay, my shoulders are rigid with tension. Nate notices and assures me everything's all right, but I notice his shoulders are strung bow-tight too.

Nice try, big brother.

In the lot, a handful of cars are parked by the restaurant's entrance. I spot my Mercedes, parked slightly crooked, and point it out. Before Nate has put the car in park, I'm out of his car and tugging on the driver's door of my own. The interior of the car blasts me with warmth.

I kneel down and take inventory of her, my heart thrashing in my chest as ice and snow rain down on my head. Talia is dressed in jeans and a sweater, and a brown leather jacket. Her hair is down, the ends curling and damp from the weather. She's cradling her wrist, her smile wan.

"I should have checked the weather app," she tells me.

"*I* should have checked the weather app," Vivian insists.

"Accidents happen," Nate says, as he opens the passenger door to kneel before Vivian. He kisses her, dropping his forehead onto hers, relief emanating off him in waves. Or maybe that's me.

Taking Talia's wrist tenderly in hand, I move it. Her yelp of pain sends a flood of concern into my system. I want to yell at her for leaving the safety of the townhouse at the same time I want to kick my own ass for not being there for her so I could drive. Instead, I ask, "Did you hit your head?"

"No." Her bottom lip trembles. "Sorry about your car. I'll pay for the repairs."

"You won't," I assure her, my tone lethal. I feel both Nate's and Vivian's curious stares on me, but I don't take my eyes off Talia. "We're going to the hospital."

"No. I'm fine."

"Wildflower."

"Kingpin." Her eyebrows lift and we have a stare-down. I'm hyperaware of the bemusement on my brother's and future sister-in-law's faces over Talia's shoulder. I don't normally bring girlfriends around—if that's what Talia is—so they haven't seen my protective side often, if ever.

"It's probably a sprain," Vivian assures me. "No need for a trip to the ER, but a doctor's appointment might be a good idea."

Talia smirks as if saying, "*See?*"

"We'll ice it at home," I tell her, grateful when she nods her agreement.

Nate walks Viv to his Tesla and then stands at the driver's side front tire of my Mercedes. "Looks drivable," he tells me. "You have a hell of a beauty mark on the hubcap."

Talia opens her mouth, I presume to say she's sorry. I shoot daggers from my eyes in a silent warning that she'd better not apologize.

"Good to see you again." He bends down and extends a hand. She reaches over her injured left arm with her right and clasps his palm. "We'll follow you a while, just to be safe."

"That's not necessary." I help Talia to her feet so I can walk her around to the other side of the car.

Proving he is as stubborn as I am, Nate smiles and informs me, "Well, I didn't ask."

CHAPTER TWELVE

Talia

Archer heeded Vivian's advice about not taking me to the ER, but he insisted on a visit to urgent care. Two hours later, he parks his dinged Mercedes at the curb.

Before I can step out of the car, he's there, helping me to my feet even though I don't need him to. I don't argue. He's on a mission.

The conclusion at urgent care was that my wrist was definitely sprained, the injury mild. They wrapped it, which I need to do for at least two more days, longer if the pain increases. The doc felt confident I'd be back to 100 percent in one to two weeks, but cautioned me about being overconfident too soon.

"I was serious about the repairs," I tell Archer as he palms my back and walks us to the entryway.

"Don't," he warns.

"I wrecked your Mercedes," I remind him. He's not reacting appropriately. The car's in worse shape than I am.

When I finally got a look at the front of it, I felt even worse for taking it out. "I should have stayed home instead of—"

At the entryway, he scoops my face into his hands, his gaze intent but soft. "Enough about the damn car."

I nod, moved by the tenderness in his voice. I turn toward my entryway, but he stops me by steering my hips toward his side of the building. "You're staying with me."

"That's not—"

"Go." He pokes my back with two fingers. I roll my eyes as I walk up the stairs and then inside his townhouse. He helps me take off my coat, navigating carefully around my wrapped wrist. I plop my purse on the island and turn, prepared to tell him I have a sprained wrist and not a broken one. That he's overreacting and doesn't have to worry.

"Archer—" I start.

He cradles my jaw in one wide palm. Then he whispers, "Shut up," before slanting his lips over mine.

I don't resist. I fist his sweater with my good hand and tug him closer, aligning my body to the length of his. His tongue is warm, his nose is cold. His fingers dive into my hair, and I lift my arms to loop them around his neck. In our haste to hold each other, he bumps my injured wrist. I whimper into his mouth, and he pulls away, his eyes sparking with a mixture of concern, regret, and anger.

"I'm fine, honest."

He holds my left arm tenderly, turning it this way and that as his eyebrows close in over his nose. "The eight-minute drive with Nate felt like an eternity. Until I saw you were okay with my own two eyes, I wasn't sure what to believe. Seeing you was like taking a big breath of fresh air after being underwater too long. Wildflower"—his voice cracks—"you scared the shit out of me."

"I'm sorry." He truly looks agonized, which I don't understand. It was a minor accident, one that could have been so much worse.

"The apologies are going to stop too." His hand in my hair, his fingers tousle the strands. He moves to the cabinet and pulls out a bottle of Advil. "Two every four hours. I'll be here to remind you. In the meantime"—he tips his chin toward the stairs—"go to my bed."

Archer

I need to slow my roll.

First off, Talia's an adult and can take care of herself. Second, I know she's okay because I have not only her assurances, but a doctor's diagnosis as well. Advil, ice, don't overuse the wrist, and she'll be as good as new.

But Nate's and Vivian's stunned—dare I say overjoyed—expressions keep replaying in my head. They're enjoying the hell out of this, probably saying to each other, *"Well, well. Look who has a girlfriend."*

The word hammers me again as I roll down the covers in my bed. *Girlfriend.* I can't have a girlfriend who lives in Miami. Talia is going home as soon as my spa opens. At the rate things are going, it'll happen sooner rather than later. Then what am I going to fucking do?

Hearing her shaking voice over the speakerphone rocked

me to the core. Honestly, that's freaking me out more than the girlfriend thing. In the past, my relationships have been casual. What I'm feeling for Talia can only be described as intense.

I frown.

"This is unnecessary," she complains as she looks down at my bed. "Unless you are going to strip me bare and make me forget my worries." She sidles over to me, raising her arms to hold me. I take in the bandage, remember the way my stomach flopped and heart nearly exploded upon hearing about the accident, and hold her away from me with my hands on her hips.

"Seriously?" she asks.

"You've been working nonstop. You're going to rest."

The heat in her eyes fades to hurt. I don't mean to hurt her feelings, but I can't make love to her right now. Not because she's injured, which we could work around. There are too many emotions swirling around inside me. Sinking into her heat with my mind on how much I don't want her to leave is a recipe for a two-tiered disaster cake.

She drops her arms and shakes her head. "I'm going back to my place. This is silly."

It's more than that, but I'm not willing to define it.

"I'll come with you."

"Archer—"

"Benji's parents died in a car accident," I snap. "It happens. Don't act like it couldn't have."

She twists her mouth in sympathy.

"I haven't thought of that in a long, long time. Until today." Fresh fear electrifies my arms as I picture what could have happened to Talia.

"I hate that for him." Her eyelids lower. "Losing a parent is hard. Losing two would be unbearable."

She seems to fortify herself then, nodding curtly as she palms my arm with her right hand. "I'm going back to my place. I can do a little work while I'm there. I want to change into something more comfortable, anyway."

"You work too much," I bark, my frustration at its peak. Her pushing me away reminds me there is a bigger goodbye hovering on the horizon like a doomsday meteor. Her mouth is taut, her eyes tired. And *tired* is a nice word for it. She looks completely exhausted. "You have to pace yourself. I have received emails this week from you with timestamps at eleven p.m., two a.m., and four a.m. It's ridiculous."

"You're one to talk," she huffs around a humorless laugh. "You work more than I do."

"You're not me."

"And you're not my father," she says sharply. "My hours are none of your business. There is a contract between us, in case you've forgotten. Nowhere in it does it say you can mandate when I do or don't work."

"Nowhere in it does it say you can borrow my car or have sex with me either, but we've done that."

"And maybe that was a mistake." Her voice is hard. "You promised not to apply pressure when I arrived here. What happened?"

She happened. She happened all over the place.

"I feel..." I swallow hard and try to come up with a way to reverse out of the argument we're having. "Responsible for you."

"I'm not your responsibility, Archer. I'm your consultant."

Such a dry way to describe what we mean to each other. Pissed about the sterile term, as well as her hinting that we shouldn't have slept together, I say, "Take the Advil with you. Two every four—"

"Hours. I know. I can set an alarm on my phone. I don't need you to remind me."

She walks downstairs. I stand in my empty bedroom, hands propped on my hips, looking at the bed we could be rolling around in if I would have agreed. I have many valid reasons for refusing her. And, hell, maybe some space would be good for us. We've gone from a long-distance working relationship to one intense, sex-filled Florida night to practically living together, all in the span of a few weeks.

I'll give her tonight to herself.

We can reconfigure in the morning.

CHAPTER THIRTEEN

Talia

I'm aware of the throbbing in my wrist moments before I open my eyes. It's sunny today, and the beams shine through the balcony doors, warming the bottom of the bed. I sit up and stretch my arms out to absorb some of that warmth, smiling in gratitude. Then I recall the argument with Archer last night and frown instead.

He told me I work too much, which tripped a trigger inside me. I heard his accusation in my father's voice, though Archer was far more commanding than Papa would have been. No, if it was Papa, he would have wound me up in cotton batting and tucked me into a corner. Archer's more the type to stand guard at his bedroom door and refuse to let me leave.

He did let me leave, though, and after I said some not-so-nice and not-so-true things to him about how we shouldn't have slept together. Sure, and it's also possible to stop a speeding locomotive with a butterfly net.

I dress in a pair of joggers and a slouchy sweatshirt—carefully, not that it matters. I wince every time I move my wrist, which happens a lot while pulling on my clothes. Downstairs, I aim for the coffee maker, figuring I will start my morning brew before pouring a glass of water and swallowing some Advil. Then I'll go to Archer's and wake him up with a cup and another apology.

I'm a big girl. I can admit when I overreact.

In the kitchen, I open a drawer and pull out the coffee filters, jumping when I see a human man lying on my sofa. Startled, I drop the filters and gulp huge breaths of air while attempting to regulate my breathing.

I didn't expect Archer Owen to be asleep on my sofa after I left him standing in his own bedroom last night. What did he do? Sneak in? Although, I guess that's not accurate given he has a key. I *tsk* under my breath, finish preparing the coffee, and swallow two Advil. He doesn't budge.

In the attached living room, I stand over his sleeping form. He's stupidly attractive lying on his back, arms folded over his chest, mouth parted slightly. He was trying to take care of me yesterday. I tried to seduce him and he told me no, as if I was too fragile to make that decision on my own. My father treats me like I'm fragile, and I resent it. But after a full night's sleep and finding a sleeping sentinel on the couch, I remind myself he's not Papa.

Archer and I have undeniable physical attraction to each other and a camaraderie bordering friendship. He was worried, and communicated it by being demanding. I was insulted, and communicated it by retreating. We both handled last night poorly.

The coffeepot sputters, the brew complete. I pull down

two mugs from the cabinet and hear a sharp inhale from the other room. He stretches before pushing himself to sitting. His shoes are off, his button-down shirt untucked from his badly wrinkled pants—his outfit is a poor excuse for pajamas. He scrubs his beard with one hand and regards me with sleepy eyes.

"Sleepwalk much?" I ask as I carry in a mug of coffee for each of us in one hand—my good hand.

"How's your wrist?" is his response.

"It'll be fine."

He takes the mug, and I sit next to him. We sip in silence before he breaks it. "Your couch sucks."

I let out a small laugh. "Well, you could have slept on your own."

"I'm sorry about—"

"Don't," I mutter in my best Archer Owen voice. "I over-reacted."

"I have no right to tell you what to do," he says to his mug.

"Vivian checked in on me last night. Text. She asked how I was and then asked if you were behaving like Nate, who she says is a worrywart."

"Protective," he corrects. "We protect the people we care about." He makes this admission easily, reaching for my knee and squeezing it. "I'll drive you wherever you need to go until your wrist heals."

"You don't have time to be my chauffeur."

"I do." His scowl is a warning.

"If I need to go somewhere, I'll call Robert."

"I'd prefer it if you leaned on me while you're here." He studies my face like he's looking for clues. "Can you do that?"

My heart buoys. He didn't command. He asked. Having options means a lot to me. I nod.

"Good. For the record, I don't think you're weak or incapable. I'd just feel better if I knew you were in good hands." His mouth slips into a sideways smile. "And we both know how much you like my hands."

Reminding me how well we fit together physically was a wise tactic. I do like his hands. All of him, really. His bossy side is fine as long as he's not trampling my autonomy.

"Thanks for staying. Though I'm not sure you'd have woken up if there was an emergency."

"I wake up for important things." He sounds mildly offended before lifting his mug. "I called a lawyer for you."

"Why?" I round my eyes. "Are you suing me?"

"*No*," he says with exaggerated patience. "A lawyer to help you set up an LLC for your new business. If you're still interested. Kathleen is knowledgeable. You'll like her."

He stands from the couch and stretches again, his shirt parting at the bottom to reveal a slice of tanned, toned belly. *Drool.*

"Are you leaving?"

"No." He watches me from his height as if debating. "You want me to?"

"Would it matter if I did?"

His lips twitch. "Probably not."

ARCHER STAYED the rest of that day at my place. He insisted on showering with me so I wouldn't be tempted to use my sprained wrist to wash. He spent a lot of time washing my breasts and ass, but I didn't complain. After, he lowered to his knees and put his mouth between my legs. I forgot I had a wrist at all.

The following day, he drove me to his lawyer's office. He was right about Kathleen. She was very cool. She had a pencil stuck in her wild blond hair and talked ninety miles a minute. She helped narrow down the ideas I had for the name of my business. We settled on Talia's Design, LLC. (Evidently, "incorporated" is something else entirely.)

My wrist healed fairly quickly. There was no need to wrap it for the remainder of the week, which was nice. By the following week, I was typing on a keyboard without issues...as long as I didn't overwork it, my wrist didn't hurt. Archer worked from home—my home—bringing his laptop and phone with him and setting up at the coffee table.

I didn't argue. I liked hearing his low voice murmur from the other room. He is becoming a staple while I'm here, but in my defense, I don't have much of a life outside of this townhouse.

The next Monday, the weather has turned from ice and snow to sunshine (albeit really cold sunshine), and Archer broke the news that he had to drive to Owen HQ in Columbus. He promised to be home by dinnertime and kissed me goodbye.

By four o'clock I'm elbow-deep in lasagna—not literally, but it's a messy process. The recipe is Lis's, and she gave me way too many instructions. I went to town—driving is much easier without the sky falling, by the way—in search of fresh pasta. I had to go to three markets, but I finally found what I was looking for.

My front door opens as I push a dollop of ricotta cheese

off the spoon and onto the final layer of lasagna.

"Present for you." Archer swaggers into the kitchen, manila envelope in hand. He doesn't say anything for a moment. He's watching me so intently, I have the irrational worry that I've chosen the wrong recipe for dinner.

"Do you not like lasagna?"

"I like lasagna." He rounds the island and palms my hip. Then he kisses me softly while I hold my ricotta-covered fingers out of the way and kiss him back. His moss-green eyes lock on mine before he offers the envelope. "Here you go."

I run to the sink and clean my hands, and then tear open the envelope with all the self-restraint of a kid on Christmas morning.

My LLC is official.

"Oh my God!" I leap into his arms, and he catches me with a laugh. He sets me on my feet, and I hold the paperwork in both hands, staring in awe and not knowing what to do with my excitement.

"I thought we'd go out and celebrate."

"Oh." I look down at my partially completed dinner. "I can finish layering and pop this into the fridge. It'll keep for a few days." I think. I'll have to double-check with Lis.

"No." He sends me a warm look that is less predatory and more familiar. "This is better. I'll be back with wine. And then I have something to ask you. Red or white?"

My mind is hooked on the what-he-wants-to-ask-me part, so it takes me a beat to confirm, "Um, red."

He leaves. I finish up the pan of lasagna and slide it into the preheated oven. By the time he returns and pours us two glasses, I suspect I know what feelings he was maneuvering around when he first walked in.

From the *how was your day* to the cozy home-cooked meal to the moment we're bellied up at the island sipping a delicious red zin, we've turned incredibly domestic.

Archer

"The last time I had homemade lasagna at home was..." I was about to say when I was a kid, but now that I think about it, that was catered for an event. "Have I *ever*?"

Talia gasps in shock. She's slouched over the island, her elbow on the surface. "That's so sad. Child abuse, really."

I laugh. My upbringing was far from abusive.

"Are you going to ask me what you wanted to ask me?" she prompts with a smile. I wondered if she was going to notice I hadn't. I wondered if I was going to actually ask her. It's a big ask.

I swallow a mouthful of red wine, which doesn't go a long way to quenching my dry throat.

"My parents are having a dinner," I announce firmly. "Vivian said I should invite you."

Talia's eyebrows lift.

"Not that I wouldn't have invited you," I add. "Although, I probably wouldn't have, but not because of you. I don't take my coworkers to dinner at my parents'. Usually." I feel like a nervous seventeen-year-old version of myself, sweating through my tux while standing on the stoop to pick up Jenny Carrington for prom.

"What kind of dinner?"

"Dad founded Owen Construction in February. We

always celebrate. Vivian attended last year, and Cristin has come for years with Benji. She's practically part of the family and has been for a decade."

Talia brightens. "Cris and Vivian will be there?"

"Yes. They are dying for you to come, according to Viv. Benji told me Cris has an epic girl crush on you. That's a direct quote."

"That's sweet."

"That's Cris." She was like a sister to me for years, and soon, I'm sure she and Benji will get married, and then she will be my sister by law too.

"And you're sure this is a good idea?" She tilts her head. I don't know if she's asking because she recalls me mentioning how I haven't brought a woman home with me since college, or for some other reason—like maybe we shouldn't cross the meet-the-parents line.

I decided while she's here we're going to enjoy each other. Sure, I had a freak-out a week or so ago—an overreaction. We've moved on.

"I want you to come. I can't keep you sequestered here for another three weeks without you going stir crazy. You need some girl time."

"Tell me about it. I ruined my one chance at an outing with Vivian by spraining my wrist." She holds up her perfectly healed arm and wiggles her fingers. At the reminder of her accident, my heart seizes. I know she's fine, but the terror of what could have happened lingers in my periphery. "Does your mom like wine? I'll bring a bottle."

"My mom keeps wineries in business with her massive stash. Just bring yourself."

CHAPTER FOURTEEN

Talia

We pull up to a house that is so huge, it can only be described as palatial. I immediately question my outfit choice. Following Archer's lead of jeans and a button-down, I opted for dark-wash jeans and a white shirt with a sweater layered over top. The grandness of his family's home suggests a formal dress would be more appropriate.

"I didn't know I was meeting the queen." I tip my head back to take in the gargantuan structure. Balconies, columns, a zillion windows...it's beautiful. The front door is both wide and tall with ornate bronze handles and detailing. Bloomless rosebushes flank the walkway, and tall, naked trees peer at us from around the sides of the house. A few proud pines are holding their needles.

"It's not a fancy ordeal," he assures me, but I have my doubts. He grew up in this environment. Fancy could be his norm.

Me, I grew up with enough, but never too much. I was

aware of how hard my parents worked for their money, and I knew it didn't come easy. My mom worked late nights at the restaurant to afford everything her teenage daughters needed. She helped me buy my first used car. My compact Chevy was an embarrassment to me when I first got my driver's license, but I smile whenever I think of that teal-blue-with-rust-holes monstrosity. I wonder what kind of car Archer drove as a teen. It's safe to bet it had no rust holes. He's spoken about how his parents haven't always been billionaires, but it's hard to picture them struggling in the face of such opulence.

The cars in the driveway echo that thought. Archer's Mercedes. Another Mercedes. A BMW. Nate's Tesla. I pause in front of it. The Tesla acted as a white horse the icy day he and Archer rode to the rescue. Archer notices my staring, squeezes my hand in his, and then places a succinct kiss on my mouth.

Behind the massive front door, Nate is standing next to a smiling, dark-haired Benji, both of them holding glasses of champagne. Their heads turn when Archer and I walk in together. I register their surprise and smile to cover for my nerves. I haven't met a boyfriend's parents since I was engaged. Not that Archer qualifies as a boyfriend, but after learning how disapproving his father has been about his past girlfriends, bringing me here seems significant.

"Late," Nate grumbles to Archer, a second before his amiable half-smile appears. He greets me next, lifting my hand. The tip of his crooked nose brushes my hand as he kisses my knuckles. I muse how attractive he is and how fitting a partner he is for sassy, take-no-crap Vivian. "How's the arm?"

"Good as new." I rotate my wrist.

"I hear you were victim to the weather, Sunshine," Benji says with a sunshiny smile.

"It came out of nowhere."

"It has a way of doing that. Glad you decided to come. I wasn't sure my brother had to balls to show up with a living, breathing woman for dinner."

"Jesus, Benj," Archer growls, clearly not wanting to draw attention to the fact he'd struggled with the choice.

"Don't feel pressured," Nate says easily, his big body resting in a casual stance. "Lainey is fantastic, and William is polite. Archer worries like a mother hen, in case you didn't notice the day you busted your wrist."

"He sneaked into my townhouse to sleep on the couch," I tell Archer's brothers, happily ratting him out.

Archer's mouth is a flat line, his eyes narrowing in a warning I ignore. Benji comes to his rescue.

"I'd have done the same with Cris. I know she can take care of herself, but we like to be needed, you know?"

"Yeah," I say with a laugh, liking Archer's brothers more with each passing moment. Men who are there for the women in their lives remind me of how much my father did for my mom, and not only at the end when she was sick. He'd always doted. What a wrong turn I took moving in with ambivalent Brandon.

"Let's get you a drink." Archer guides me away from his brothers and deeper into the house. He's a wall of stone at my side when we pass an enormous, gleaming white-and-gray kitchen. The floors are marble, a winding banister staircase leads to the upper floor, and tall, arched doorways mark each room.

We step into a sitting room with plenty of cushy sofas and chairs and what appears to be a fully stocked bar off to one side. Vivian and Cris smile and stand from the sofa when they see me, excitement evident in their postures.

They're both wearing jeans as well. *Phew.* Cris's are black with a stylish tear in one knee. She paired them with flat black shoes and a lightweight pink sweater. Vivian manages to look elegant in dark-wash denim like mine, her silky-looking shirt emerald green, knotting at one side to showcase her slim waist. She's chosen sky-high heels, which I've noticed is her usual.

"Yay! You brought her." Vivian sweeps over to greet me and kisses me on the cheek. She rubs Archer's upper arm in an approving way. "She's probably been bored out of her mind trapped in the tower you've been keeping her in."

I laugh. It's not accurate but not hard to imagine him keeping me locked up for my own safety.

Cris gives me a quick greeting, hers a half-hug instead of a kiss to the cheek. "I want to hear about Archer's project," she tells me, her gray eyes going wide with excitement. "He mentioned a spa but left out the fun details. I'm an excellent secret keeper too, so maybe we could stop by the facility and I could have a teensy peek?"

"Easy, Firecracker." Benji enters the room, sliding an arm around her and kissing her temple. She's petite, my sister's height if not a bit shorter, coming up to Benji's chest. They make an adorable couple. "Talia might want a night off."

"I love to talk business. I rarely take time off," I say, hearing Archer's muttered, "That's the truth," behind me. Nate, who walked in with Benji, flicks his fiancée a look like he's surprised Archer knows that about me.

"She's officially an LLC now." Archer's hand presses my back. His arm stiffens when he adds, "Soon she'll be doing other projects and raking in her own billions."

"I don't know about that," I add with a nervous laugh. "Billions seems like a lot of responsibility. I'd rather start with thousands and see how I do."

"Handling it is the same," Benji says with a shrug. "Just more zeroes."

Cris dismisses the Owen brothers collectively with a wave. "Don't listen to any of them. They're out of touch."

"Hey!" Vivian pouts. "I'm not out of touch."

Cris lifts the edge of Viv's shirt and mutters a designer name I've heard on fashion reality shows. Viv curls her lip but gives up and laughs shortly after.

"Champagne, Talia?" Nate asks. "Since Archer's not going to offer, thought I'd better."

"Fuck off," Archer growls.

"Be right back." Nate chuckles, as if the F-off isn't unusual for them. Before we can launch into more conversation, an older couple strolls into the room.

"I see we have a guest," the woman announces. She's dressed in a little black dress, the skirt knee-length, the fit tailored to her lithe form. Her heeled shoes aren't as high as Vivian's, but whose are?

"Lainey Owen." Archer's mother approaches with her arm outstretched. I take her hand and shake. Like the man behind her, her hair is dark, and her skin is olive-toned. Italian heritage, I'd bet. Though there could be a touch of Greek in there, like on my father's side. My mom's side is Mexican.

"This is my husband, William."

Archer's hand flinches at my waist, a subtle reaction, but I notice.

"Talia Richards, is it?" William's green eyes match Archer's. His suit and tie are a touch formal, and I wouldn't be surprised to learn that he dresses this way most, if not all, of the time.

"Lovely to meet you." I shake his hand. Archer inches closer, a wall of protection at my left side. So far, I'm not picking up any vibes other than polite ones from his parents.

"You're helping with the spa, I hear," William says. So he does know about the project. I wondered.

"Some of the finer points of design and aesthetics."

"Interior design," he guesses incorrectly.

"Not specifically. My position is hand-crafted."

"Like mine," Cris chirps, standing on my other side and beaming up at Will. I didn't notice he was looking at me with intensity until I witness his face smoothing when he turns his adoring gaze to Cris.

"Benji made up my title, though I've refined it through years and years of careful observation," Cris tells me.

"Well, at least one of you is observant," Nate, king of one-liners, quips as he hands me a glass of champagne. "Cigars tonight, Will?"

"Absolutely. If the ladies allow."

"Because we have *so* much say." Lainey rolls her eyes. Nate offers to pour her a flute of champagne. She shoos him off, saying she'll pour it herself. Once everyone has a cocktail in hand, the men split off to one side of the room and the ladies to the other. Small talk ensues, but it mostly revolves around where I'm from, my family, and how I came to know Archer. I was unsure how much to share.

Vivian picks up on my hesitation and fills in the gap beautifully.

"She was at the Heart-to-Teen fundraiser last spring. In Florida."

"It's a wonderful charity. Do you have a connection with adoption, Talia?" Lainey asks.

"I had an interest in Archer," I say, opting to tell the truth instead of fabricating a story I'd likely forget the details of later. "He helped me with a grand opening of a spa in Miami for the company I used to work for. He's incredibly talented."

I feel Archer's gaze on the side of my head and peek over my shoulder to smile at him. His lips soften, letting me know he both overheard and appreciated my seal of approval. It's so interesting to see him like this. He's never been anything less than confident and self-assured with me at home. In his parents' home, his tension is like an uninvited guest in the room.

Dinner is far from catered lasagna. A waitstaff of two serves mussels in white wine sauce and triangle toast points with caviar to start us off. The waitstaff is informal, but Lainey doesn't ignore them in cliché rich-folk fashion. She asks them about their families and thanks them when they deliver her plate. Spring mix salad with goat cheese and sundried tomatoes comes next, and for dinner we are given a choice: lamb chop lollipops, pineapple glazed chicken thighs, or filet mignon.

I chose the lamb chops. Though they are delicious, Calista's are better, but I keep that observation to myself. During dinner, Archer mentions my sister is a chef, and the conversation runs on that bit of steam for a while. William asks about her restaurant, and I tell him she doesn't have her own yet.

"She should. She could franchise later. Have a line of sauces and condiments packaged for sale in markets all over the country."

"William," Lainey scolds. "No business talk at the table."

Benji singsongs the word "busted" under his breath, and Nate piles on, warning William he "knows better." Archer, I notice, is resolutely quiet during the exchange, even though Will takes the teasing from his other two sons easily.

After the meal, the men retire to the portico for cigars. The ladies meander back to the sitting room where a fire is crackling. Vivian pours after-dinner drinks—port wine in tiny stemmed glasses. I sink into the settee nearest the fire, full from dinner and happy to be away from Archer for a few blessed minutes. He's been so intense since we arrived, I swear I've caught it. I have to mentally remind myself to pull my shoulders out from under my ears.

"Lainey, where's your port?" Cris asks.

"Hot tea for me. It's been a long day of dinner-party planning." She offers me a warm smile. "I'm glad you joined us tonight, Talia."

"So am I," I say, and it's the truth. Archer might be stressed out, but so far I haven't seen evidence that his parents are unbearable. I wonder if William and Archer have simply chipped away at each other over the years. Kind of like the way crashing waves beat shoreline rocks into craggy, jagged edges.

"Do come see us again." She touches my shoulder in an elegant but motherly way. Even though she's nothing like my own mother, who was more boisterous and outspoken, Lainey

143

obviously loves her children and makes it a point to show support with her presence.

"I love her," Vivian says after Lainey leaves the room. "It's nice to have a mom again." To me, she adds, "My mother is no longer living."

"Neither is mine." I share a sad smile she returns.

"Lainey is the best," Cris agrees, plopping down next to me with her own wee glass of port wine. "My mom is alive, she's just...uninvolved in my and my three brothers' lives."

We sip from our glasses and watch the fire, the moment passing in silent ode to the loss of our mothers in some form or fashion.

"What's up with William and Archer?" I ask, fishing for details after the beat of unplanned silence.

"You noticed that, huh?" Cris asks rhetorically. "Rumor has it Will wasn't fond of any of Archer's past girlfriends, though I haven't seen him with a woman I'd consider a girlfriend in a long time." She pauses to regard the ceiling. "Maybe not ever. He rarely brings a date anywhere, and to a dinner of this magnitude? Unheard of."

"You're making her nervous," Vivian says from her seat on an armchair across from us. "Will and Archer butt heads about work. I've overheard them bickering. Will wishes Archer would have built churches or something."

"Churches?" I ask with a giggle. "A far cry from nightclubs."

"Not really. There is dancing, and usually God's name is mentioned." Viv gives me a wry smile. "Have you been to Club Nine?"

I shake my head. "One of Archer's?"

"Vivian and Nate were engaged there," Cris says. "Will

and Lainey were there that night. Will's not totally reluctant, I think he's just worried."

"Well, that runs in the family," I say before I take another sip of my port. It's sweet and smooth and delicious. I notice both women leaning in, as if waiting for me to continue. "Archer and I... I'm not sure what we are to each other. After I wrecked his car he refused to leave my side. I sprained my wrist, not even a break, and he checked on me every five minutes."

"Which was fairly easy since you were next to him in bed." Viv smirks at me. My cheeks grow warm. I blame the fire and the wine.

"That did make it more convenient," I say.

"Well, I just love this!" Cris slaps her thigh with one hand. "Archer seems happy. You seem happy." Her eyes glaze over with the sort of hope reserved for the lovesick around the globe.

"We are enjoying each other's company while I'm here," I say carefully. "One of the reasons I secured an LLC was because I want to continue working for myself, hopefully based closer to home where my sister and father live."

Vivian nods, but her expression is careful. "So, it's fairly new? He hasn't been hiding your relationship from us since last spring?"

"It was strictly professional until recently." I decide to avoid mentioning him punching out my ex-boyfriend or sexing me up, down, and sideways during the rest of that lovely Sunday. "There was a lot of email-flirting leading up to that, though."

"Well, he's into you. It's obvious." Cris shrugs like she's said something impossible to argue with. I don't, not wanting to turn our dessert-wine chat into an intense speech about how I'm not looking for permanence. The last time I tried for permanence, I was engaged. The consequences were too steep to mention.

"We're good friends. His concern is touching." *Lame, lame, lame.*

Neither Cris nor Vivian argue, but their disappointment is evident in their tight smiles.

"Who, uh, who helped with your LLC?" Cris asks, clumsily but blessedly changing the subject.

"Kathleen Stapleton."

Cris nods with familiarity. "She's great."

"She was knowledgeable and friendly. Both of which I appreciated." The turn of topic is tepid, but I settle in and focus on the company.

"When did your mom pass?" Cris asks, her tone gentle.

"Shortly after I graduated high school." I force a smile to let her know it's okay to talk about, even though talking about her ushers in a fresh wave of guilt. I reach for the bottle of port on the coffee table and top off my glass. "It was a long time ago."

"I've lost both my parents," Vivian tells me. As if sensing my discomfort, she throws in a detail I didn't know about her. "Maybe you've heard of my father, Walter Steele."

I gasp before I can stop myself. Cris jokingly lumping in Viv with the uber-wealthy Owens earlier tonight makes much more sense now. Walter Steele swindled a lot of people out of a ton of money. He went to prison for it. I read he passed away in there. A biopic about his life is coming out next year. I saw a trailer online.

"There's a television show on the way. I'm not in it, thank

God." Viv's tone is easy, but her posture stiffens, revealing her true feelings on the topic. She's not comfortable talking about her infamous father. Who would be?

"I'm sorry," I tell her.

"I'm not watching it," Cris states with finality.

"Don't be sorry," Viv says with more forced ease. To Cris, she adds, "And you'd better watch it. I'm counting on you for a summary of events. I want to know how much they butchered since I refused to consult on the project."

"That sucks, though," I say.

"That's life sometimes." Vivian offers a warm smile before waving a manicured hand. "Anyway, it's the past, and it's not even *my* past. Nate has helped me understand that I'm not responsible for my father's actions. I worked for him, but I had no idea what was going on under my nose." She changes the subject abruptly, the topic of Walter Steele having run its course. "Tell us about the spa."

"It's unique. And now that I'm involved, it's going to be the premier hangout for twenty-five- to forty-five-year-olds in Clear Ridge. Mark my words."

I paint in broad strokes, not wanting to bore them. I describe my vision for the spa in the most general terms. At Cris's encouragement, I go into more detail. I'm glad I do when she chimes in with her own ideas. Vivian offers some truly priceless input, as well, and I relax into my seat and listen.

The Owen brothers have similar taste in women, I think to myself as we animatedly chat and pour more port. Strong, opinionated—these women could never be overshadowed by a powerful male presence.

I fit right in with them.

CHAPTER FIFTEEN

Archer

Nate, Benji, and I are standing on the covered porch near one of two tall space heaters. The heat and cold battle each other, but hovering in between both isn't a bad sensation. My brothers are chatting about a new restaurant that just opened at Grand Marin, and how slippery the restaurant business can be. I understand. Nightclubs come and go too. I've had to close the doors on a few when profits turned upside-down.

Dad steps outside to join us, a pair of unwrapped cigars in hand. Rather than insert himself in conversation with Nate and Benji, he offers me one of the cigars. I accept, wary, still waiting to have a pseudo-conversation ending in heated debate like every other time I come to dinner.

"When I started Owen Construction," he says, "I envisioned it differently than it exists today. I thought it'd be...bigger."

I can't help chuckling as I clip the end off my cigar.

"Bigger than a multi-billion-dollar company with its hands in various projects?" Nate's live-works, my nightclubs, and soon, spas. Dad heads up projects of his own, including and not limited to shopping malls, amusement parks, and restaurant franchises.

"I thought I'd be retired by now." He lights his cigar. I light mine. We puff in silence, watching the smoke mingle with the chilled night air. Nate laughs, the big sound echoing off the ceiling of the large portico. He and Benji are facing away from Dad and me, maybe to avoid our pending verbal scuffle. Or maybe it has nothing to do with me and they're content keeping each other's company. "I'm too involved in Owen Construction to retire."

His tone is self-effacing, and I allow my shoulders to relax. I know I've bitched about us butting heads, but my dad's a good guy. He is a blood/sweat/tears guy. He created Owen Construction with a nest egg and a dream, and here we are. It's damn impressive.

"If I was better at delegating, we'd be all over the country instead of the Midwest and East Coast."

"You have time, old man." The stars are out in droves tonight, pinholes in a navy blue sky. I inhale the crisp, cool air, content to stand here in silence, when he drops a bomb on me.

"Talia Richards. She's pretty."

Tension returns in a blink. An old reaction from former circumstances. Back when waves of disapproval rolling off him sent me into a tailspin. And, if you remember my mentioning, that happened whenever I showed up with a woman on my arm.

"She's more than pretty," I say, my tone a warning.

"You've known her a short while. I've only just met her. How can you know?"

"Because I know. If you don't trust my judgment, look around. Everyone likes her," I tell him. "Even you. Admit it."

Talia swept in here tonight, her head high, her smile bright. I remained close to her side so she'd know I was here for her, but honestly? She's here for *me*. I've been on a razor's edge with her in tow. She's important, and I refuse to allow my father to categorize her as anything less.

His eyebrows lift in a show of surprise at my reaction. "Why wouldn't I like her? She seems lovely, and Vivian and Cris think she's the best thing that's ever happened to you."

That comment draws my attention. I watch him carefully, but his eyes are where mine were a moment ago—on the night sky.

"Is she?" he asks.

Yes.

"She's an asset, for sure." I try for casual, redirecting the topic to business since I am in no position to admit that whopper aloud. "Once we open the night spa, she'll return to Miami. I might hire her to work on another if the wellness industry expands like I expect."

"It's a red ocean, but then you've always been a risk-taker."

The dig is subtle, but I'm triggered. By "red ocean" he means bloody, like a hungry shark in a herd of seals. It's his way of saying the industry is overcrowded. It's a speech I've heard before—how tough it can be to stand out, to stay alive in that environment.

"Growth requires risk. A night spa is a good idea." That came out more defensive than it sounded in my head.

"A *night spa* is a glorified bar." He inhales his cigar, the warm orange glow highlighting his bone structure. He's getting older. I've noticed before, but tonight his age stands out in sharp relief. In the fan of lines at the corners of his eyes, and the brackets around his mouth. He's still good-looking, with a nose slightly larger than mine, his build a touch wider. The gray at his temples is thicker than ever. While he doesn't look fragile, there is something softer about him. I can't put my finger on it.

It should be the end of the conversation. Could be if I let him have the last word. I could stand here, smoke, ignore the tension strung between us. But I don't.

"Why the hell do you bother commenting on what I do, anyway?" I snap, earning a curious head tilt. He doesn't seem angry—not yet. "My passions have never been your priority. I can't gain your approval no matter how great my earnings are or how much positive publicity I lend to this company."

"This isn't about approval, Archer," comes his stern reply. "It's about you finding a niche worthy of who you are. Nightspots are—"

"Save it. We've had this discussion how many times? You don't like what I do. I get it. But you also haven't kicked me out of the company yet, so you must be A-okay with the money I bring in."

He faces me, his arm rising, cigar scissored between his fingers. He looks angry now. I square my shoulders, ready for a standoff. "Son, this has fuck-all to do with money. It has everything to do with how much I love you."

I flinch, shocked into momentary speechlessness. I swallow past a dry throat a few seconds later and recover.

"You don't come to my grand openings." I hear the hurt

in my own voice. I didn't mean to reveal how much that hurts, but it's impossible to miss. "You attend every opening Nate has ever had." I'm aware of my brothers' sudden silence —almost as loud as Nate's laughter was a few minutes ago. I can tell without turning my head to check, they're both listening. "You don't let a day pass where you're not bragging about Benji's math wizardry and how he keeps this company afloat behind the scenes. Hell, at dinner tonight, you said we'd have folded if it wasn't for him."

"Archer," Dad warns.

"I don't want you to stop supporting them," I continue, on a roll now. "But would it kill you to throw a bit of praise my way? I'm here for you, Dad. I'm here, at Owen, because of you. I didn't start a competing company and go off on my own. Maybe I should have, but I didn't. For years I've tried to prove I'm worthy. It's like you think because I'm not building exactly what you'd like me to, I'm failing."

"I don't think you're failing. I *know* you can do better!" he snarls.

"Hey," Nate interjects. "Let's not do this tonight."

"Mind your business," I tell Nate, my eyes locked on Dad's. My father's gaze hasn't wavered. He's the picture of stubbornness, his mouth tight and his cheeks pulled. If I'm not careful, that'll be me in a few decades. "I don't need your praise. I want it, but I don't need it. If you can't find a way to be proud of your first son"—I tap my chest—"then fuck you."

I stub out my cigar in the wide ashtray standing between us and turn and walk into the house.

BEHIND THE WHEEL of my Mercedes, I reverse out of my parents' drive, my arms straight, hands wrapped around the wheel at ten and two. Talia is sitting in the passenger seat, loose-limbed after plenty of port wine with Vivian and Cris. She's wearing a slightly wonky, completely captivating smile as she watches out the windshield.

When I came back into the house after dropping the big F-you to Dad—a first for me, in case you were wondering—I didn't rush into the sitting room and grab Talia's hand to lead her from the house. I didn't want to ruin her night. I also didn't want to talk about how angry I've been with William Owen for years.

I don't want to talk about it now.

"I had a really great time," she tells me. "Your mom is reserved, but so sweet. And your brothers—they're funny and interesting. And protective." She pokes me in the arm. "You all are. Your dad's a good man. He reminds me a lot of you."

My arms stiffen so much I worry I might tear the steering wheel off the dashboard.

"You look like him. The same green eyes. Though you do have your mother's nose," she amends. "Did you know you and your father stand in exactly the same position? It's funny. The same lean on one hip, the same stubborn fold to your arms." She laughs lightly. "Are you sure he doesn't approve of what you do?"

"Yes, Wildflower," I answer, impatience evident in my voice. I blow out a breath and try to calm down. "I am positive he doesn't approve of what I do. Like I said to you before, and like I told him tonight in so many words, I don't need his approval."

She's quiet for a while. The only sound in the car is the

heat blowing and the occasional swipe of the windshield wipers as it starts to rain.

"I've been going against what my father wants for me for years," she tells me when I expected her to argue about my father's approval. Instead she's sympathizing. "You have to do what's best for you in the end, no matter what he says. You have decided to be the king of nightlife. I have decided..." She trails off, unwilling to finish her sentence. Then she sighs, a heavy sound. I instantly regret bringing the mood in the car down to my level. She was happy a minute ago. "I hope I can make this LLC work."

I spare her a glance as I turn right at a traffic light. "Where the hell did that come from? Of course you can make it work."

"I'm not as good at rebelling as you are. I hear my papa's voice in my head warning me to be careful and keep my safe and secure job. I've tried that. *Many* times. It's not for me." She shakes her head, frustrated, but I'm not sure if she's frustrated with herself or her father. "I don't exactly know what I'm doing."

"You're doing your thing." I reach over and squeeze her hand, resting her fingers in mine against my thigh. "I'm doing my thing."

"And what are we doing to each other?" Her tone is light and teasing. She's not asking about the future—only the immediate future.

"Honey, I'll do whatever you'd like me to do to you tonight." I smile for her benefit, easing into flirting with her. Smiling feels a hell of a lot better than being pissed off at my dad. Focusing on now feels a lot better too. God knows we can't guarantee each other more than that. No matter how much I want her to stick around, I have no right to clip her wings. Her father's been demanding she behave a certain way her entire life. I can relate to that sort of pressure.

"Don't listen to what anyone wants for you but you," I tack on.

"Are we still talking about sex?" she asks cheekily as I park in front of my townhouses.

"Definitely not. Well, in the bedroom, you should listen to me," I amend. "I always have your interests in mind." I put the car into park. She leans over and kisses me, doing wonders for my decaying mood. As my lips tug and sip hers, I shove the evening's events aside, including my father's shocked expression and my brothers' worried ones when I left. Instead I focus on what's going well. Talia. In my arms. Clinging to me as I lead her up the steps to my townhouse.

I lose myself in her and try hard not to think of when I might lose her altogether.

CHAPTER SIXTEEN

Talia

E*ureka!*
    I finally find the loungers I want for the pool area at the night spa. They're within budget, thanks to a motivated salesperson, and after a quick phone call to Jarod for approval, I type in the credit card information on the website to finalize the purchase.

That only took *a month*, I think with an eye roll. For a hot second, I worried we'd have to do the grand opening with lawn chairs from the discount store instead.

The pieces are coming together. I was personally involved in choosing the statue for the meditation room and, after going back and forth a dozen times, I opted for a golden Buddha. I nearly chose a koi fish statue instead. In the end, a smiling Buddha seemed more on theme, and Archer agreed.

It's done nothing but rain today. I'm in the wading pool room, perched on the edge of one of the sampler loungers that helped seal my decision. It's wrapped in plastic and is going to stay that way until we open. The seat is cream-colored and I don't want to risk it getting dirty. My neck is bent over my brand-new laptop—a splurge, but I needed it—as I make a detailed list of tasks that need to be done before we open. Fat raindrops beat the windows, matching my rhythm as I peck the keys. Number one on my list? The wading pool needs water.

"Wildflower, you done?" Archer's voice bounces off the empty pool sides as he steps into the cavernous room.

"Almost."

Like whenever I hear his voice, chills run the length of my body. He's become my partner in several senses of the word. In business, in the bedroom. Having a partner in either area is a strange yet welcome dynamic. I try not to focus on how strange or how welcome it is.

He looks good today—but then, he looks good every day. I should've grown used to his presence by now, but am almost taken aback whenever I see him. He's so attractive, it's alarming. You'd think I'd be accustomed to his bearded, muscled hotness since he struts into my townhouse daily with barely a knock to announce himself. Not so. Each morning, my belly drops, my nipples tighten, and my breath catches.

I've been sleeping at his house on and off. He's slept at mine on and off. Not every night or anything, as neither of us is particularly clingy. He's traveled for work some and stayed overnight in Columbus twice. Those nights I retreated to my laptop, designing business cards or tinkering with the website I've yet to launch. I contacted Prisha to ask for help with it. I'm fantastic at spotting what looks good, but HTML and CSS are outside my wheelhouse. Hers too, she admitted, but her boyfriend, Malik, is a web designer. He's been a huge help.

It's starting to feel real, the LLC. Every time I think about the possibility of it working out long-term, my insides jump with a combination of excitement and fear. Excitement because trying something new is enthralling and motivating. Fear because I've grown acquainted with failing miserably over the years and would rather not repeat the experience.

"You up for an adventure?" Archer folds his arms over his chest and regards me with an expression I can't quite read. He also makes my insides jump—for exactly the same reasons as the LLC.

We don't do anything particularly *adventurous*. Our business dinners out end up with us in bed together. Private dinners at home end up in the same place. We haven't put a label on what we're doing, and I'm finding it necessary not to label it right now. Labeling leads to planning, and planning leads to thoughts I'd rather not entertain. As I said, I'm acquainted with failing miserably. What Archer and I have is uncomplicated. I'd like to keep it that way for as long as possible.

"What'd you have in mind?"

"Depends." He smirks. "How much energy do you have?"

I close my laptop and stand. "This sounds like a trick."

"I thought we could go out and celebrate."

"Celebrate?"

"Yeah." He shrugs, and then gestures around the nearly empty pool room. "We're almost done."

"The list on this laptop says we are very much *not* almost done."

He takes the computer from me and kisses my mouth. Automatically I lean in for more, but he leaves me hanging. "You have to celebrate as you go. You need a break. I need a break. Plus, I thought you'd like to see how the nightlife kingpin earned his name."

I bring my folded hands to my open mouth, trying not to look or sound too excited. "You're taking me to one of your clubs?"

I've been asking, but he keeps telling me we'll go "later." In his defense, he is involved with a lot of projects at one time. I understand how it might not be relaxing for him to visit a nightclub. Kind of how it's not relaxing for my sister to visit a restaurant.

"Club Nine. That was the request, right?" He hoists a knowing eyebrow.

I nod. Ever since Vivian mentioned it, I haven't been able to stop imagining going there.

A few hours later, we enter Club Nine. I'm as excited as I was when I went on my first trip to Disney World. It's almost as big of a spectacle as Disney World, with its neon lights and gaudy fake palm trees outside the building. Inside, music thumps from unseen speakers in the fog-filled room.

"Finally, you in your element," I call to him over the noise. It's nine thirty, early by club standards, but the place is packed.

He has a hold of my hand and pulls me to him. "Drink?"

He smells damn good. Faintly of teakwood and eucalyptus. After we left the spa, we changed and went out to dinner. I was vocal about how good his ass looked in the black pants he has on, and demonstrative about my appreciation of the navy blue shirt with a slight sheen to the fabric when I ran my hands over his chest. Bonus: the collar is open, showing his delicious neck leading up to a beard I can't imagine him without.

I consider biting his neck when he leans closer to give me his ear. I debate a beat before answering, "Surprise me. But not with bourbon."

"No bourbon?" Lights from the dance floor lend a twinkle to his green eyes, but the mischief there is all Archer.

"Not tonight."

A dab of seriousness leaks into his expression before he mutters, "Shame." Then the music changes, and he tucks me close and shuffles me into a few quick dance steps. He's good. Much better than I am, and expending half the effort.

He lets me go to slide behind the bar and make our drinks. Interested patrons gawk at him, maybe because he's not dressed like he works here, or maybe because he's impossible not to admire.

I rest my forearms on the bar top and watch him. Like his dance steps, his movements are smooth. He flips a cup, catches it. Fills it with liquor, flips the bottle, then shakes a metal shaker. The crowd around me whistles. He grins. It's blindingly beautiful, and my heart squeezes. I'm totally turned on and somewhat possessive when I notice a few other women around me salivating over him.

While he makes drinks, he converses with the bartender. I'm seeing yet another side of Archer I haven't seen before tonight. In his element, he's light. Almost, dare I say, *frothy*. A group gathers in front of the bar as the other bartender yells something into Archer's ear I have no prayer of hearing thanks to the loud music. I shuffle to the side as a gaggle of women push their way to the bar to order. Archer leans over the bar, cups my jaw, and says loud enough for me to hear, "Wait for me in the VP lounge. *Pumpernickel* is the password."

A drink is pressed into my palm. He holds up an open hand and mouths, "Five minutes," then points at the upstairs deck where, I assume, the VP lounge is located.

He then dives into the gathering crowd, taking orders, preparing drinks, and serving them with both flair and a smile. I watch, awed for a minute, before crossing the dance floor to take the stairs to the area overlooking the club. A bulky guy at the door steps in front of me. I open my mouth to say pumpernickel, but he speaks first.

"I saw you with Archer. Go on in." He steps aside, and I walk into a virtually empty room.

Five people who appear to be together are grouped in a sunken area with a sofa and a tiny dance floor. Three women are dancing, the two guys settled on the sofa, beers in their grips. There is a private bar up here with a female bartender behind it. Her nametag reads, "Shauna." Shauna welcomes me to "the VP" and instructs me to hang out wherever I like.

It's quieter up here than downstairs, thanks in part to a solid wall of glass behind the bar facing the dance floor below.

I meander about until I come to a low metal divider preventing VP guests from toppling over the edge. It's like a privacy panel with decorative holes in it that you can see through. I settle into one of a pair of cushy red chairs, which gives me a perfect bird's-eye view of the bar.

Archer mixes drinks while the other bartender takes cash. He leans forward and offers an ear to the group of women who approached as I walked away. One of them touches his arm and keeps her hand there, obviously flirting. I frown.

I imagine this is what his life was like back when I met him at the fundraiser last year. The idea of being one in the long line of women he flirts with is unsatisfying.

I sip my drink, trying to push away feelings that have no business lingering. I had no claim on him back then, and even though I have ended up in his bed, I don't have a claim on him now, either.

After fifteen minutes of irritating contemplation over whether or not I was claim-worthy to him, I order a drink from Shauna—vodka cranberry this time since I have no idea what Archer mixed up for me. She slides the short glass across the bar, complete with lime wedge, at the same time a broad hand warms my back.

"Bourbon for me, Shaun," Archer says. She nods, pours, and hands the glass over. He steers me to the same cozy corner from where I was watching him before.

"How did you have time to finish a drink *and* pull your bartender out of the weeds?"

"I have skills, honey. Bonus points for using restaurant lingo," he praises before admitting he "lost" his drink after diving in to help Randy. "He was down a bartender, but Michele showed up after all."

"Is it your habit to hop behind the bar and pour drinks?"

"Pour drinks, take orders, repair the sink."

"Repair the sink?" I try to picture him repairing a sink. Like him eating cookie dough on my couch, the visual takes me by surprise.

He shrugs and drinks his bourbon, his delectable throat

jumping as he swallows. "Whatever it takes. I don't mind dirty hands."

He leans back in the fat red chair caddy-corner to mine, his legs spread, his elbows resting on the arms of the chair. Nightlife Kingpin on his throne.

"What are you smiling about?" he asks, a budding smile tickling his own lips.

Instead of answering him, I tip my head toward the floor below where the women I noticed earlier are standing in a circle. They're young and thin and coiffed. I remember my club days, and the attitude I had back then. Those ladies are on the hunt tonight. "Your fan club misses you."

He tilts his head to see who I'm talking about, then gives me an admonishing look.

"Is that sort of attention typical?"

He leans back, getting comfortable once again. "Yes."

"Oh." I sip my drink from a pair of skinny cocktail straws and try not to look inconvenienced by this news. I was hoping for an answer like *nah, they have no interest in me* to assuage the bizarre feeling of inadequacy that cropped up out of nowhere. Since I can't seem to shake it, I lick my lips and ask the other question rattling around in my brain. "Do you... often take girls like that home?"

"Often?" His eyes go overhead like he's counting as heat climbs my neck. "Not too often."

"Oh."

He's watching me closely now, so I take another sip of my drink and pretend not to care. One side of his mouth pulls slowly to one side, then the other follows the same path. What started as an impish smile is now a full-on tooth-baring grin.

He sets my drink aside and takes my hands, pulling me onto his lap. Then he turns me so I'm sitting sideways. I loop one of my arms around his neck and cross my legs over his. His hold is loose, one arm at my back, his other arm draped over my thighs.

"That's better," he decides. "What did I tell you about my bed at home?"

"You don't sleep in it."

"And?"

"That's all I remember," I lie.

"You asked if it was reserved for sex, and I told you I didn't bring women there."

"But you brought me."

"I did." He closes in on me, his nose nuzzling mine. "Jealous of those girls, Wildflower?"

"Why would I be jealous?" My voice catches when he licks my earlobe and then suckles it into his mouth. "You're here with me."

Smug satisfaction lingers on his handsome face as he lifts my hand and kisses my knuckles. "You don't have to worry. Since I bumped into you at that fundraiser, I've been on...a break."

"A break?" I cant one eyebrow.

"A *break*," he repeats, his voice dipping. "Sweet buttercups like those," he says of the circle of women below, "can't stand up to a feisty wildflower like you."

I know the cheesy compliment shouldn't work, but I'm totally melting. That rogue sense of jealousy—fine, I was a smidge jealous—flickered away the moment he touched me. *Claimed* me.

"I've never liked being claimed," I inform him while tracing the line of his beard to his neck.

"Not claiming you." He applies the slightest pressure to my back. I bend and cover his mouth with mine. His kiss is slow and deliberate, the hand around my back climbing higher until it's curved around my ribs, very close to my right breast. My tongue touches his, sliding warm and soft into his mouth. A spike of electricity zaps my spine and sends tingles shooting through my fingers—fingers now wrapped around the column of his neck.

He scoops my hair up and pushes it to one side. I'm lost in moss-green eyes sparkling with challenge. "You're in a good position to claim me, though."

So I am.

Properly motivated, I tilt his head back, lower my mouth to his throat, and take possession of what's mine.

CHAPTER SEVENTEEN

Archer

G od in Heaven.

I can't speak right now, so I only say it in my head. Talia's teeth scrape the side of my neck before the flat of her tongue licks a path along my Adam's apple. My hands tighten —one around the length of her hair and the one resting against her ribcage. I haul her closer, sliding the hand from her ribs to her ass. My back is facing the only other guests up here, and even then, we're half hidden behind a divider. The bar laid out below is visible through the grate, but everyone down there is too busy with their own lives to sneak a peek of my hand on Talia's perfect rear end.

I squeeze her ass cheek, slipping my hand around as her head moves so as not to impede her progress. She slides off my lap and presses both hands on the arms of the chair, hovering over me. Her eyes go over my head, to the side, and snap back at me as if she's checking her surroundings. Whatever she saw must please her because she attacks me again.

This time she grabs my ears as her mouth covers mine aggressively.

When she scoots back into my lap, she encounters a roadblock. I grunt, shifting a massive erection out of the way. Her head shoots up, her smile both delighted and surprised. But she doesn't stop...no, no. She covers my dick with her palm and begins to massage it. I keep my eyes on her, the thumping of bass vibrating the floor matching the pulse pounding mercilessly against my fly. She leans in and bites my earlobe —payback, I'll bet—and then offers a husky, "I have a naughty idea."

"Yes," I croak.

"You don't want to know what it is?" Her grin is mischievous and bright, beautiful and beguiling.

I don't need to know what it is. I have seen the preview. "I'd rather you show me."

She slides off my lap, deliberately bumping my rigid cock, and sashays across the VP. She makes a "wrap it up" motion to Shauna, who looks over at me for permission for whatever Talia just asked.

I'm going by instinct here, but I assume whatever my vixen instructed Shauna to do or not do is going to be as fine as frog hair with me. I give her a thumbs-up. And a nod, just to be safe.

Suddenly, there's a lot of movement. Shauna leaves the bar and shuffles to the other VP guests. Over my shoulder, I watch her escort them out. Shauna follows. I hear the barred gate slide closed, low murmuring from the security guy.

When Talia returns to me, she sits primly on my lap. My arms wrap around her curved hips. "Straighten things out?" I ask.

"I asked for privacy for an *urgent* matter." She cups my junk when she says "urgent" and smiles down at me. "We have ten minutes. Can you handle that?"

"Fuck, yes."

I don't hesitate.

I scoot her off my lap and stand, spinning the chair so that it faces the now-empty bar. This corner is my favorite, and out of view of security cameras. Anyone looking up into the VP area from the ground floor *might* see a shadow or a hint of movement, but not much else. I'm going to have to leave her dress on just in case. Not my preference. I'd love to set my mouth to her perfect tits.

I pull my belt open and sit before unzipping my fly, revealing the "urgent" matter she teased me about. Her eyes go hungry and wide. I skim my hands under her dress along the creamy skin of her thighs, swallowing a groan. On my return trip down, I come out with a pair of lacy black panties. Daintily, she steps out of them, sending one furtive glance at the bar below, then back at me.

That smile. God help me.

Straddling my lap, she rests her arms on my shoulders and leans down to kiss me. I palm her pussy, gliding through her wetness with my middle finger.

"My girl," I growl against her lips. She smashes her mouth into mine, presumably to thank me for the attention I'm paying her down below. Stroking her clit with my thumb, I slip my middle finger inside her. Then out. Then *in*. She whimpers her approval into my mouth. "Come, Wildflower. Right now. Right on my hand."

She bites her lip, squeezes her eyes closed. She liked that command. I cup her breast over her dress and find her nipple through her bra. Give it a pinch. Stroke into her again while continuing to play her clit with my thumb. She makes a desperate whimpering sound as her fingernails dig into my shoulders.

I slide once more, and she comes.

While she's attempting to hold in the cry that climbed her throat, I shift my cock and plunge deep. One fast, smooth thrust, and I'm sunk into her heat to the hilt. Hands tight on her hips, I fuck her with single-minded focus, the sensual slide of our flesh causing sweat to bead on my forehead. Then I hold her there, desperately trying to recenter myself before I blow early. The tip of my dick pulses angrily. Every instinct within says to pound hard and fast until I black out from pleasure. I huff a tortured breath as her forehead conks onto mine.

"I have a surprise for you," she murmurs, lifting off my member and taking me in again. Then again. I'm going to lose my fucking *mind* if she keeps this up.

"Whatever it is"—I pause to endure another intoxicating slide—"I love it."

"I'm protected." The pupils of her lust-soaked eyes are round and dark, the irises thin rims of color—blue today, thanks to the neon lights. She licks my upper lip and purrs, "I'm on the pill. No condom tonight, Kingpin."

I was right. I love it. I don't know why she waited to tell me until right now, but I don't care. I begin moving with more urgency, having no idea how much time has passed, but it goes damn fast. She's riding me, kissing me, using my mouth to muffle her cries. I swallow every last one.

She returns the favor minutes later when she draws my release from me. I come inside her, grappling onto her back and hugging her to me. I bury my face in the front of her dress, let out a hoarse sound that might have been a roar had I not muzzled it. I don't black out, but there are spots behind my eyelids while I attempt to catch my breath.

She strokes my hair once, twice. I open my eyes and meet hers. She watches me for a beat as lights swirl around us and muted bass adds to the buzz in my veins. Then she slips off my lap and places a kiss on the side of my mouth. "I'll be right back. Button up."

Dazed, I do as I'm told. She walks toward the restrooms beyond the bar. I sit on the red chair staring into space in the empty room, my mind a million miles away. From my periphery I become aware of the gate swinging open, Shauna returning to her station at the bar, and the guests who stepped out bellying up to receive the free drinks I assume were promised in exchange for their compliance.

A moment later, Talia swaggers from the ladies' room, her long brown hair flowing in waves behind her, her gait even and confident. I'm grinning like an idiot when she sits down and palms her drink. Had she not told me to do up my pants, I might still be sitting here, my mind on another planet, my schlong on my thigh.

I am so fucking *weak* for this woman.

Talia

"I've never done that before," I confess as Archer takes my hand and helps me out of the car. The night is clear but cool. I brace against a particularly chilly gust of wind.

"Proud to be your first time," he replies casually.

I don't feel casual. I feel... I don't know how I feel. Nervous, I guess. I was caught up in him at the club. Being caught up scares me. I don't know where my rational mind went. All I knew in the moment was that I wanted him. I wanted to take him, then and there, and give him an unforgettable experience.

"I need a shower." I'm a little jumpy. Not because we had sex in a semi-public place. I trust him. He wouldn't have agreed if he wasn't sure we'd have privacy. Again, the idea of how I forgot about the rest of the world for a while swirls back into my consciousness. I lost myself in him tonight. If I look back over the past few months, I bet I'll find I've been losing myself in him for a while.

Losing myself isn't what I signed up for. I think of my former life—and note how it *feels* former. I don't like that either.

He angles us toward his townhouse.

"What are you doing?" I pause at the alcove rather than follow him in.

"You said you need a shower. I happen to have a big one." He waggles his eyebrows. "As you know that's not all I have that's big."

"I'm tired from dancing. I'll probably go straight to bed after." After fantastic sex in the VP room, we stayed at Club Nine for another hour or so. We finished our drinks and danced downstairs until we were sweaty and exhausted. I knew he could move his hips, but I was beyond impressed by his ability to keep the rhythm. By the time we collected the car from the valet, I was hot and bothered all over again.

Now, I'm just bothered.

"I have a big day tomorrow," I continue my one-sided argument.

"Take the day off." He frowns.

"I can't."

"Sure you can. I'm your boss. I say so."

His authoritative tone is as abrasive as a dry loofah. I pull my hand from his. "No, *I'm* my boss. I know what needs to be done. I need to do it." Aware I'm overreacting, I fold my arms and look away. "I'm sorry. I'm cranky. It's been a long day. I should..." I trail off as I point to my own breezeway.

Rather than let me avoid him, he stands so close to me his chest nearly touches mine. His tone is gentle, his voice softer than before. "I'll give you room to sleep, but you're doing it in my bed. In my space. I'm not letting you out of my sight after the stunt you pulled tonight. You want to shove me away, you don't do it after doing something to me that's never been done before and in a place I've never done it in."

"Well, you can't tell me what to do," I reply haughtily as I slowly process what he just said. My stomach buoys and then sinks like I went over the first big hill of a roller coaster. "Did you say 'never'?"

"Never. Never cleared the VP room in any of my clubs. Never had anyone clear it for me. Never met someone like you, who made me...lose myself like that." His tone is achingly sincere when he mutters, "Sorry, sweetheart. You made a lot of promises tonight."

He lost himself too? The jittery feeling in my chest expands to the rest of my body. I've crossed a line with him, and I never saw it coming.

"Will you be able to sleep without me?" He doesn't wait

for my answer before adding, "Knowing I'm next door, awake without you?"

I picture him, as lost as I will be without him next to me tonight. I'll lay staring at the ceiling unable to understand what's happening to me. He'll be watching TV alone or maybe standing on the balcony in front of a fire.

Never met someone like you.

"What if I did to you what you did to me? Slipped you off my lap and cleared the VP room with a snap of my fingers." He leans in the scantest bit closer, reminding me of how we were glued to each other at the club. "Gave you a ten-minute time limit. Then drove us home, dropped you at your door, and went to bed by myself. How would you feel?"

"I'd feel...fine," I hedge, feeling anything but.

"You wouldn't feel used? Discarded?"

"Not at all," I mutter, even though he's painting a not-so-pretty picture. Why does it sound so much worse with our roles reversed?

"No?" His eyebrows lift.

I offer a meek shrug with one shoulder and lie again as I try to make myself believe it. "I would be fine with you taking time to yourself."

He sighs at the night sky. Nods once to whatever god is up there, and then says, "All right. I'll walk you up."

His hand pressed into the small of my back, we start in the direction of my townhouse.

Shit.

I have a terrible feeling I've hurt him. I pause at the foot of the steps leading to my front door. The door I no longer want to walk through. "I might..." I trail off before having to gather the courage to start again. "I *might* be disappointed if you were in a hurry to escape me."

"Do *you* want to escape me?"

"No. I don't know. I'm just...overwhelmed. My business is new, and I don't know what I'm doing yet. Calista is paying for the apartment by herself, and I feel so guilty. I tried sending her money, but the payment still says 'pending.' She's not making it easy for me to assuage my guilt." Before he can say he sympathizes with the idea of a woman making life difficult, I continue. "And my father is on medication. I've called him a few times this week, but he's been busy with work and couldn't talk. When I'm home I can check on him. When I'm not—" I shrug. At a loss, and not entirely sure what point I'm trying to make.

"You can talk to me about this shit, Talia," he growls, his eyebrows a pair of angry slashes. "How long have you been holding this in?"

"I'm not holding it in. I'm just—" I lift and drop my arm. "I'm tired."

"I can help with the business questions. So can Vivian. So can Cris. You can lean on the people around you, you know."

Why does that sound nice and alarming at the same time?

"If you want to fly home to see Papa Richards, I'll book a jet."

I'm already shaking my head. "The spa..."

"You need time with your family, take it. You're not being held captive here." He pushes my hair off from my forehead, the tip of his finger tracing my eyebrow. "Much as I'd like to hold on to you indefinitely."

My heart crushes like an empty aluminum can. That was sweet.

"I'm sure Papa's fine. I'm just worrying. Thank you. For listening." I scrub my forehead with my fingers, starting to catch a chill from the breeze, or maybe my own oddly icy demeanor. I'm not entirely sure what caused my epic freak-out. Too many cocktails? Sex that should have been dismissed as dirty, but seemed to mean so much more? Archer reminding me I'm a special part of his life?

All of the above, I answer myself.

"Want me to tuck you in?"

He's too much. How can I say no? Resisting him has proven futile for a while now. I'm not sure if drawing a flimsy boundary around not staying in his bed with him is going to help or hurt matters at this point.

I wrap my arms around his neck and press my breasts to his chest. "You *do* have a nicer shower than mine. Am I still invited?"

"You're still invited." He kisses my nose. Takes my hand. We walk back to his townhouse. He angles me with a look before opening the door for me. "In the meantime, you need to be careful."

I turn and face him. I'm inside his townhouse, he's outside, just over the threshold. "Careful about what?"

"Careful not to make yourself unforgettable if you're hoping I'll forget you in the end." He steps inside and shuts the door. "I'll start the shower."

He walks away. I stand frozen in the foyer.

I wonder if he's as afraid of needing me as I am of needing him.

CHAPTER EIGHTEEN

Talia

Three days later, I'm standing on the balcony of my borrowed townhouse soaking up the sunshine. The weather is chilly, but there's no rain, no clouds, and the sun is actually *warm*. I was beginning to wonder if the Midwest was under a constant gray cloud cover.

I have Calista on speakerphone. She's yammering on about her latest recipe. I misplaced my earbuds. I think they're in my office. *I think.* There's an outside chance they're in the cup holder of Archer's Mercedes. I'll have to look later.

She wraps up her story about fried octopus and in the same breath says, "I miss you!"

"I miss you too." It's good to hear and feels better to say. We're not away from each other much. The distance has been challenging. "I see you finally accepted the money I sent."

"I'm holding it for you. I only accepted it because I

received nine text messages from the transfer company and nine more from you. I was tired of being harassed."

I smile, knowing I'm never going to accept if she tries returning the cash.

"I wish you could come home," she says, but not for reasons I would have thought. "I have a few days off and I need your palate and unbiased opinions."

"My opinions are totally biased," I remind her. "I'd love to see you, but I'm expecting more than one delivery this week, and I need to be here to oversee the details." It was nice of Archer to offer to fly me back to Miami for a few days, but with all due respect, he's not the one overlooking the minutiae of this opening. I am. It's not that I don't trust the guys finishing up the interior of the spa to accept a delivery. It's that I know they *don't* know the difference between "moss" and "eucalyptus" and "sage." When the window coverings arrive, I'm going to be there to reject or accept on the spot. A photo sent to my cellphone while I'm in Florida isn't going to cut it. "Why don't you come here instead?"

She gasps. "I can do that?"

"Why couldn't you?" I didn't clear it with Archer, but I'm sure he doesn't mind if I have people over. It'd be good to have my sister here. I miss her like crazy. And I miss her cooking almost as much. "You have a few days off, I have the space. Plus, the kitchen—"

"I love that kitchen," she states, her awe palpable. "I'll check into flights. Maybe I'll luck out and find an inexpensive ticket. What's the closest airport to you?"

"I'll fly her here." Archer is standing on the neighboring balcony, bedroom doors open, sunglasses settled on his nose.

One of the nicest suits I've seen him wear, steel gray in color, is stretched over his broad shoulders.

"You're in Columbus," I tell him. I could have sworn he'd said he'd be there until morning.

"Columbus airport?" Lis asks.

"Um, sorry, no. Not you. Archer says he'll fly you here." I turn off the speaker and bring the phone to my ear. "He has a jet."

"Your boyfriend is going to fly me to Ohio *on his jet*?"

"Company jet, but yeah." I feel Archer's steady gaze, and I'm secretly glad he didn't hear the boyfriend comment. We've tiptoed around enough landmines lately.

Since the night at Club Nine when I agreed to sleep over, he hasn't warned me against being unforgettable. I've also calmed down. Him wanting to sleep with me is not a decent reason to flee in the opposite direction. It hasn't escaped my attention that he now knocks and waits for me to answer the door rather than rapping once and letting himself in.

Luckily, we both enjoy distracting ourselves with sex. It's amazing what a soapy, orgasm-y shower can do for morale.

"In that case, I'll pack my bags." I hear the grin in my sister's voice.

I can't see Archer's eyes because of the sunglasses. I can't read his expression because he's Archer. If he doesn't want anyone to know what he's thinking, they won't. "Text me the dates and I'll set up your flight and send over the details."

We say our goodbyes, but not before my next-door neighbor disappears inside his townhouse.

No sooner do I hang up than my cell phone jingles in my hand.

"Papa. Hi."

"How are you, Tallie?"

Relief slumps my shoulders. He sounds tired. It's the first phone call I've had with him without people shouting in the background or large machinery drowning out his voice.

"Fine. I mean, good. I'm keeping busy." I walk inside, through the bedroom, and down the stairs.

"When are you coming home?"

"After the spa is open, which is coming up fast." Almost too fast. I'm both ready to leave and not ready to leave. I'll miss it here. Archer's company, mostly, but I can't let missing him mandate my decisions.

"What will you do for work when you're back?"

"Well, my contracted work has turned into a business of its own. I have an LLC now. I'm official." Nervousness creeps into my voice, and I laugh uneasily. I know he won't approve. I remind myself that, like Archer doesn't need approval from his father, I don't need it from mine either. Doesn't keep me from wanting it, though.

"Businesses can be unstable. It's nice that you've experimented with this, but when you're back, you are going to pick up where you left off with Lotus Leaf."

"I can't do that." I stop pacing through the living room, too shocked to keep moving.

"Yes, you can."

"Papa, I dumped green juice on Ed Lambert's head."

"Tallie, Brandon is offering your job back. He's willing to overlook everything that happened. Including the man you're working for physically assaulting him," he adds. "He said to call him when you come back to Miami. You know as well as I do the business you began on a whim might not work out.

179

Besides, you might find you and Brandon are more compatible than you were before. You need stability."

I'm too angry to think straight. What point do I argue first?

"Archer hit him because he insulted me, Papa. I'm sure Brandon didn't tell you that when you called him. I'm assuming you called him?"

"I always liked Brandon."

"Well, I don't. I'm not working for him again, and I'm sure as hell not dating him again." Restless energy propels me from living room to kitchen to office and back again.

"I want you to be happy, and happiness means not working yourself half to death in a career you won't make work."

"How the hell do you know it won't work?" I snap.

"Because I know!" Rare is the occasion my genial father yells. We both fall quiet. My heart rate escalates, making me worry about his heart rate. I instantly regret losing my temper, even though it was completely justified. Work for Brandon again? Really?

"Are you all right?" Concern is a heavy blanket on my shoulders. "I didn't mean to upset you."

"I'm helping," he says, and I figure he believes that.

"I can't date Brandon, Papa. I'm dating Archer Owen. For the moment."

"The man you work for."

"I work with him, yes."

"Is he coming to Miami?" I hear the spark of hope in his voice and nearly laugh. He wants me taken care of—by Brandon or Archer, and it doesn't seem to matter which one.

"No. *I'm* coming back to Miami, though. And when I'm

there, I'll be living with Calista and building Talia's Design until I can afford an apartment of my own."

"Talia—" he starts, but a knock at the door saves me.

"He's here. I have to go." I'm guessing, but who else could it be? I open the door and find Archer standing there. He changed from that delectable suit, looking no less edible dressed down in worn jeans and a maroon Henley. "Love you," I say into the phone, my eyes on Archer. I don't miss the flicker of surprise in his eyes as I end the call. "That was Papa Richards."

"Uh, you mentioned the sink." He holds up a small red tool chest.

"I thought you'd call a plumber." I texted him about the minor leak in the kitchen earlier.

"You're looking at him." He kisses me, stamping his mouth over mine while hugging me close with his free arm. My phone, still in my hand and trapped between our bodies, buzzes against his chest and mine. "Papa again?"

"Yes." I ignore the call. "I'm not talking to him right now. Wine?"

"Sure."

I go to the bottle on the countertop, and twist in the corkscrew, my hands shaking. He wanders away to "shut off the water" and then returns. After a bit of wrestling, I toss the corkscrew, the mangled cork speared onto the tip, next to the bottle.

He grabs two glasses for us from the cabinet. I glug wine into my glass, spilling some in the process. He takes the bottle from me, kisses one of my shaking hands, and completes the task for himself.

"Want to talk about it?"

"Not yet," I mumble at the edge of my glass.

Fifteen minutes later, the cleaning supplies beneath the sink are encircling Archer, who is lying on the floor, twisting and puttying and whatever else it takes to seal a leak. Apparently it's happened before, and as such, he knew exactly what to do.

My father doesn't call again. He texted a stern parental message that read *Call me, Talia Elise.* I can't ignore him forever. After alternately texting him back that I would, checking my email (twice), and ogling the slash of belly revealed by Archer's rucked-up Henley (four times), I've chosen my favorite activity of the three. Watching Archer work on the sink, I lean on an elbow and finish my first glass of wine before splashing some more into the glass.

He grunts, swears.

I smile.

He twists something, swears again. His shirt rucks higher.

I smile bigger.

"That oughta do it," he finally says, shoving himself out from under the sink with less grace than you might expect. He knocks over window cleaner and a box of sponges, kicking a can of degreaser while he's at it. "Damn it."

He makes quick work of stashing the cleaning supplies beneath the sink and then stands, his face slightly red, his hair slightly disheveled. Insanely beautiful man. I offer his wine. He takes the glass, sips, and sighs. Incredible. He looks good in a suit, better in a Henley.

"Now you want to talk about it?" He rakes a hand through his hair.

"He called Brandon."

Archer's frown mirrors my earlier disposition. A low, growly, "Why?" comes next.

"To get my job back for me, since I can't possibly make it on my own." I pour more wine. We're going to have to open a second bottle at this rate. "I'm more than capable of taking care of myself." I pause and add, "Leaky sinks excluded."

"You knew to call me. Owning a business doesn't mean doing everything yourself. It means you know who to lean on when, or before, there's a crisis."

"Do you do that?" I ask, genuinely curious as he settles onto the stool next to mine.

"You're here, aren't you?" He's not smiling, but the lines around his eyes are. "I asked for your help. Best decision I ever made."

As angry as I am with my father for trying to shove Brandon back into my life, I'm equally grateful to Archer for giving me another option. "If it wasn't for you, I'd be begging for my job back from Brandon."

"You wouldn't have begged."

"But I might still be working there." A small inner voice whispers that Lotus Leaf would offer a more stable income than working for myself. It sounds suspiciously like Papa. "I relate to you not having your father's approval. It's frustrating."

"You're closer to receiving approval than I am."

"Papa would like me to give Brandon a second chance." When Archer's eyes narrow, I continue teasing him. "Do you think I should?"

"I showed you what I thought when I hit him. If you need me to show you again, I can fly down there and pay him a visit. I'll fly back with Calista."

I nudge him with my arm. He's warm and strong, sexy and funny. "Thanks for offering to fly her here."

"No big deal."

"But it is." I smile, easing toward him when he leans forward to kiss me. Another small voice whispers I shouldn't become accustomed to him solving my problems. Soon I'll be back in Miami, where my problems will once again be my own.

CHAPTER NINETEEN

Talia

"Lis!" I'm jogging toward the jet, arms outstretched as my sister steps off the plane with a huge smile on her face. I embrace her around her purse and jacket, hugging her tightly to me. "I can't believe you're here. I'm so glad you came."

"Oh man, me too." She laughs in my ear. Her hair smells like pineapple and coconut. Like summer. Like *home*. She holds me at arm's length and says, "Where can a girl get a drink around here?" before looking over my shoulder at the shiny Mercedes and exclaiming, "Nice wheels!"

"It's Archer's. He lets me drive it."

She's already circling the car like a hungry shark. "It's *gorgeous*."

"Let's start at the townhouse and we can decide where to go from there." I pop the trunk on the Mercedes, and an attendant loads her luggage.

At my Ohio home, Lis settles in to one of the spare

bedrooms. She's yet to stop remarking on how "freaking gorgeous" the house is. She's accused me of being blasé about the opulence, and I assured her that my jaw was on the floor for the entirety of the first week I was here.

"So. This is your life now." She's in the kitchen, sitting on a stool at the island which gives her a primo view of the fabulous stove. "Little Orphan Annie has found her Daddy Warbucks."

I wrinkle my nose. "I'm not an orphan and I do *not* think of Archer as Daddy anything." I repress a shiver. Barely. "I call him Kingpin."

"And you're Wildflower," she says without any teasing in her voice. Cradling her glass of pinot grigio, she props her head on her hand and gives me a wistful smile. "You guys are stupid cute."

"No, we're not."

She sips her wine and hums the affirmative before expressing in words, "Yes. You are."

"Papa called, by the way."

"Good. I told him to call you back. That you were worried." Of course she did. "Anything new going on?"

I lean my elbows on the island, my glass of white wine between my hands. "Yes, actually. I have very interesting news. I can have my old job back, thanks to Papa and Brandon working out a deal."

Lis's eyes widen. She didn't know, which makes me feel a bit better that she and Papa weren't conspiring against me.

"Papa would love it if Brandon and I started dating again."

"He didn't," she says, her voice packed with alarm.

"Oh, but he did." I swallow the remainder of my wine and tip more into my glass.

"Did you tell him you have a boyfriend? A life? A modicum of pride?"

"In so many words. I'm avoiding him until I can explain I'd like him to stay out of my life without swearing."

"Well, good luck with that." She pauses to bite her lip and stare at me as an unpleasant sensation creeps up my spine. "You're different with Archer. And he's..." She gestures around the house as if at a loss for words.

"Rich?"

"I was going to say he's taking care of you. I knew you'd make a face when I said that." She points at my face, which is screwed into an expression like I just smelled a skunk. "It's okay, you know, not to be independent all the time. I'm proud of you for living here."

"This house is in my contract, Lis. I'm not being taken care of. I'm being subsidized for my work on a project."

"Whatever you have to tell yourself. But you're different. Subsidized or no. You're sleeping with him, but are you sharing more than that? Are you sharing meals? Beds? Obviously, you're sharing a car."

"Are you trying to freak me out?" Because it's working. Each detail she points out causes my shoulders to lift. Now that they're nestled under my ears, I have to admit the thing I didn't want to admit. And with my sister watching me, alert and knowing, I have no choice but admit it. "He likes me."

"Duh." She rolls her eyes.

"I'm afraid he likes me so much he'll want me to stay here. Like, indefinitely. I'm not moving to Ohio."

"There's no sunshine here, so it's understandable."

"There's also no *you* here."

"I'm here now. I'm a jet's ride away. I'm positive if you two were a thing you'd be in Florida routinely. He has work there too, right?"

"Yes." My shoulders curl a little higher.

"You don't like the idea of him being in Florida?"

"In my experience, everlasting relationships are anything but."

"Your high school boyfriend and a premature engagement don't count." The reminder of Estevan lands in the center of my chest, pointy end first. "We both know Brandon was my fault. You couldn't afford the flat alone after I took off on you."

"You didn't force me to pack my things and shack up with Brandon Lambert, Lis. That's on me."

"And he's ruined you for other men?"

"No. I'd never give him that much credit. But I'm not going to lie and say I haven't set up boundaries to make sure I don't screw up again."

"What about Archer?" she asks sadly.

"What about him?"

"Have things changed since you've been here?"

Great question. "Yes. Sort of, I guess. We went out one night to his club and...uh, danced a lot." I choose not to share what else we did in his club—what I did *to him* in his club. Lis wouldn't judge me, but it feels private. Just for Archer and me. I blink, considering how he and I have secrets. That's new. I tell Lis everything. "Anyway, I came back here and told him I was going to my bed alone, and he insisted on me coming home with him."

"Did you?" Her expression is the picture of hope.

"I did. He thought I was trying to avoid him—which of course I was—and then he told me to stop being unforgettable if I expect him to forget me later."

My sister's hand goes over her heart. "Talia. Seriously. What on earth do you not like about this guy?"

"I like everything about him," I mumble to my wineglass. "That's the problem. I've never liked any guy I've dated as much as I like Archer."

She grunts, thoughtful.

"What was that for?"

"I was thinking about how I like *everything* about the guys I date, which is likely the genesis of my problems."

I chuckle. "There's no rule that says you must be half of a couple. Being unmarried isn't a problem. Papa just makes us feel like it is."

"Yeah, but..." She tilts her head. "Don't you want to be half of a couple? Have someone to cook dinner for? To go to events with? To look for in a crowded room and know they're looking for you? To curl up by a cozy fire with and cuddle in bed and drink coffee with in the morning?"

As she makes her list, I realize Archer and I have done all of those things. I've cooked for him. We've gone to see his parents. I watched him through a crowded club, and he sought me out after. I've curled up in front of a cozy fire and cuddled with him in bed—a bed he didn't sleep in until I slept in it with him. Not to mention the coffee thing. I've brought him countless mugs.

"Your face is sheet-white," my sister points out. "What's wrong?"

"I think..." I swallow thickly as the reality of the situation descends. "I am already half of a couple."

189

Lis, not caring about my impending aneurism, grins and holds up her glass. "Cheers to choosing well, my sister. Does he have any single brothers?"

Archer

Nate and I are standing in the center of the lobby at the night spa. The construction part is finished, the interior nearly finished. Large fans blow on the freshly painted walls. The furniture arrived, wrapped in plastic to ensure the painters didn't accidentally add a splatter pattern to said furniture.

"I took down a wall like this with a sledgehammer once to spite Vivian," my older brother joked when he first stepped inside. It's a long story—I'll let him tell it. Now he has his hands in his suit pants pockets and is strolling through the place for the first time. I follow, curious to hear his opinion. He has an eye for detail, and if he sees something amiss, he'll tell me.

"Never thought I'd see the day you entered the wellness industry." He pauses and offers me a half-smile. "This is nice, Arch. I'm impressed."

"The industry is crowded, but not too crowded. Plus, wellness is exploding right now. It's a wise investment. This one won't be my last."

"If Talia is responsible in any way, shape, or form for how nice this place looks, you'd better hire her for each one of them." He arches one eyebrow when I rub my bottom lip in thought. I don't know if I can hire her because I'm not sure she'll be around to be hired. "I'm not trying to make you nervous, man," my brother says, calling me on my shit. "But I recognize what it looks like to meet the woman who stops time."

"You chased Vivian hard."

He chuffs. "I had to. She wouldn't stop running away."

"You never could take a hint."

He laughs before giving me the side-eye. "William liked Talia, you know. And Lainey *loves* her."

"That's new. Dad hasn't liked any woman I've brought home. How do you know he liked her, anyway? He tell you?" I step around him and lead us to the wading pool. He follows. "Pool guy came out yesterday to fill it. We can't swim for a few days, but there she is."

Nate doesn't let me change the subject. "He did tell me. Right after you dropped an F-bomb and stomped off the portico."

"He had it coming."

"You don't know how good you got it, kid."

I glare at my brother. I respect his opinion on my work, but I don't like when he talks to me about how lucky I am. And I really don't like it when he calls me "kid."

My glare bounces off his hard jaw. "You have a dad who isn't a piece of shit. Who didn't sell your furniture out from under you because he had to get high one more time. I'm not trying to tell you I had it worse than you—"

"Really, because that's what this is sounding like." I bend and swish my hand in the water, simply to expel some of my agitated energy. "You had a shit childhood, and Will and Lainey found you and shined you up. You're whole. Congratulations."

"You know damn well I'm not the golden boy in this family."

"No, that's Benji."

"That's you, dumbass."

I stand and shake the water off my hand, consider hitting Nate, and then reconsider. He's taller than me by a few inches and wider by a few more. Not that I'd actually fight him. The last time we had a physical altercation was when he first came to live with us and borrowed my bike without asking. It ended with both of us grounded, and worse, we had to share a bedroom until we didn't hate each other anymore. We reconciled fast.

"This isn't about favorites." He shakes his head. "You don't understand because you've only had one dad, but Will's a good one." I open my mouth to argue, but Nate cuts me off. "He's also wrong."

That caught me off-guard. I snap my jaw shut.

"Nightclubs, night spas, hell..." He waves a hand like he's trying to think of a third thing, and then he does. "Night *gyms*. You do what you love because you love it. It's admirable. If Will wasn't constantly trying to hew you into a perfect replica of himself, he'd see that too. You're your own person, Archer. A damn good one."

I swallow thickly, weirdly emotional after hearing such bald approval.

"What women have you brought home?" Nate asks.

"What are you talking about?"

"You said Dad hasn't liked any woman you've brought home. Who have you brought home?"

"Monica. Jennifer. Leslie," I rattle off, annoyed he can't remember them.

He lets out a boom of a laugh that bounces off the walls. "The girls you dated in college?"

"Why's that funny?"

"Because you dated them for about three and a half minutes each. You weren't serious about them. They sure as fuck weren't serious about you."

"Thanks a lot."

"You know as well as I do those girls were dating you because you bought them nice things."

"There's nothing wrong with buying women nice things," I argue, petulant.

"Listen." He faces me, nearly eye to eye since we're close to the same height.

Nate's an intimidating guy if you don't know him. That crooked nose confirms he can take a punch, and the sheer width of his shoulders suggests he could maul you without trying. I know him. Well. He's upfront, straightforward, and confident enough in his own actions to do what he wants. I've always admired that about him.

"You like to do things for the women in your life," he says. "So do I. I blame a twisted kind of white-knight syndrome, stemming from me not being able to take care of my family when I was a kid. Making up for it now, I guess." He shrugs before adding, "Vivian fought me at first."

"You won her over." I point out the obvious.

"Took some doing. Talia is the independent sort, but she's also the family sort. The women you dated in college didn't care about anything but what you could buy them. The reason our parents, Dad in particular, were grouchy about the girlfriends you brought home was because they weren't good enough for you."

"Dad said the same thing about my clubs."

"Yeah, but he's wrong about that. He was right about the girlfriends. I remember one of them asking Lainey how much her shoes cost, and then asking to borrow them."

I wince. I'd forgotten.

"Monica." It's coming back to me now. "I ended up buying her a pair exactly like Mom's." I was proud to afford a gift she wanted, but as I remember the way she bragged to her friends, my stomach flops. We broke up shortly after. She met someone else.

"Yeah." Nate nods but doesn't wait for an explanation. "Talia's not as easily bought. She might be staying in your townhouse and driving your car around, but she's also working her ass off, isn't she?"

"Nonstop."

"After she approached you at the fundraiser, she didn't go home with you that night. She's a challenge, Arch. You like that about her."

"She didn't approach me. I came to her." I smile at the memory of the mystery woman wearing a necktie and pinstriped pants, her long, long hair a temptation I couldn't resist.

"You're different with her. I don't know if you want to hear that or not, but there it is. When she wrecked your car, you were a mess."

"Was not," I growl, not liking that word. "I was concerned."

"Concerned." Another loud *ha* escapes his chest. "You were *a mother hen*. I've never seen anything like it, and neither has Viv. *Concern* is reserved for the people you don't fall in love with. The sort of bone-chilling worry you were expressing is reserved for the woman who's wrapped around your heart and squeezing."

A visual of Talia's long hair coiled around my heart pops into my head. Rather than argue with him, I say, "She's leaving Clear Ridge after we open the spa."

"Did you ask her to stay?"

I don't answer, which is an answer in itself. I didn't ask because, frankly, rejection with her is almost guaranteed. I hate being rejected. I like sure things. But as I glance around the spa I have built with Talia's help, I realize this isn't a sure thing, either. It's a risk, and it's made me feel more alive. Then again, if it tanks, I'll feel awful.

That also parallels what I have with Talia.

"Her family is in Miami."

"Go to Miami."

Like it's that simple.

"My family is here," I counter. We have a miniature stare-off that ends with him calling my bluff.

"Sounds settled, then. She's leaving. You're moving on." Without taking me to task further—which is both a relief and completely irritating—he walks down the corridor and calls over his shoulder, "This way to the massage rooms?"

CHAPTER TWENTY

Talia

"I have an idea." I hold up my fork, a light bulb blinking over my head. "I'll add catering to my business plan and you can work for me. That would also require you to be my personal chef. Once I make my millions, I refuse to suffer through my own mediocre cooking."

Calista laughs as she plates up another perfectly fried rectangle of tofu. She marinated them, topped them with a sheet of nori—aka seaweed—then deep-fried the entire thing to make something called "tofish."

I take a bite, shocked when it reminds me of fish. I've learned my lesson: don't knock tofu until someone who can cook well prepares it.

She piles oven fries on the plate in front of me while I take another bite of the tofu "fish" and shake my head in wonderment.

"You're a genius."

"You can cook too, Talia. I know it."

"I'm too busy to cook."

"That sounds more like you." She settles in next to me, forcing a scoop of coleslaw onto my plate I was going to ignore in favor of the fries. "I need an honest opinion. Adding an item like this to the menu is going to take a lot of convincing. Julio is resistant to me changing anything."

"Meanwhile you want to change everything, suggesting you should start your own restaurant." I chew thoughtfully before saying, "What if you crumble some of the nori into the marinade as well?"

"Yes. Great idea." She reaches for her little chef's notebook and scribbles something down. "And a touch more seasoning in the batter. It's a little bland."

I take another bite and confirm with a nod. "Not much. But maybe..."

"Tarragon," we say at the same time.

"Told you you can cook," she says after writing that down as well.

I hear a knock at my front door and wait for Archer to let himself in. When the knock comes again, I blink at my sister. "Well. That's unusual."

"I wouldn't know. He's been avoiding me since I arrived." She sounds offended, and she probably is. Lis likes to have company and likes people to like her. She swore to me earlier she'd take over her best dish and wiggle her way into his good graces. I assured her he likes her just fine, but he's trying to give Lis and me space.

I open the door to find Vivian. "Hi."

"Hey, lady. I was in the neighborhood."

"How are you?" We embrace in a brief hug. I feel closer

to her since we had time to hang out at the Owen household. "Come in. You can meet my sister."

In the kitchen, Calista is on her feet and pulling another plate from the cabinet. I do a quick introduction as she plates Vivian a portion of her latest creation. "I'm recipe testing and I won't take no for an answer. So far we have confirmed we need more tarragon."

Vivian takes a bite of tofish and chews, her eyes narrowed. "Wow. This is"—she examines the golden-fried food on her plate—"surprisingly good. I eat tofu with curry, but I never knew you could do something like this with it."

"Tofu is the ultimate blank canvas. It's just waiting for a talented artist." Lis bats her lashes. "I need to convince my dominant male boss it's worth putting on the menu."

"You managed to finagle your crepes on the menu," I remind her.

"Yes, but we already had crepes on the menu. He's never served anything like this at Mango's."

A calculating expression crosses Vivian's face. "Explain to him that while vegans don't make up a majority of the population, they are usually dating an omnivore who has to please two different palates. Couples with different preferences are always looking for restaurants both of them can enjoy. Further explain that fish, especially fresh fish, goes bad quickly and can cost a lot of money. Tofu does not. I'd recommend a snazzy menu name paired with a price point deserving of this sort of unique take."

"I love you," Lis replies earnestly before turning to me. "I love her."

Vivian laughs, and Lis grabs her notebook again, presumably to take down Viv's advice.

"You both have to come to girls' night. I'm ordering from this posh restaurant in Grand Marin that just opened. Everything is made in-house, from the soups to the salad dressings to the condiments. If you are vegan, I need to know so I can order appropriately."

"I eat everything," Lis answers with a wave. "But if you wouldn't mind ordering some vegan dishes, I'd love to compare notes."

"Sure thing," Viv answers with a smile. "I'm hosting at mine and Nate's place. Cris is coming too. The boys are converging at Benji's. I'm glad to meet you, Calista. More glad that you're coming."

"I wouldn't miss it."

Vivian eats another bite of the tofish and chews slowly. "Tarragon, for sure. Did you consider adding chopped capers to the marinade?"

"Capers. Vivian. Will you marry me?" my sister asks.

"Sorry, toots. I'm spoken for." She hops off the stool. "I have to run. Saturday. Eight o'clock. We have plenty of spirits but, Tal, bring your favorite Archer Owen story. We're sharing *all*. Goodbye, ladies."

"Bye, Viv."

She leaves, and Calista shakes her head. "She could be your sister-in-law if you play your cards right."

"Do not start."

"When's Archer coming home today? I have a plate of bribery to take him." Lis munches on a fry.

"For the third time, you don't have to bribe him. Honestly, I don't know his schedule this week. He has a lot going on." I pay attention to my lunch.

"You should take it to him. Men like to be brought dinner. Besides, you've been avoiding him this week."

"I have not."

"When have you spoken to him?"

"Other than cc'ing him on a company email?"

She folds her arms and gives me a know-it-all smirk.

"Fine. I'll take over the tofish." I roll my eyes for effect, though I am slightly nervous. Maybe it was Viv's inference to bring a story about him, like I'm already part of the family.

"Don't tell him it's not fish. I want an honest carnivore's reaction. Also, if you return home late, or not at all, you will owe me a massive amount of gratitude. And, at your discretion, lots of details. I haven't been laid in a few months. I'm afraid I'm forgetting how to do it."

I chuckle at her plight. "You mean in your desperation you didn't call Webber?"

She wrinkles her nose. "Ew. Are you sure there's not a spare Owen brother floating around?"

"Pretty sure the Owens are done adopting boys who grow into gorgeous men."

"What about a stray cousin?" She refills her wine glass. "Or a good friend who's like a brother and is also a foodie?"

"With an ass like Julio's?" I prompt. She deserves it for what she's putting me through with Archer. She blushes. *Got her.*

"With an attitude like Julio's, he has to have a great ass or he'd be unbearable." Her frown is tepid, if it's a frown at all. "He'd better let me put this faux fish on the menu, or I will have his balls."

"He'd probably like that too," I tell her, and she wads up her napkin and bounces it off my nose.

Archer

I change into jeans and a Henley and pace into the kitchen to find dinner. Nate and I grabbed a late lunch after we visited the spa, but somehow I'm hungry already. I pop open the fridge where there is leftover Chinese food, a couple of apples, and a bag of salad mix that has seen better days.

I shut the fridge and uncork a half-full bottle of wine I opened last night. *Alone.*

I didn't want to drink alone, but I wasn't willing to bust in on Talia's sister time with Calista. I survived many a lonely night without Talia before she lived next door, and I should be able to do it again. The bitch of it is, I'd prefer her here all the time, which makes me worry unnecessarily about her leaving when the spa opens.

"Find your balls, man," I mutter as I pour myself a glass of red. Halfway to the living room to watch TV I most assuredly won't enjoy, I hear the door open and a sweet voice say my name.

"Hi." Fresh-faced, smiling Talia, her hair wavy and every-where at once, is standing in my kitchen with a container in her hands. "Lis cooked dinner. She wants you to try it."

"Perfect timing. I was about to resort to delivery." I walk over, soaking in her beauty and trying to read her face. Other than a few emails, I haven't talked her to while Lis has been here. "I thought you were avoiding me."

"Me?" She makes a choking noise to express her offense. "You are the one avoiding me."

"I don't want to be pushy."

"Since when?"

"Wine?" I offer. Now that she's here, I want to give her as many reasons to stay as possible.

"Sure." She settles on one of the barstools and props her chin in her hands. I deliver her a glass of wine, stealing a kiss as I do. She tastes like Talia—in other words, heaven.

"Nate came by the spa today."

"What did he think?" She sits straighter, perking up at the mention of work. On the clock. That's my girl.

"He thinks we're a good team."

A trickle of alarm slips into her eyes but quickly vanishes.

"I might have to hire you again if this works out." When she's silent, I continue. "Have you thought about what sort of projects you'll take on? How's the website coming along?"

"Prisha is a godsend. I swear if I can make this work, I'll hire her on as my assistant."

"*When*, Wildflower," I correct. "When you make this work."

She blushes prettily. "When."

I can't resist her for another minute. "I've missed you like crazy. How long are you here?"

"I promised Lis we'd watch this cooking competition show on TV. Want to come over and watch it with us?"

"Can we make out the whole time and ignore the show?"

"No." She laughs, the easy sound going a long way to soothing my earlier worries. I hate to admit it, but Nate wasn't far off with his "mother hen" comment.

"Can we make out here before I have to let you go home?"

Heat blooms in her dark eyes, a nonverbal *yes*. "I'd like that."

"Yeah, me too." I offer a hand and help her up. When she's standing in front of me, I cup her jaw and rest my lips on hers. One kiss and I'm already planning on taking her clothes off. A taste of her isn't enough. It never has been. After I met her at the fundraiser, she rarely wasn't on my mind.

My dinner forgotten, I walk her backward to the living room, my mouth sealed with hers. She doesn't resist, fisting my shirt and stroking into my mouth with that talented tongue of hers.

"She'll know if we have sex," she says between kisses.

"So?" I lay her down on the living room sofa. Her butt hits the remote and the TV blinks on, some cop show rerun.

"Archer." She sighs my name. I love that sound. I love the way she claws at my hair when I kiss her neck. I love—

I cut off the thought and start pulling off her clothes. Her mild protesting seems out of habit more than anything. I know she doesn't mean it when she starts undressing me. Within minutes, she's rolled over the mute button, and I'm settled between her legs to have an appetizer I've been dying for all week.

I part her with my thumbs and stroke her clit with the flat of my tongue. She tugs my hair and encourages me until words fail her entirely. Then there's only moaning and writhing, and the honey-sweet taste of her on my tongue.

"Hurry," comes her request after an orgasm shakes her luscious body. I obey, wanting to be inside her as badly as I wanted to taste her. Okay, worse.

When I slide home, she has her hands wrapped around my biceps and her hazel eyes glued to mine. I hold her with my gaze, taking her hard and fast. Her breaths are truncated and interspersed with high, tight noises making it impossible for me to hold back.

So I don't.

When my mind goes blessedly blank, the tension from the week ebbing with my release, I finally relax. My rigid shoulders soften, and she notices, lightly scraping my back with her fingernails. Up, down. Up, down. I pull my face out of her hair, intending to say something akin to "I knew you wanted me," but instead three words crowd my mouth.

Three words I'd be an idiot to say.

Three words I refuse to think.

And so, I think of three different words that aptly sum up my emotional state. Want to know what they are?

Fuck. I'm screwed.

CHAPTER TWENTY-ONE

Archer

Guys' night at Benji's is underway. Four of us round a poker table in the basement. A really nice basement—fully finished with its own gym. He also has a massive shower and bathroom (complete with towel warmers), a wine-tasting room, and a cellar. If anyone is hosting indoors, Benji's house is a good choice.

"Fold," says the guy sitting next to Nate. His name's Heaton Taylor, and I haven't seen him since he was a scrawny mathlete sitting next to Benji on that televised math competition, *Divide and Conquer.*

"I never should have invited you," Benji jokes with a laugh. "We're not getting any of your money tonight."

"Hell no, you're not." Heaton laughs, his straight, white smile miles from the crooked teeth I remember him having. His hair is a sandy, reddish color, kind of like Nate's. That's where the similarity ends. Heaton is younger, like Benji, and leaner with muscle, like me, though I have him outweighed.

"What's the use of having it in the bank?" Benji asks. "Spend it."

"I'm new to the wealth game, man. I've spent plenty."

"Worried it'll run out?" Nate, a cigar between his teeth, asks.

"Kind of."

"Noobs," I mutter, but Heaton takes the insult in stride.

"What say you, Nate?" Benji prompts.

Nate hums, his big arms folded over the table. One eyebrow is craned so high his forehead crinkles.

"Cut the shit. You have no poker face." Benji grins.

"You're one to talk," I tell our youngest brother. "That smile is the only face you got."

Heaton laughs. "Isn't that the truth. When I ran into you the other day, it'd been, what...fifteen years since I saw you? You look identical to how I remember you back in the day. Except back then you had no game."

"He still didn't, until very recently," Nate mutters, wearing his tough-guy face.

"All part of my charm. You and Archer could learn something from me," Benji tells Heaton. "Woo yourself a woman or two."

"Pass," Heaton says, hinting there's a story behind his resistance.

"Just what I need," I chime in.

"Someone telling you what to do," Nate and Benji finish for me in unison. It's my go-to line whenever the topic of my singleness is broached. It rings less and less true the longer Talia is in town. After the couch quickie that never should have made her mean even more to me, it sounds like pure bullshit.

"Call." Nate takes the unlit cigar out of his mouth and sets it aside before throwing in a handful of chips representing a whole lot of money. To me, he says, "Talia isn't the type to tell you what to do, is she?"

"You have nothing, and you just doubled the pot," I say with a head shake.

"We'll see." Nate holds his cards close to his chest—literally, in this case.

"Talia does her own thing. She's not interested in doing anything else."

"Except move to Clear Ridge to dedicate herself to your night spa," Benji says.

"Sounds like she likes you," Heaton observes.

The turncoat.

To Nate, I say, "Let's see 'em."

They reveal their cards.

"I will be damned!" Benji exclaims. "You dick! You took me for a ride."

Nate grins. "Now who has the best poker face?" He scrapes the pot toward him like a greedy troll. "Technically, the best face, period."

"If you're into the crooked nose thing." I toss my cards on top of the chips he's scraping in.

"I don't need to be into it, but Vivian is."

Heaton and Benji make a show of saying, "Aww!"

"Shut up, both of you," Nate says. "Benj, you guys decide if you or Archer is going to be my best man?"

"He refuses to choose," Benji tells Heaton before raising his glass of bourbon. "Obviously, the best-looking one of us should be best man."

"So, me," I conclude.

"You two are ridiculous." Nate grabs a red chip. "Winner is the best man. No arguing. Ready?"

"*This* is how we're deciding?" Benji asks, affronted.

Heaton folds his arms and sits back in his chair. "This I gotta see."

"Just pick your favorite brother." I pull my hands across my chest, watching as an angry storm cloud forms over Nate's head.

"Unless you want to cage fight each other for it," he growls, "I'm flipping a chip. Aside, cage fighting could permanently change the outcome in the best-looking-face contest."

"Fine." Benji narrows dark eyes at me. "Ready to lose?"

"Heads or tails?" Nate shifts his gaze between us.

"Heads," I say at the same time Benji says, "Tails."

"At least that wasn't a struggle." Nate flips the chip, letting it land on the pile of chips he's accumulated from his winning hand. It hits with a *plink!* Heads.

"The universe is wise," I brag.

"The universe is against me for taking years to realize I was in love with Cris," Benji grumbles. "Be forewarned."

"You're a slow learner," I throw in. I'm helpful like that.

My younger brother's laugh brings his smile back like it never left. Nate joins in, stacking his chips into neat columns on his side of the table.

"Guys. It's been real. I have an early day tomorrow, so I'm going to head out." Heaton stands, shaking each of our hands. "Benji, we'll do it again. At my mansion the next time." I can't tell if he's kidding about the mansion. He slaps my shoulder and congratulates me on the best-man win, and then he leaves.

"You think *I'm* a slow learner?" Benji lifts thick eyebrows in challenge, picking up where we left off.

"I know it's hard to believe with your smarts and all, but yes. It took you nearly *ten* years to realize Cris was your perfect other half."

"He's got you there," Nate agrees.

"It didn't take the *entire* ten years," Benji argues, stacking his small pile of remaining chips as I scrape the cards toward me. "And once I realized how I felt, I wasted zero time telling her. Nate, same way. He admitted to Vivian he was a goner. You, not so much. You're standing there with your dick in your hand."

"My dick is not in my hand." I give him my best fuck-off look and flat-out refuse to admit I'm in deeper than I expected. Bottom line, it doesn't matter. I'm not going to do what Nate did: drop an I-love-you bomb and end up screwed over when she tells me she doesn't feel the same way. It worked out in the end for Viv and Nate, but what are the odds of that happening twice?

"You two are neck-deep in the ocean of love," I continue as I shuffle the cards. "You're not seeing things clearly. Talia and I have a shared attraction. That's it. Sometimes relationships are temporary."

"We know," Nate and Benji both answer, and the bitch of it is, they *do* know. They used to date women with expiration dates before they each found women who were perpetual.

"Don't wait too long, Arch," Benji says, looking serious for a change. "I love Cris with everything I am. Denying it meant wasting years."

"It wasn't wasted. She's your best friend," I argue,

because there has to be a silver lining for me and Talia. There has to be.

"Yeah, but we could have been having sex that entire time. It's Nate's fault, anyway."

"Me?" Nate asks. "What the hell did I do?"

"You came to my house that night blubbering over Vivian—"

"I don't blubber."

"—after you confessed your undying love for her and she rejected you."

"Yeah, well, at least I put myself out there. Which is more than I can say for The Art of Stoicism over here." He gestures at me.

"I'm not in love with Talia," I say loud enough to stop their bickering. I hate how those words tasted. Like something sour I had to spit out of my mouth. I hate how untrue they sounded too. It'd be a fuck of a lot easier *not* to love her. "I like her. A lot. That's it. There's nothing more to say."

Neither of my brothers are intimidated by my growling. They exchange looks that communicate they're giving up. Fine with me. I don't need a proper surrender, just silence.

"Give me the cards," Benji says.

"Forget it. I'm dealing." I tip my chin. "Someone front me more chips."

"You good for it?" asks Benji, the smartass. I don't answer him.

"What's wild?" Nate asks.

"Nothing. We're playing it the way it's intended to be played, where every card is exactly as it appears."

If only the rest of life worked that way too.

SINCE I DROVE Nate to Benji's house after dropping off Talia for her girls' night, I take him back too.

"I do not know what to do with all this money," he humble-brags as he counts the bills. "Here." He stuffs a one-hundred-dollar bill into the cup holder. "Buy your girl something nice. I have an embarrassment of riches."

"You are an embarrassment *to* the riches."

He slaps me on the arm as he laughs at my lame joke. We ride in silence for a moment before he says, "Glad it's you. I mean, if it was Benji, I'd be glad it was him, but...I'm glad it's you."

I don't know what to say. A tsunami of hectic feelings has been pummeling me lately. I swallow past a bowling ball lodged in my throat. Hopefully he stops talking before I embarrass myself.

"When Vivian and I were planning the wedding"—he starts, definitely *not* done talking—"she said something I'll never forget. She said, 'If you wouldn't have been brave enough to give me your heart, I'd have held on to mine for safekeeping forever.'"

Damn. You'd have to be a heartless bastard not to feel the sentiment behind that. It's one of the sweetest fucking things I've ever heard, and I'm *not* a sap.

"I believe if you feel it, you should say it," Nate continues. "That hasn't worked out well for me always, given my birth mother is a piece of work, but for the most part, being clear about what I want, when I want it, has served me. If Talia is it for you, she's worth putting your ass on the line."

"And if she believes she's not for me?" I shift in my seat,

not sure I want to hear the answer. I'm not accustomed to heart-to-hearts with my brother about the women I'm dating.

"Then I recommend Benji's house for shots. He has a comfortable guest bed."

"You were a miserable son of a bitch then, Nate." I glance over at him. He watches out the window, offering a solemn nod as if he's remembering how dark those days were. "Your hindsight might be clear as a bell now, but if you knew it wouldn't have turned out, would you go back and risk it again?"

Rather than admit I'm making a damn good point, which is irritating even though I didn't expect him to, he says, "I am who I am, Arch. And maybe that's the takeaway here. You do you, bro. You're the only one who can."

He grins like he knows he's way too old to use the phrase "you do you." We arrive at his place, and I park in the driveway. He walks in ahead of me, and the second the door is open, I hear a lot of female laughter, and one delicate snort.

In the living room, on the large, slouchy couch, Vivian is doubled over, Calista leaning into her, laughing just as hard. Cris is on the floor holding her stomach, Talia is next to her, tears running down her face, and in a fit of laughter as well.

"What's this?" Nate asks, a smile spreading his lips as he goes to Vivian. I'm smiling too. I have no idea what's so funny, but these overjoyed women are contagious.

"Hi, honey." Viv swipes her eyes. "Nothing we can talk about. Girls' night is sacred." She purses her lips for a kiss he doesn't hesitate giving her.

"Hi, *honey*," Cris echoes to Nate. "No kiss for me?"

"You think I won't?" He pulls Cris to her feet and places

a quick kiss on her cheek. "You can't drive yourself home if you've drunk yourself into a laughing stupor."

"We switched to water a long time ago." She shoves him, but he doesn't budge an inch. "Besides, I'm not sleeping without Benji. I can't stand to be away from him now that we live together."

I pretend to gag. She gives me an evil eye that is unintentionally adorable.

"Bye, lovelies!" She waves to the girls. "Lis, text me."

"I will," Calista promises.

When Cris reaches me, she springs to her toes. I offer my cheek, expecting a kiss, but instead, she yanks my earlobe and whispers, "Do *not* lose this one, Archer. I like her."

"Okay, okay, ow!" I rub my ear, and the petite blonde spears me with a hot glare. Hopefully my agreement won't hold up in court. I was being tortured, technically.

After Cris leaves, Talia eyes me curiously. I help her off the floor, and she stands to her full height, chin up. I deliver the kiss she's wondering if I'll give her despite our very attentive company. I can't think of anything except how badly I want her in my bed, in my life, in my *world*.

Damn Nate. Blaming him feels better than blaming myself.

Talia's eyes twinkle, her smile soft. "Hiya, Kingpin."

"Hey, Wildflower." I wrap my hand around her neck and tangle my fingers into her fantastically silky hair.

"Seriously not fair. No one is kissing me hello. Why don't you have a fourth brother?" Calista aims the question at Nate.

He shrugs. "Three Owens are enough Owens."

"Sometimes too many," Viv adds.

"Well, if we decided anything tonight, it's that we need men for one thing and one thing only." This ushers in another round of laughter. My brother and I both shake our heads.

"Assuming that one thing is a ride home," I tell Talia and her sister.

"We could have called Lyft for that," she says pragmatically, once again an arm's length away. I'd be a certified moron to admit what I'm feeling to her. She'd cut me off at the knees and wear my shoes around her neck like a prize.

"But we'll take you up on it, since you're here and all." Calista hugs Vivian goodbye. Talia does the same, thanking her for the fun evening. Viv stands to see us out, but as the ladies walk outside to the car, she stops me at the threshold.

I groan. "Don't tell me you have advice for me too."

"She's great. Incredible. And Calista, oh my God. She rocks. And she's a good cook. She brought over a whole pan of marshmallow and fudge brownies that are to die for."

"She made fish out of tofu," I tell her. "I'm sort of angry about how good it tasted. It doesn't seem right."

Vivian laughs and then leans on the doorway while Nate, whistling, prepares himself a drink at the bar cart in the living room. "Talia has her reasons for being gun-shy. Don't go off half-cocked before you find out what those reasons are. Some women need more space than others."

"If memory serves, you needed a couple of states' worth of space."

"Very funny." She gives me a bland blink.

"Viv, nightcap?" Nate calls out.

"Sure thing, babe," she calls back. Then to me, "Be patient."

"Patient's my middle name," I tell her, not bothering to

214

ask her to decipher the coded message. In the car, I turn over the engine. Talia and Lis chat on the way home about everything and nothing. Two peas of the same pea pod.

At the townhouse, I open the car doors for them. We all walk to the building, only at the alcove, I turn for my townhouse, and Lis and Talia turn for theirs.

"If you two wanted to..." Calista gestures between her sister and me. "You can hang out longer if you want. I'll probably go to bed and read a cookbook. My life is *so* exciting."

"I'm good," I tell her, saving Talia from having to refuse. "I might have a cigar on the balcony instead of reading a cookbook, though."

"Sounds nice." She sends Talia a careful glance, gauging her sister's reaction.

Talia brightens with a smile, Benji-style. "*Totally* up for reading in bed tonight. Don't we have some homemade ice cream to check on?" She loops her arm in Lis's, throwing over her shoulder, "Thanks for the ride, Kingpin."

"Anytime, Wildflower." Then I head inside to find a cigar.

Talia

"You two are ridiculous," Lis says around a mouthful of ice cream. "Why don't you go over there and fuck him already? He clearly wants you to."

I nearly choke on my bite of chocolate brownie ice cream.

"Calista!" I scold her rather than admit I'm miffed he

didn't invite me over. Not that I'd have gone over anyway. It's my sister's last night in town.

"I haven't been out of the game too long to believe sitting here and eating ice cream with me is better than sex." Her brooks-no-argument tone reminds me way too much of Mom.

"It's really good ice cream." I smile. She's sitting on one side of the living room sofa, and I'm on the other. I poke her with one stockinged foot. "I want to spend as much time as possible with you before you leave tomorrow. I'm not going to go over to Archer's for a booty call while you're here."

"I would," she says to her bowl.

"Go on. He might take a substitute."

"Yeah, right." She doesn't laugh. "He's totally nuts about you, Tal. He's not going to accept *any* substitute. I also haven't been out of the game too long to recognize a man over the moon for you when I see one. Brandon never looked at you the way Archer did tonight."

"Archer chose a cigar over me, Lis."

"Well, you chose ice cream over him." She shakes her head. "You're being impossible, and I can't figure out why. What are you afraid of?"

Him stealing away my attention when I should be paying attention to my dad's health or my newfound career.

Luckily she doesn't wait for me to answer.

"He told you he'd be smoking a cigar on the balcony so you'd know where to find him if you changed your mind."

"I doubt that."

"Whatever." She finishes off her ice cream with a few more agitated scrapes of her spoon. "You are as stubborn as Papa."

"Am not." I frown, but it feels true.

"*Are to*. I'm going to bed," she announces, pushing to stand from the sofa. "Beignets tomorrow, and then back to Florida for me. Night, babe. You have fun friends."

She rinses her bowl in the kitchen sink. I follow suit, tucking our silverware and bowls into the dishwasher and turning it on before climbing the stairs to my own room. Once I'm there, I peek out the balcony window to check if he's out there. He is. A fire glows in the stone fireplace, his handsome profile catching the light.

Tonight, when Nate walked over to kiss Vivian, I felt a longing so acute, I had to catch my breath. Then Archer came for me. I realized in an instant how much I liked him coming for me. How much comfort he offers. How can something so dangerous feel so damn right?

Grabbing a throw from the chair in the corner of the room, I wrap it around my shoulders and step outside. The March wind is fierce, kicking my hair around my head. I shiver. His head turns like he heard me, or maybe he was expecting me.

"Hey," I call out. No sense in pretending. We both know he's the reason I came outside.

"Hi, gorgeous," he calls. "Can't sleep?"

"That's my line. You're the insomniac."

He stands and approaches the wall the same as me, and now we're facing each other, arms leaning on two separate ledges, enough space between to be daunting. How apt.

"What had you in stitches when I picked you up tonight?" he asks.

"I'll never tell." I doubt it'd be as funny out of context. We were laughing about womanhood in general. It started with long lines at public restrooms and ended with us joking about men and their appendages.

"Your sister in bed with her cookbooks?"

"Yes." I don't know what comes over me, but I blurt out, "She thinks I should be over there having sex with you."

"I knew I liked her." His smile is a flash of white in the dark. A pleasant thrill trickles down my body, warming everywhere it touches. Keeping my walls up with him is becoming harder and harder. "You miss me, don't you?"

I roll my eyes rather than admit he's right.

He makes a show of looking over his shoulder at the fireplace. "Cozy over here, Wildflower. Why don't you sneak out and pay me a visit?"

A smile curls my lips before I can stop it. My excuse of spending Lis's last evening with her seems lame since she's already gone to bed.

"I have to be home to enjoy homemade beignets tomorrow morning," I say, the weakest caveat ever.

"I accept those terms." He pushes away from the ledge, walks inside, and returns with the electric blanket. As he's unspooling the cord, he says, "Come on over. What do you have to lose?"

So much, Kingpin. So much.

I go over anyway.

CHAPTER TWENTY-TWO

Talia

"I don't know why you fight me." Archer peels my sweater over my head and tosses it onto his bed.

"I'm not fighting you," I lie, my voice small.

"Not now, but you were." His hands slide from my waist to my ribs to cup my breasts. I didn't bother with a bra since I changed to come over here. Who am I kidding? I knew he'd have my clothes off the second I set one toe inside his townhouse.

He thumbs my nipples as a rich, decadent shiver climbs my spine. "You have a bad habit of pushing me away."

I trap his hands over my breasts so I can focus on what he's saying. "*You* have a bad habit of being mercurial."

"And you're not?" His brows pinch in thought before he tugs his hands out from under mine and unsnaps my jeans. "After the VP room of Club Nine, you couldn't get away from me fast enough."

He smells too good. His hands feel too good. I'm capable

of resisting him, I just...don't want to. Tipping my chin, I intend to set my lips to his for a kiss. He halts my movement, his knuckle under my chin and his thumb close to my bottom lip.

He angles a glance at me through narrowed eyelids. "Tell me what you're afraid of."

I tuck my hands beneath his Henley, tracing the bumps and ridges of his abs before encountering the crisp chest hair encircling his incredible pectorals. "The usual. Spiders. Public speaking. Loss of control."

"You're safe here. Spiders fear *me*."

I offer a half-smile.

"And public speaking is a learned skill." His grin is honey slow. "So is surrendering control."

He grips my wrists and pulls them behind my back, holding them in place with one of his larger hands. Then he slides his other hand into my jeans and past my panties. I suck in a breath and wiggle, but his hold only tightens.

"I'll let you go if you want. Or you can let go of some of that control of yours. You'll like it." He is convincing, kissing me senseless while tucking his fingers into my panties. By the time he's gliding his middle finger back and forth in my wetness, setting me off like a book of lit matches, I stop trying to get free and simply enjoy myself.

His talented fingers play and wander. I close my eyes, at war with the instinct to close off, protect myself. Something's changed between us, but the warning bell in my mind sounds flat. Either that or I can't concentrate while he's touching me like this. He confines his exploration to my clit, lowering his head to pull my nipple into my mouth at the same time.

"Almost," he breathes, his warm breath covering me as he

switches breasts and drives me out of my mind. I fight his hold, not to escape him, but because I have to touch him or I'll die.

And so comes my impatient request. "Let me touch you."

"Later," he murmurs, giving me his full attention. He watches my face as he continues his languid strokes. He doesn't let me go. He doesn't look away. Overcome, I give in to the release surging forward. My shaking legs lose their strength, but he catches me and releases my wrists. I collapse like a bag of flour onto the bed.

He tugs off my jeans and shoes, throwing aside my panties as well. I'm dazed when he lies down next to me a minute later, naked, on his belly, his hands folded in front of him. His hair is a mess from removing his shirt. All I can think about is having sex with him for hours.

Dammit. I am so pathetic.

"You're potent. Did you know that?" I grumble.

His half-smile suggests he does, but what he says is, "Not to everyone. Just you."

He cups my jaw and leans in to kiss me. He's watching me, and for a second I fear a pending pronouncement. There's definitely something lingering in his eyes. I realize what we've shared has been intense, which for me is uncommon. In moments like these, it's harder to remember why I don't want more from him, but the instinct to flee is alive and well.

"Wildflower," he murmurs, but what follows isn't what I expect. "Get on your hands and knees."

It surprises me so much I burst out laughing. He doesn't. "Why would I do that?"

"Because. I'm going to grip those thick hips of yours and

tenderly fuck you from behind. *Slow*. Then fast. Until you're screaming my name. His voice grows lower as he speaks, ending on a whisper. He punctuates it with a grin of challenge. "Don't you want a few more of those big Os you like so much?"

I resist moaning *yes, please*. Like I said: pathetic. Trying to hold on to what dwindling control I have left, I shrug and try for nonchalant. "I can live without them."

He shrugs too, with his mouth and beard. "As you wish."

Gauntlet dropped.

I crane an eyebrow. He rolls to one side and props his head on his hand like he's in no hurry to persuade me. My eyes wander to his naked chest and torso, to his cock, at a healthy half-mast between his legs. I'll show him a thing or two about control.

I roll over and kiss his mouth, taking my time. His hands move to my back, but he doesn't hold me in place. His beard tickles my lips as I lick to his throat. As I suckle his pulse point. It doesn't take long for him to wind a fist into my hair. I kiss my way down his chest, to his stomach, and earn a tug. Just enough to let me know he's steering. I whimper with pleasure. I am within sucking distance of his incredible thickness when he pulls my head up. A second later, I'm flat on my back.

"Nice try," he praises, on top now. "My turn." He slides down my body the same way I did his, only he stops at my nipples, distracting me for way too long. Then he's circling my belly button with his tongue, freeing his hand of my hair to take hold of my thighs.

Like every time I've been naked with him, I cede control. He laps at my folds, inserts one finger and then two, while I lift my feet to his shoulders. One of his hands comes up to pinch my nipple as he continues to pay delicious attention to my body. Whatever argument or challenge I fought to win moments ago is forgotten. I whisper his name, interspersed with the "yes, please" I wouldn't allow myself to say earlier. My hips buck when he hits that perfect spot. I come on his fingers not long after he starts.

A wash of color bursts behind my closed eyelids as my entire body sizzles and pops like oil in a hot pan. I can't open my eyelids, as if they're weighed down by sandbags. His arm loops my back, and he flips me. Now I'm dead weight, flat on my stomach.

Finally, I pry my eyes open and peek through a curtain of my hair. He drags my hips back, my ass colliding with his muscular thighs.

"What do you think you're doing?" I ask, hoarse.

"*You.*"

Using what little strength remains, I push onto my hands and knees and back into his thighs. I collide with his rock-hard erection as it slides through my wet folds. He twists my hair into a long rope and tosses it over my shoulder.

His thumbs coast over my ass before his fingers tickle along my seam. Then he's in, his cock sinking deep as he draws a long, sated moan from my throat.

One powerful thrust, and I'm unable to hold in my reaction. A loud, approving "Oh!" escapes my lips. He doesn't let up, slamming into me with enough force to push my breath from my lungs. Still tingling from my last orgasm, I shout—yes, *shout*—his name. Encouraged, he picks up speed.

I continue praising him as another orgasm slams into me. I lose the strength in my arms and collapse facedown on the pillow. Fingers gripping my hips, his release takes him a moment later. He spills inside of me, each pump shoving me higher on the bed until the pillow is under my chest instead of my cheek. I laugh, effervescent and damned satisfied as waves of electricity buzz along my limbs.

He folds over me, his breathing not yet regulated. His chest warms my back, reminding me of that first time over the kitchen counter, when he took me under his control, and I was more than willing to let him do whatever he wanted.

He shoves my hair aside, since it's rearranged itself of its own free will, and kisses my neck. "What you do to me, Wild-flower," he growls into my ear before pulling out and rolling to his back.

My hips sink to the bed. I have to make a pitstop in the bathroom, but what I wouldn't give to fall into a deep sleep right where I am, coasting to dreamland on a wave of spent hormones.

"I like that smile." He leans over and kisses my mouth. "Clean up. Come back." He delivers a sharp, fast slap to my ass, and my head snaps up.

"Hey!"

He grins. I touch the corner of his bearded smile with one finger. "Why don't you smile more?"

"Gotta keep my guard up. People want things from me."

"Spine-exploding orgasms?" I guess.

"Money. Favors. Not the sexual kind, sadly."

"I have a hard time believing that. You're very, very good." It's my parting line. I go to the bathroom and then return and start collecting my clothes. He pokes the bed next to where he's lying.

"Ass in here," he commands.

"Sorry, Kingpin. I have to go."

"Don't make me bring you back here. I'm very convincing when I need to be." He pushes up onto one elbow, looking like the best gift I've ever unwrapped. All that golden skin and taut muscle, manly hair, and sparkling green eyes. "As you keep reminding me."

"Do I?"

"Afraid I'll win you over? Make you want to stay?"

I blink, not knowing how to respond. Maybe because he's right.

"Ass. In. Bed." He pokes the rumpled sheets with his pointer finger as he says each word.

We're running out of time. The spa's nearly done, the grand opening looms. I can spend the remainder of my time here in his bed, in his arms, or I can spend it trying to draw boundaries I end up ignoring and crossing anyway.

I surrender and crawl into bed, curling against his furnace-hot skin. I hum in my throat, the post-orgasmic glow returning the moment I touch him.

"Admit I'm right." He hugs me close.

"About?"

"You want to be here." He kisses the top of my head. "I just can't figure out why you're playing hard to get."

"I'm going back to Miami," I murmur, reminding us both.

"Yeah, I know." He goes quiet for a long while before he sighs. "But you're here now."

I am, but there are things he doesn't know. I back away from him and slide my hands under my cheek on my own pillow. "I have my reasons."

"For sleeping with me?"

I smile. "Well, yes, but I mean for leaving. I've been caged by the men in my past before."

"Not trying to cage you, Wildflower. You're completely in control of what you do and how you do it. This"—he gestures at the bedroom—"was a choice. I invited, you came." His lips hitch. "Several times, if memory serves."

He takes me there faster and more often than any man I've been with. My heart lurches. I like him so much. Too much.

"You can't blame me for trying to change your mind." A shadow of seriousness slips over his face. "Everything's better with you here. In my house, my bed. Hell, just knowing you're next door makes me happy."

I might hyperventilate.

My smile trembles. His stiffens.

Stepping up what we have could be dangerous for everyone. I've never had a relationship work out, and the ones that looked like they might were doomed.

"Wedding's in May. I want you there."

My heart stops for a second before realizing he's talking about Nate and Vivian's wedding, not proposing to me.

"I'm the best man." He shoves one arm beneath his pillow, facing me. "Nate flipped a coin. Well, a poker chip. I won. Or lost. Depending on who you ask."

I have to chuckle, knowing there's no way he thought he "lost" by being named best man. "Do I offer congratulations or condolences?"

"Either. Both," he says, his dry humor making an appearance. "He was sappy on the ride home. It was irritating."

I stretch an arm over his chest and rest my head on his

shoulder instead. Burying my nose in his incredible neck, I inhale and shut my eyes. "Stop being so likable."

"No way." His fingers take their places in my hair. "Especially if it means you're starting to like me."

He barely tugs, and my mouth lands on his. While I'm kissing him, I know three things for certain:

I'm not going back to my townhouse tonight.

I won't soon forget him telling me everything is better with me around.

And what I feel for him? It's *way* more than like.

CHAPTER TWENTY-THREE

Talia

Two weeks later, I'm inspecting every corner of the night spa and preparing for the opening. Today is the final walk-through, then we, or rather *he*, can alert the team to fix the crooked molding in massage room three, or hang the warning signs required by law in the wading pool room. They were designed to be stylish and quiet instead of big, bold, red-lettered eyesores.

Everything I started months ago—from dumping green juice over Ed Lambert's head, to launching my own company, to starting up with Archer, is beneath this one over-arching goal.

We've been hanging out nearly every night since Lis's last night in Ohio, when I sneaked over and slipped into his bed. The following morning I woke next to him. I left him snoozing, the rain pattering the windows and patio door in the early hours. I intended to have breakfast with my sister before she left that afternoon. When I opened Archer's front door, guess who was standing there, beignets in hand?

Lis, who was thrilled I'd stayed the night with Archer, barged in with breakfast and made her presence known by shouting up the stairs, "Get your butt down here, Kingpin!"

Predictably, Archer didn't spring out of bed bursting with sunshine. I went upstairs to wake him, which he resisted, instead pulling me into his arms, burying his beard in my neck, and mumbling something I couldn't understand but assumed was a sexual request. When I told him my sister was downstairs with donuts, he cupped a handful of my butt and squeezed, and said to give him five minutes. Then he climbed out of bed, shut the bathroom door, and turned on the shower.

Since our beignet-and-coffee filled morning with my sister, he hasn't mentioned what will happen after I return to Florida. He doesn't shy from telling me he likes me in his bed or in his life, but he's careful in the way he goes about it. I'm glad. If he turned up the pressure, I'm not sure how I'd react.

Will he want to continue flying back and forth to Florida if seeing me means travel? Or will we go back to email-flirting with the occasional request of advice? Will he chalk us up as temporary, moving forward with his life as usual?

Will I?

Whenever I think about "us," my stomach clenches in fearful anticipation. What if I changed my mind about leaving? I can't afford the townhouse next door, but he could rent it to me. When I think of moving in with him, I want to throw up. I made a similar decision with Brandon, and it was so clearly the wrong decision. And what about Calista? She can't afford a place of her own. What's she supposed to do? Move in with Julio? Or worse, *Webber*?

The bell dings over the front door as Archer and I emerge from the long corridor of the pool area. A woman wearing a butter-yellow pantsuit and carrying a fat leather handbag smiles in greeting.

"Mr. Owen. Ms. Richards." The event planner, Carmella Fortova, is here to finalize the plans for Saturday night. She's older, fifty or so. Her hefty build is balanced on a small frame precariously. She has the energy of a hummingbird. "Ready to wrap this baby up?"

"More than ready," I answer and feel Archer's eyes at the side of my head.

"Wonderful. In here?" She gestures to the lobby, where a massive round glass table sits in the center of a circle of couches and chairs that are stacked with fat, fluffy pillows. Rather than ratty magazines on the table, there is a collection of shells in the middle. Guests will be encouraged to bring their drinks from the bar, whether it's wheatgrass juice or a peach Bellini, and congregate.

Carmella takes the chair while I lower onto the couch. Archer sits next to me, his hip touching mine. She pulls a leather binder out of her bag and takes a pen from the loop. "I didn't see a sign out front. No name for your spa yet?"

"It has a name," Archer says.

Pen set over paper, her eyebrow wings upward.

"It's a surprise for the grand opening," he says.

"Even I don't know what it is," I tell her. Archer wanted to guarantee interest in the spa and thought a surprise "reveal" would garner attention and lure in guests. He's a genius at this sort of thing, so I default to him.

Carmella hums and scribbles something down. "Well, everyone knows the address, and the neon flashing 'Open' sign outside should alert them if they don't. Now, about the guest list..."

An hour and a half later, she has arranged our ducks into a neat row. She wishes us the best of luck for the grand opening. Unlike Archer—or me, apparently—she doesn't oversee her own handiwork, instead promising to send a staff of three to the actual event. She's efficient and smart. There's an air of power surrounding her. As I watch her hasty walk to the parking lot, I sigh wistfully.

"I want to be Carmella when I grow up."

"Sorry, Wildflower, you're too tall." Archer, just over my shoulder, cups my hips from behind and murmurs into my ear. "Let's try the pool. It's heated to the perfect temperature and no one's here for the rest of the day."

Tempting. The clouds are low, and while the sun hasn't set yet, it's nearly dark from a day of rain. I've been chilled to the bone all afternoon. A heated pool sounds like heaven.

I spin in his arms and hook my hands around his neck. I fiddle with the longer strands of his dark hair. "You need a trim, Kingpin."

"You don't like it?"

"I do." I like him every way. Dressed, undressed. Bossy, quiet. Smiling, frowning. There isn't much I don't like about him. As if he senses this, he places a kiss on my mouth that lasts longer than either of us expect. I lose track of time, and of where we are, wrapping my leg around his and curving my back to get closer to the part of him I enjoy most.

But that's a lie, isn't it? There was a time when I liked him for what he could do to me in bed, but over the past few

JESSICA LEMMON

months, that's changed. I also like to talk to him. About everything. Business. Family. The weather.

I pull my lips from his, and he hums low in his throat,
cupping the thigh of my leg still looped around his. "Is that a
yes to the swim?"

"I brought a swimsuit, just in case," I murmur, touching
his beard with one finger.

"Did not."

"Did. I've had swimming in the pool on my to-do list
since I set foot in this building. I can't resist."

"Like you can't resist me?" he fishes.

My smile is brittle.

"You don't have to go home right after we open, you
know."

"I know."

He nods, studying me quietly. Carefully. "Make your
decision. You can tell me after the grand opening on
Saturday."

I don't have to wait until Saturday. I already know I'm
going home after the grand opening. But I don't tell him that.

He leads me to the wading pool, which is finally complete.
I'm so proud of this part of the night spa. The vibe is less
chemicals and concrete and more spa getaway. Lush loungers
with large square pillows and oblong ones for back support
line one side of the pool. Between each lounger is a table with
rolled towels on the bottom shelf and jar candles on the top.

He releases my hand and goes to a tall cabinet, coming
out with a pair of stick candle lighters. Wordlessly we light
the candles at each of the tables. He extinguishes the overhead lights and dims the pool's interior lights as it starts to

rain again. Outside, the trees sway in the wind as rivulets of water slide down the curved glass walls.

We strip off our clothes and he takes my hand, walking with me into the zero entry until he's chest deep. The water is a liquid blanket, soothing tired muscles and coating me in its weightlessness. He lifts me into his arms. I wrap my legs around his waist.

"Nice work, Wildflower. This room's my favorite."

"Mine too." My hands are in his hair, my lips magnetized to his. Whatever room he's in is my favorite. I'll miss him when I go home. But I can't stay. I can't. It's a mantra that's been looping in my mind for so long, and there is so much fear surrounding it, I'm not sure I fully understand my urge to leave.

"You really should stick around longer. We can do this again." He looks admiringly around the softly lit room. It's a fantasy come true, this place.

"Don't you want to see a profit report first?"

He shakes his head, his eyes on mine. "Don't need to."

I debate saving my news for Saturday. Wouldn't it be best to pad the blow? "I have to tell you something."

He stiffens, and I smile to try and ease his worry.

"I have a job lined up. I've been calling around like you suggested."

"With who?" His eyebrows pull to center.

"A company turning a gym into a wellness center," I hedge. "I'll be working in Miami again."

"Congratulations." His voice is monotone. "When?"

I can't look at him when I say, "In two weeks. They're in a hurry to open a new gym-slash-spa, so I'll be busy for a few months nonstop. But at least I'll have my first job on my own."

"This spa was your first job on your own," he reminds me. His eyes narrow. "You don't want to do this new job, do you?"

"How did you—" I shake my head. "I have to. With a brand-new business, I have to take what comes."

"No. You don't. If this offer doesn't fit into your life right now, turn it down and find another."

"I don't have your reserves in the bank," I tell him quietly.

His hold on me tightens. I sense everything he doesn't say. He would give me the money I needed if I stayed here with him. I could live next door indefinitely.

"I want to be close to my family."

He quietly accepts that truth.

"Have you looked into this company? Checked out their financials?" he asks. "Do you know their values?"

I nod but remain silent.

"What are you not telling me?"

Clearly there's no concealing the truth. I let go of him, untangling from his hold to break the news. "The gym is owned by Lotus Leaf."

His expression is lethal. "Not Brandon."

"Not directly."

"Goddammit, Talia. We did not walk out of there for you to crawl back, especially when you don't have to."

"I'm not crawling," I snap. "I'm taking a good-paying job for my company."

"I offered you more work here."

"I don't need you to make up something for me to do. I want to earn my way, on my own merit. I can't depend on you to keep my business afloat." I wade farther away, warm water lapping at my shoulders. "I don't mean I can't—you're very dependable. What I'm trying to say is..."

"You don't want me to help."

"Right."

"Why the hell not?"

Because nothing lasts forever. Because when this ultimately ends, I'll be on my own. Using him or his money as a safety net will do nothing but cripple me in the future.

"I have to stay focused on what's important," I say instead. "I'm responsible for my own income now. I can't stay here and play house." I realize the moment I say it that I made a mistake. "I didn't mean that the way it sounded. This is coming out wrong."

He lets me off the hook and reminds me gently, "So set some boundaries. But consider staying, flying back and forth on weekends."

I laugh, the sound echoing off the walls. "Boundaries? I've set almost zero boundaries when it comes to you."

His face pinches briefly, like my remark hurt his feelings. I lift my dripping hand to my forehead. Water trickles down my cheek. "I knew you'd be upset about my working with Lotus Leaf. That's why I wasn't going to tell you."

His face is hard, but he looks more hurt than angry. "You don't have to choose between me and your family, Talia."

"I don't have a good track record with balancing both, Archer," I whisper.

He turns his head on that fantastically sexy neck of his and watches the rain outside for a beat. A more volatile storm ripples over his features with each passing second. "It's late. We should go back."

He wades to the zero entry and walks out, grabbing a

towel and his clothes. Then he walks down the connecting hall to the private changing rooms, leaving me in the pool alone.

I handled that wrong, but I doubt the news of my taking a job with Lotus Leaf over Archer ever would have settled well. With a sigh, I climb out of the warm water. I towel off and collect my cell phone from my purse. Needing to ground myself with the reminder of why I'm making the hard decision rather than the convenient one, I dial Papa's number. After the second ring, he answers, sounding tired and harried.

"How are you feeling?" I ask. I listen while he tells me about what he's been up to lately, fortified by my decision.

I'm doing the right thing.

CHAPTER TWENTY-FOUR

Talia

The afternoon of the spa's opening, Vivian showed up at my townhouse with Cris in tow. We went to Grand Marin to shop for outfits to wear that night. An endeavor made less stressful when one has a billionaire boyfriend. Though I suspect Archer would offer to foot my bill, I'd die before I let him. He's done enough for me already, and since that tense evening at the spa's pool, we haven't exactly been on the same page.

Vivian has expensive taste, the stores we shopped at *way* outside my comfort zone. I tried pretending none were my style, but when I slipped into a black sheath with an open back and twin gold chains crossing the deep V, Vivian informed me she was buying it. Cris advised me not to argue with Viv because it never worked. I argued anyway, but quickly determined Cris was right. It wasn't going to work.

Viv mentioned paying it forward, followed by, "If you

knew about all of the clothes Nate bought me, you'd let me do it."

Cris chimed in, "She's truly spoiled. Let her do it."

After, we ate dinner at a restaurant in Grand Marin. Martinis and pasta. Cris asked Vivian how the wedding planning was coming along, and I turned into the Tin Man, sitting rigidly in my seat while I ate. Instead of asking if I was planning on coming, Vivian reminded me the black dress was perfect for guest attire.

I've grown so close to Vivian and Cris in the short time I've been here, I honestly planned on flying back to attend. But I doubt Brandon will be as magnanimous about giving me time off to fly home for an Owen wedding. When I called him to tell him my father was mistaken about me wanting my job back, Brandon offered to hire me, but not as an employee of Lotus Leaf. He further explained that Ed crossed a line. Then he admitted he crossed one too, and apologized for acting like a jealous jerk. "Jerk" was putting it mildly, which I let him know. He told me there was no sense in turning down good money close to home. Then he asked if I missed Papa and Lis, and Miami.

I did. So, he had me there.

I talked to the site manager, Tom, yesterday about the design job. They want a spa built onto the back of an existing fitness center, and they need to pivot their focus from barbells and bulky guys to a softer, more welcoming environment. I mentioned introducing meditation, yoga, and the requisite massage, and Tom told me I could do whatever the hell I want, so long as he finished the job on time and earned his bonus.

Not the passion with which I run my business, or Archer

runs his, but at least I have control over my part. My wheels haven't stopped turning since.

Now, Vivian, Cris, and I are lingering at the bar of Archer's unnamed night spa. Guests showed up—nearly everyone invited. They're mingling, drinks in hand, as scratchy, upbeat, lo-fi music plays over the speakers.

"You are a million miles away," Vivian tells me. She's bathed in lavender light, lending her dark hair a purple sheen. Her black gown is shorter than mine, and sparkly. Cris wore red, which reminds me of the night I met her at the fundraiser. Red is her color.

"Sorry. I just want everything to go perfectly tonight."

"You can breathe easy," Viv says as another of Carmella's underlings sweeps by to straighten a vase of flowers. The three assistants she sent are efficient and nearly invisible, but I've spotted them re-fluffing pillows whenever someone stands from the sofa, and collecting left-behind wheatgrass shot glasses or champagne flutes.

"When is the big reveal, anyway?" Cris asks. "I can't believe he wouldn't tell us the name of the spa. I understand the subterfuge with the public since he wants to lure in the fancies, but he could have told *us*." I assume by "fancies," she's referring to the celebrities in attendance. A young actor and actress in the latest sci-fi film are here and, remarkably, half the cast of *Hamilton*. Archer never ceases to impress me.

"I'm sure we'll find out soon. He can't keep it a secret forever." Viv and Cris attempted to shake details out of me at dinner, but I finally convinced them I have no idea what to expect either. I haven't talked to Archer since he passed by, drawing his fingers along the bare skin of my back. I've spotted him behind the bar, in the lobby, and mingling with a few suited men I don't recognize.

Since the awkward ride home from the spa after our argument, we haven't talked about my leaving. And while we've shared kisses and spent time together, I've noticed the careful way Archer holds himself when he's around me.

As if on cue, a loud whistle cuts through the air. The music quiets as every guest's head turns toward the lobby, where Archer is standing in front of a large square *something* wrapped in Kraft brown paper and tied with jute twine.

"You are pioneers," he announces. "Embarking on the first night spa in Clear Ridge, Ohio!" Applause paired with lots of smiles erupts in the room. "Thank you for being here for the grand opening. I couldn't have done this without my incredible staff." He rattles off names and points out people in the crowd. They are incredible; he's not exaggerating. "Talia Richards, come up here."

I shake my head, but Viv and Cris literally push me in his direction.

"Come on, Wildflower. This is your baby as much as it's mine."

Reluctantly, I step up next to him, awkwardly shy about being singled out. Odd, since that's what I strived for when I worked at Lotus Leaf. I didn't take this job for kudos, though. I did it because I was hungry for an adventure. I'm not disappointed. I've enjoyed every moment of it.

"Talia designed this spa, and I've begged her to stay and do another. She's going to give me her answer tonight."

My cheeks grow warm.

"And now, the reveal you've been waiting for." He rubs

his hands together. "I'm going to tell you the name of this place."

More applause, mine included. I step back as he pulls a pocketknife from the pocket of his dark trousers and slices the twine. He turns to me and gestures to the large, wrapped sign. "Go ahead. Tear it open."

Hands sweating, I fumble, ripping at the paper fruitlessly before making a hole big enough to poke my finger through. I tear it away, discarding the pieces and revealing thick letters made up of green and blue and yellow flowers. I see the word in its entirety, its meaning sinking it slowly. When I realize what it means, it's like the air is suctioned from the room. I back away as Nate and Benji each lift a corner of the sign.

"Welcome to Wildflower Spa," Archer calls out. The cheers are deafening, the music is loud again, and I...I stand stock-still staring at my nickname—Archer's nickname for me —painted on the sign for his new night spa. He points at a blank wall and tells his brothers, "It goes on those nails right there."

Nate and Benji hang the sign, all eyes on them. Including mine.

Archer startles me by wrapping his hand around the back of my neck, leaning close to mutter, "If you're looking for a sign to stay, Wildflower, there it is. You and I make a great team. Proof is all around you—the building you're standing in."

I'm numb, overwhelmed. Unsure what he's asking...or *if* he's asking. I'm saved from replying by two late-arriving guests. Lainey and William Owen step through the front door and steal Archer's attention.

"We'll talk later," he tells me.

I force a smile. I need a minute, and with Archer distracted by his parents, I take it.

Archer

I will be goddamned.

My father steps through the front door of my night spa, dressed in a suit as per his usual, my mother on his arm. I never imagined he'd show, and the sight of him startles me for a truncated moment. Adrenaline is still pumping through my bloodstream after having surprised Talia by naming the spa after her. Seeing Dad here sends an echoing tremor down both arms.

Nate is the first to greet them, but Mom waves to me after receiving a hug. Dad's gaze snaps from Nate to me, his jaw tightening as he offers a curt nod. I nod back, and then put one leaden foot in front of the other.

"Mom." I kiss her cheek. "Dad."

"Son," Dad says, taking in the atmosphere. The lavender lights, the modern music, Mom's prize roses in clear vases dotted throughout. "How about a tour?"

"You two go without me. I want to say hello to Vivian and Cris. And your Talia, if she's here." Mom squeezes my arm and winks at me.

My Talia. If only. She's as much mine as the wind. Or a cloud passing by in the sky.

After Mom walks away, Dad and I pull in big breaths and inflate our chests. Without my brothers as buffers, I wonder how long it'll take for this conversation to devolve into an argument. He speaks first. "Congratulations."

"Thanks for coming."

"Well, I had the evening free." He purses his lips. "I wanted to see you in action. Lainey expects her first massage to be free, but I told her I'd pay for it. You are aiming to turn a profit here, are you not?"

"That's the idea." My chest loosens at his light tone. He's trying. I appreciate that.

I extend an arm toward the corridor. "You mentioned a tour."

We walk through the kitchen, the meditation room, and end up standing over the wading pool. No one's back here, but the candles are lit, lending the room a warm ambiance. The still water reflects the flames. The last time I was in here, Talia was telling me her family mattered more than me. What I didn't say, and what I planned on telling her tonight before my parents showed up, was that I can be her family too. The distance separating us is less Clear Ridge-to-Miami and more her refusal to let me be more. I want to mean as much to her as she does to me. How do you ask for something like that?

"Son, I apologize," Dad starts, his voice rigid.

I lift one eyebrow. His gaze flits over and then away.

"Did Mom put you up to this?"

"Of course not." He frowns. "Kind of, but my apology is sincere."

I'm not accustomed to heart-to-hearts with him, as reflected in every line of my stiff posture. He reaches out and squeezes my shoulder, and I have no idea what to do with my arms.

"I've done nothing but second-guess you for years," he continues. "I hate that you felt I supported your brothers but overlooked you. I don't have to form you into who I want you to be, Archer. It's good enough for me if you're happy doing what you're doing."

"What's going on? Are you dying? Trying to make amends?" I can't help my suspicion. This conversation is alarming, to say the least.

"God, I hope not." Hands in his pockets, he studies the room. If I'm not mistaken, his smile is proud. "Night spa."

"Why not?"

"I couldn't picture it when you told me about it. Now that I see what you've created... It's a damn good idea."

"Thanks." My throat is packed with emotion. From the rush of Dad coming to my grand opening to both praise my efforts and apologize, and the uncertainty over Talia's panic after she revealed the sign with her nickname on it.

"You don't need me," he says, looking down at the water. "It's time I accepted that."

"Of course I need you." I don't want him thinking that. I know firsthand what it's like not to be needed. A certain brunette keeps reminding me of it.

"No. You don't. Benji and Nate, they seek my counsel often. I'm honored to teach them. But you want to do everything on your own. Like me." He chuckles. "I'm surprised you let Talia as close as you did. You've never dated anyone like her before. Someone worthy of you. Someone you can have a future with."

Worthy of me. I remember Nate's similar assessment about my past girlfriends and how they weren't good enough for me.

"Is she going to be around?" Dad waves a hand. "To help you build some more of these?"

"I don't know yet." I shake my head, the weight of the last several days pulling my shoulders.

He hums low in his throat. "If I were you, I'd work on convincing her."

"Beyond naming the spa after her, you mean."

"Well"—he laughs, the twinkle in his eye suggesting he might have done his fair share of crazy things to win over Mom—"that's a good start, son. That's a good start."

Talia

Cris finds me in a corner away from the crowd and hands me a glass of champagne. Her gray eyes are wide with a deep sort of understanding I don't expect. Shouldn't she be grinning from ear to ear and congratulating me like everyone else has?

"So, Archer really, *really* likes you." Her eyebrows bend gently, then she takes me by the arm. She's strong for being so little. She leads me past the lobby, down an alcove, and straight to the meditation room. Then she shuts us in and slides the dimmer switch to lighten the darkened room.

"This is a better place for you to collect yourself." She's genuinely interested when she asks, "How ya doin'?"

And because it's Cris, as I know how sweet she is, and I desperately need someone to talk to, I tell her the truth.

"I'm kinda freaking out," I say through a laugh.

"You didn't know about the name of the spa, did you?"

"No. And there was zero percent chance in my mind

Archer would do something like name it after me." I let out a stuttering laugh and rub my forehead with my fingers. "I am definitely freaking out."

Cris pulls a meditation pillow out of the corner and drops it in the center of the room, pointing at me to sit. She's the picture of Zen with her curly blond hair encircling her head like a halo. Obediently, I sit, my knees together, feet splayed to the sides awkwardly thanks to my dress and high heels.

"Remember our girls' night out at Vivian's house? How Viv and I joked that we thought we wanted an alpha guy until they became too alpha and bossy and possessive. Then we're like"—she holds up a palm—"refund, please."

I smile. I remember.

"The very thing you like about Archer is also what's driving you crazy." She smiles gently. "He's coming for you, Talia, and I'm fairly certain you don't want to be chased."

"It's not that I don't want to." I frown. The truth is complicated. "I just have to go home. He knows that. Instead of respecting my decision, he's trying to talk me into being here with him. He made me like him too much."

"That *jerk*," she gasps, her sarcasm evident. She pulls up another meditation pillow and sits in front of me. "What if he's trying to show you the version of the future he sees in his head? And, for the record, Archer isn't all that likable." A pleat dents her forehead and I have to laugh, remembering her and Vivian's warning to me at the fundraiser last year. "If he's likable to you, you must like him."

"I used to have a very simple goal. I wanted to move up the corporate ladder and have a job I love. Now, look what I've done. Uprooted my life to start a business—I barely know what I'm doing, by the way. I left Papa and Lis alone in Florida. I'm overwhelmed. Out of my element. I've never had a relationship last longer than two and a half minutes, so what gives me the right to think Archer and I might make it?" I blow out a breath after my mini tirade. I had no idea that was in there.

"There's no reason to think that you might," chipper Cris answers. Her smile paired with harsh news is confusing. "None of us really know. Vivian and Nate had their own brush with doubt. Benji and I flat-out broke up."

"You did?" I had no idea.

"Uh-huh. I was miserable and crying and my brothers threatened to beat him up in my honor."

"That's sort of sweet."

"It sort of was." Her smile falls. "You have a right to leave."

"What the hell am I supposed to do about a spa being named after me?" I lift my hands and drop them uselessly, which is similar to how I'm feeling in the moment.

"How about nothing?" She shrugs, like it's just that easy. "Your time is up soon. You're going home. Unpack your bags. Settle in. Make a decision about your future you can live with, and without pressure from Archer. You can't make the wrong decision. There's no wrong decision to make. Everything just *is*. So let it be."

She emulates the Buddha statue behind her, touching her middle fingers to her thumbs and closing her eyes.

"Just be," I say, feeling weirdly better about everything.

She opens her eyes and takes my hands in hers. Squeezing my fingers, she says, "Sometimes we mess everything up by trying to fix it. It doesn't sound like you have anything to fix."

CHAPTER TWENTY-FIVE

Archer

We're driving home from the grand opening. I can't read Talia. I decided to wait and talk to her about everything after we left. She was deep in conversation with Vivian and Cris when Dad and I finished with the tour. Something told me the timing wasn't right.

I park by the curb and we pause between townhouses. Indecision is a habit we have cultivated. Does she come to me? Do I go to her?

"I have bourbon," she tells me. "If you want a glass."

Bourbon. It's a bit of a symbol for us. I nearly proposed to her at that fundraiser when I asked what she had in her glass. Then, I was joking. Now, I have no idea what I'd say if she flipped that script on me. After she avoided me for the rest of the night in her namesake spa, I doubt a proposal is forthcoming. Probably the opposite. I'm fairly certain she'll take me inside and explain why she's leaving. I'm too fucking scared to hope for anything else.

"I'll take you up on a bourbon." I follow her inside, slipping off my suit jacket and draping it over a chair in the living room.

"No bourbon for you?" I joke when she pulls a wine glass from the cabinet alongside a short, square glass for me.

"Hello? Have we met?"

I should know her preferences. I thought I did, but she changed on me. She went from a woman who fantasized about having me to someone who had me and lost interest. Do I sound as pathetic to you as I do in my own head?

"Huge success tonight," I say to fill the space in the room. "Not a bad first gig for a brand-new LLC."

"I couldn't have done it without you." She pours a few inches of bourbon into the glass and pours herself a splash of wine next. "To us."

"To us." We tap glasses and then drink. I lock eyes with her.

She's silent for a long beat. Too long. I can't take it anymore.

"You don't like the name of the spa."

"I like it," she says, her tone high and nervous. "Why did you do it?"

"For you." I shrug. Because *duh*. "Your stamp is in every room of that spa. I can't look anywhere without seeing you there." Or here. Or in my own townhouse. When she leaves, I'm going to be a mess. I can feel it.

"You hoped the sign would change my mind about leaving," she says, not meeting my eyes. "I'm sorry, Archer. It didn't change anything."

"Why not?" I growl. Feeling pissed-off is better than feeling sad and pathetic. "You expect me to believe you're excited to work for Brandon Lambert? You expect me to believe you don't recognize what we have? This isn't normal, Talia. What we have isn't something you find every day."

"Archer, stop." She's begging, her hands in prayer pose in front of her. I don't care. I've come this far, and I'm not turning back now.

"I love you, Talia, and I can't figure out why that's so goddamned hard for you to accept." I'm frowning at her. Her mouth is hanging open like she's mortified. I can't think of a single other word to say.

Fuck. I'm so bad at this.

"It's impossible for me to accept," she whispers.

"Why?"

"My mother." Like those two words took the strength from her legs, she collapses on a barstool. I remain standing, hands flat on the counter. I'm too agitated to sit. "Remember when I told you I was engaged?"

I nod grimly, not liking where this is going already.

"He proposed to me after graduation. On a football field at our high school, surrounded by our friends. We sneaked in. We were still wearing our caps and gowns. He arranged to have the lights turned on. The field was lit up like game night." She smiles, but there's no joy in it. Only regret. "I was supposed to go home after the graduation ceremony. Mama was too sick to attend, so Lis and Papa baked a cake." A tear slips from her eye, and my heart shatters. "I chose Estevan over her. I told myself I deserved a night with my friends, with my boyfriend. My *fiancé*. I chose him over my family, Archer. To devastating consequences. I never told her good-bye. The last words I said to her were 'I know' when she reminded me to take photos for her."

"There's no way you could have known," I say, my heart breaking for her.

"Yes, but I should have been there. I was supposed to be there. I allowed myself to be distracted. You're a distraction, Archer. I found out before I came here that Papa was on medication for his heart—I don't know how long he has. Maybe years, maybe minutes. Lis needs me even though she won't admit it. I need to be there for her, to listen to her problems with Julio or Webber or whoever she's dating. I started a business, and I'm terrified I'll fail if I don't hustle my ass off to keep it afloat. I can't stay here. My entire life is in Miami."

I stopped hearing anything she said after she told me I was a distraction. I'm too angry to put together a halfway decent sentiment to tell her how sorry I am she lost her mom and how I don't want her to worry about anyone. About how I'll move them all up to Ohio and put them in mansions with bubble-wrapped walls to ensure their safety so she never has to feel that way again. Instead, my hurt feelings and my unreturned pronouncement make me say something totally different.

"For the first time in my life, I have something real and true to come home to. *You* are the person I don't want to miss out on, Wildflower. I have given you every reason I can for you to stay."

She draws her chin up, my tough girl. But she's not mine. She never was. I should have known from the start I wouldn't be able to keep her for myself. I should have known she'd resist being planted in cultivated, stable soil. She was born to do her own thing. She was born to be free. I've been telling myself a fairy tale, convincing myself she'd fall in love with the life we were creating and want a piece of it for herself.

"You're the first woman I ever dated who didn't want anything from me. Not money, not gifts. You're also the first woman I've offered my heart to, but you don't want that either, do you?"

The gentleness in her eyes is killing me. She cares about me, I know she does. Just not enough for her to choose me in the end.

"I didn't mean to hurt you," she says woodenly. "I understand if you want to change the name of the spa."

I don't acknowledge that unbelievably hurtful remark. I grab the bourbon by the neck and the slide the bottle off the counter. "Assuming you won't be needing this, so I'll take it off your hands. Good night, Talia."

I walk out.

She lets me.

CHAPTER TWENTY-SIX

Talia

I left Clear Ridge, Ohio a week and a half ago. I packed my bags and emptied the closet. I texted Archer and asked him to book the jet for my return flight home at his earliest convivence. He booked it for that afternoon. He drove to the airport, loaded me onto the jet, and hugged me goodbye. No kiss.

I told myself that's what I wanted. A clean break.

I was wrong.

I'm at brunch with Papa, at Mango's. Lis is working today, so I asked if he wanted to come out for huevos rancheros. He agreed. Halfway through breakfast, he asks how Brandon is doing.

"I don't know. I work with Tom on this project," I answer as I pick at my food. It's delicious I'm sure, but my newfound regret has made everything taste like sawdust.

"I know." He waves a hand of dismissal. "But Brandon gave you that job. You should be grateful."

Brandon should be grateful to have me, but I don't say that. The timeline is demanding, and the job is behind schedule and much less organized than Archer's night spa. I'm stressed. I'm overworked. After this lovely breakfast, I'm heading to the building, hence my professional pantsuit rather than a flouncy top and shorts and sandals.

"I always liked Brandon." My father offers a wistful smile. "You never know. There could be hope for you two kids to reconcile."

"There's no hope, Papa." I don't have a right to be frustrated with him. He doesn't know how I feel. Hell, I haven't admitted to *myself* how I feel.

"There's always hope, Tallie."

"I'm in love with someone else," I blurt out.

Papa puts down his fork.

"Archer Owen."

"The man in Ohio?"

"Yes."

He takes it well, his thick eyebrows lifting as he absorbs the news. "Then why are you here?"

"Great question."

Hours later, after a long day of work, I trudge into the house to find Calista at the stove, stirring something in a pot. "Still at it?" I ask, noting the time on the stove. 10:37. I'm about to drop.

"I was craving caramel sauce. I'm going to put it on the homemade ice cream in the freezer." Her mouth twists. "You look like you need it."

"I've been thinking a lot about the night Mom died," I say, bypassing any pleasantries or talk of dessert.

"Oh, Tal." She stops stirring, ignoring my warning not to.

Caramel is a full-time job. You can't stop stirring or it will burn and clump. "I can make caramel anytime," she informs me as she flips off the burner. Her arm wrapped around mine, she drags me to the sofa.

"I chose Estevan over Mama. I missed her last breath," I sob. I've never said the truth aloud or in such stark terms. Lis's arms close around me as I continue, my voice thick with regret. "I came home late that night, overjoyed. I couldn't wait to tell you I was engaged...and then I saw your face. Papa told me I missed her by twenty minutes."

A thick, choking sob prevents me from saying more. Lis is crying too, the sound daintier. She plucks two tissues from a box, handing me one of them.

"The worst part," I continue after I blow my nose, "is that it didn't matter. Estevan and I weren't married and didn't live happily ever after. It was all for nothing. I'll never forgive myself."

"Tallie." Lis hasn't called me that since she was a little girl. "Honey, you were eighteen. How could any of us have known the exact moment Mama was going to pass? You sat by her bed every night that week, remember?"

I blink. Sniff. I'd forgotten.

"Mama told you to go to your own bed whenever you stayed at her side too long. And the night of your graduation she told me she hoped you were having the time of your life with your friends." Lis takes my hand and shakes it as if to snap me out of my stupor. "She wanted you to be happy, Talia. Not at her bedside in tears."

"I should have been there." I'm unwilling to be let off the hook so easily.

"It wouldn't have changed anything."

"But I could have been there for her final moments."

"*She* wasn't there for her own final moments. She was unconscious. I fell asleep on the floor, leaning on Papa's leg. He was asleep on the armchair. None of us were 'there' for her last moments, Tal."

I didn't know that.

"Is this the real reason you came back to Florida?"

"Not...entirely."

"Archer is the man for you," she states, her voice firm. "He was in love with you and offering you the kind of life you dreamed of before Mama died. You can't control everything. Embrace the unknown, Tal. Live a little while you still can."

"But Papa—"

"He's fine. I'm fine. Do you know who's not fine? *You* are not fine. I refuse to let you ruin your love life because of some misplaced sense of duty."

"I hate how right you sound," I tell her, wadding the spent tissue in my hand.

"I want you to be happy too. And Papa is delusional."

"Actually, at brunch, he told me to go back to Ohio and settle down with Archer." I roll my eyes.

"Finally gave up on you and Brandon, huh?"

I laugh, startled by the sound. I haven't laughed since before I left Ohio.

"When I find The One, I'm not going to resist when he offers me a gorgeous townhouse with a dream kitchen, that's for damn sure." She sighs. "You don't have to do this, you know."

Part of me knows that, but the resistance within is strong. I've carried the guilt over missing saying goodbye to Mama for so many years it's like a pet on the end of a chain, and that chain is attached to a shackle around my ankle. I want to be free...I just don't know how.

"I should go to bed. I have a long day tomorrow." I give my sister a wan smile.

"You need to stop punishing yourself." She is sounding wiser by the moment. "You own your business. *You* call the shots. You have a home here with me, no matter what. You'll never be homeless. And you have Archer if you decide he's who you want. If you draw a line and take off this weekend to, oh, say, go to Vivian and Nate's wedding, there's nothing wrong with that. If Brandon fires you for it, then fuck him. But not literally."

She makes an *ew* face that squeezes another thin laugh from my chest. Then she lifts the tissue box and hands me a cream-colored envelope. "The wedding invitation arrived yesterday. I was trying to decide whether to tell you or not. You've been so sad, and I didn't want to make you sadder."

"Impossible." I tear open the invitation. The heavy cream card stock matches the envelope, the bold purple trim reminding me of Vivian. I hand her a smaller envelope and card. "You're invited as my plus-one."

"'Bring Lis. We'd love to have her,'" she reads. "'That's so nice.'" She loses her smile when she hands the card back to me. "Go without me. I have a feeling you'll be busy begging the man you love to forgive you for leaving him."

"What about the work I'm doing with Lotus Leaf?" I ask, clinging to the unreasonable sense of duty Lis mentioned a few minutes ago.

"I suggest you prioritize. You can either stay here and work for Brandon in an attempt to prove yourself to the one man who doesn't deserve your consideration, or..."

"Or?" I prompt when she doesn't continue.

"Or you can enjoy your life. You don't have to prove anything to the people who love you. Papa, Archer, and I already know you're perfect."

Archer

I plunk Benji's tux onto his kitchen countertop, announcing myself with, "I'm here. Thanks to me you have a tux to wear to the wedding!"

He appears from the direction of his office, happy as ever, completely unaffected by my terse tone. He doesn't rile as easily as when we were kids, and now that he has Cris, he's almost bulletproof.

Annoying.

"Thanks, bro." He claps my back. "Last-minute best men, aren't we?"

"*I'm* the best man, and I've had my tux for a week. You might want to try it on."

"It fit in the store except for one minor alteration. Unless the tailor went crazy and made the pants into Bermuda shorts, I think I'm good."

"We are now the proud owners of yet another tux." I shake my head, picturing the formalwear lining my closet. Sometimes being rich is a pain in the ass.

"Should've expected Vivian to be specific about what style we wear," he says, peeling back the zipper and taking a look. "Damn, it's nice, though."

It is. We're going to look better than we have ever looked. Sadly, there's no one there for me to impress.

I turn to leave. "See you Saturday."

"Wait, wait, wait. You didn't offer to do this under the guise of hanging out with me? We could play basketball."

"Have you improved since our game of one-on-one after you stepped in it with Cris?"

"No. But since you find yourself in a similar predicament with Talia, I thought you might want to talk."

"I'm good," I lie, turning for the door again. *Good* is a big overstatement. But I'm stable. I don't need to play basketball to prove it.

"Even though you were zero help to me back then, I'm willing to give you advice. It includes a beer." He's already at the fridge, cracking open two longnecks. I shut the front door, giving in.

"I'll take a beer, but this feels like a trick."

"You have to tell me what happened. I'm hearing second-hand from Cris, who talked to Talia, so who knows what's real."

"She talked to Talia?" Just saying her name hurts. I develop a serious case of dry mouth and take a deep pull from my beer bottle. My brother leads the way to his back patio. Next to his heated swimming pool, we settle onto a pair of chairs. I close my eyes, soak in the sunshine, and let the breeze ruffle my hair.

Doesn't help. I'm as miserable today as I was the day I drove Talia to the airport and hugged her goodbye and pretended I wasn't dead inside.

"Cris talked to Talia the morning before she flew home.

She told me she hasn't heard from her since. Is she coming to the wedding?"

"No." I can't imagine a scenario where Talia would voluntarily come back, no matter how much she likes Vivian. "She's busy with work."

"That's a lame reason to give up on her." He tips his beer bottle to his lips.

"Unlike you, I confessed everything. And unlike Nate, it didn't work out in the end."

"It didn't work out for him at first, either," Benji reminds me. Irritatingly.

"She has her reasons. A long time ago, she prioritized a boyfriend. Her mother died while Talia was being proposed to on a football field. She never forgave herself for it."

"Ah." That one syllable says it all. My brother, the orphan, understands where Talia's coming from. "I wasn't there when my parents died. I felt guilty for years for not being in the car." He gives me a sideways smile that is packed with grief. "I didn't realize what I was carrying around with me. I mean, I was ten. Stomachaches at age ten could mean too much sugar or growing pains. They're not typically caused by survivor's guilt."

This is the part of himself Benji hides well. There is a serious, caring side behind the happy-go-lucky facade. As much shit as I give him, his exterior is as resilient as rhino hide. He had to be tough. He left the only family he knew to live with strangers. He is an Owen through and through now, but it took years for him to feel at home with us.

"I'm sorry, man," I say, meaning it. "I can never understand what you and Nate have been through." All my whining about how they were given preferential treatment back when I was a kid looks like spoiled-rotten teenager shit now. They never had anything over me. They were starting from scratch. "I could have been nicer to you when I was younger."

"Archer, you and Nate are the best brothers I never knew to ask for. You guys cared about me and you didn't even have to. Who was I? Some kid you didn't know placed in a family that was yours."

"If you tell me you love me, I'm going to punch you in the face." I earn a hearty laugh. I like that sound much better than the distraught tone in his voice.

"You can drop the tough-guy act. I saw you with Talia. You were pure mush." He pauses to take in the swaying trees and the ripples on the surface of his swimming pool. "You miss her, don't you?"

My eyes on the beer bottle dangling from my fingers, I admit, "Yeah. I do."

"Have you thought about going to her?"

"A million times. She considers me a distraction. I'm trying not to distract her."

After a long, silent beat, he says, "Shit. I thought I'd know what to say. Turns out I'm as bad at giving advice as you are."

"And you wonder why I didn't come to you," I grumble, but my comment has no venom. I feel my mouth smiling and look up to find Benji smiling back.

"Maybe staying away is a good idea," he reconsiders. "If you put yourself out there and left nothing on the table, you have no regrets. Talia has been on her own for a long time. She and Calista are cut from the same independent quilt. She'll find her way."

"Back to me?" I ask, hating how hopeful I sound.

"If we're lucky," he says. "If not, you're going to be a miserable son of a bitch, and that'll be hard on everyone."

After our beers are empty and the topic has shifted to work and my next endeavor, we walk back inside. As I'm dropping my empty bottle into the recycling bin, Benji says, "I proposed to Cris last night."

Even at the height of my misery, I can't hear this as anything less than good news.

"She said yes."

"No shocker there."

"I want you to be my best man, Arch. I already talked to Nate, and he said he wouldn't want it any other way."

The lump in my throat doubles a size. I attempt to swallow around it, to keep myself in check before I dissolve into an embarrassing puddle of man-tears.

"He would say that," I manage, my voice scratchy. "Just to show me up, the asshole."

"I'll take that as a yes."

"Yes. Of course it's a yes. I'd do anything for you, and you know it."

"I'd do anything for you too," he says with a jovial sparkle in his eye. "Remember that the next time I do something you don't like."

"You don't have to buy yourself into my good graces, Benj," I say as I stroll to the front door. "Thanks for the beer."

"Thanks for the tux."

I leave, my focus on surviving the day. I have to wake up tomorrow and survive that one too, so I'm going to need to reserve some strength. One day at a time. It's as much as I can manage at the moment.

CHAPTER TWENTY-SEVEN

Archer

Nate and I are sitting outside in the gardens at the art institute, surrounded by lush greenery. He and Vivian are getting married today. He's as relaxed as I've ever seen him. I feel as jittery as if I drank a pot of coffee, in spite of limiting myself to one cup.

"It's a warm one today," I say blandly, tugging at the neck of my tux. It seemed the safest comment since misery has taken up permanent residence. I don't want to ruin his big day. "You're lucky it didn't rain."

"Lucky?" He lets out a derisive laugh. "Vivian threatened the gods. Loudly and frequently."

I smile because I can't help myself. As miserable as I am about my own life, I can't begrudge Nate his joy. "Gotta give it you, man. She is a catch. Beautiful, sassy, strong. She's a good friend, trustworthy. Only meddles when absolutely necessary. Cares genuinely about her family. Loves you, for some reason." That earns me another of his rolling laughs. "You did right by proposing to her. It's an honor to stand at your side when she becomes your wife."

His smile fades, his eyes narrowed over his crooked nose. He sounds uncharacteristically humble when he says, "Thanks, brother." True to form, he busts my balls next. "Jealous?"

"Not pulling any punches today, are you?"

"Sorry. It's my big day. Giving the woman I love her third and final name change. A name she can be proud of this time around. Nothing better in this world."

I figure he's right. I wouldn't know, since I haven't had luck like my brothers in the romance department. Or maybe it has less to do with luck and more to do with timing. Or maybe neither of those things. Shit. I don't know.

"I am jealous," I admit. "Where the hell's Benji, anyway? How am I here early and he's not?"

"He and Cris had a last-minute errand. Said he'd be along well before the ceremony starts."

"If *errand* is their code word for sex, they could have planned better. Are they holed up in the courtyard where they keep Mom's roses?" I look over my shoulder in the direction of the museum.

"They'd better not be. That's mine and Vivian's special spot."

"I don't want to know what you did in there with her, either."

He grins. Happy bastard.

Rows of chairs are lined on the pristine lawn facing a white arch. Everything is draped in white fabric that blows in the gentle May breeze. Roses, whatever Mom managed to cultivate, plus extra from the florist, decorate every square inch not draped in fabric. Mostly white and pink, but Nate told me Vivian's bouquet is red "to match the bottom of her shoes."

"I have time, you know," he says.

"Time for what?" I turn my attention back to him to find him staring at me.

"You want to talk about it?"

"Talk about what?" I ask my shoes. I know what he's asking about, and no, I do not want to talk about it.

"How about a drink? It's your favorite bourbon." He produces a flask from his jacket pocket, twists the top off, and takes a swig. When he offers it to me, I take it and do the same. I should probably tell him I'm leaving. If he notices I've gone AWOL in the middle of the reception, I'll never hear the end of it.

"After I give the speech, I have to go," I tell him.

"You have to go?" His forehead scrunches. "You have somewhere pressing to be?"

"Yeah. Miami."

"Business or pleasure?"

"It's not business, and I don't know if it's pleasure until I'm standing in front of Talia. She might tell me to fuck off. If she does, I'll turn around and fly back here to take liberal advantage of your open bar."

"Benji said you were giving her space."

"Did he now." Leave it to my younger brother to rat me out.

"It worked for me." Nate shrugs, looks over my shoulder. His eyes grow warm, his smile right behind them. "Hey, beautiful."

"Hey, babe." I turn to find Vivian swishing toward us wearing a slim, white, sleeveless gown. What is it about a bride that takes your breath away? She's ethereal in the golden sunshine. The red roses pinned in her dark hair match her red lips.

"Hey there, big brother," she greets.

"You have another hour or so before it's official. Change your mind yet?" I tease.

"Never." I like how certain she sounds. That spike of jealousy in my heart drives deeper.

"You are stunning. And deserve a lot better than this idiot." I shoot a thumb in Nate's direction.

"Don't I know it." She beams at him. "I can't help it. I love him like crazy, you know?"

"Yeah, he's sort of irresistible." I stand and move out of the way when she bends to kiss her husband-to-be. They murmur I-love-yous, and I swear I hear my own heart cracking. I have to fly to Miami today and find Talia or I'll lose my mind.

If I don't track her down and beg and plead and offer to do everything within my human capabilities, I'll never forgive myself. At least I'll know I tried everything. I've given her as much space and time as I'm willing. I've lost too much sleep while in limbo. Either she needs to shoot me down with a bazooka or admit she's in love with me. There is no in-between for me.

"I'd better sneak back before your mom finds out I'm over here." Vivian lifts her dress to tiptoe through the grass. "She's a traditionalist and believes it's bad luck to see each other before the ceremony. I lied and told her I was going to the powder room." She winks, her grin as bright as the sky. "See you up there, big guy."

"I'll be there," Nate promises.

When she's gone, I retake my seat on the bench and tip the flask for another nip. "You are marrying up."

"Aren't we all." His eyes stay pinned over my shoulder for a beat before returning to mine. "So, you're going to Miami to find Talia, and then what?"

"I'll tell her how I feel. Deal with the consequences. Whatever they may be."

"Can't wait 'til tomorrow?"

"No." I give him an apologetic head shake. "It can't. Some best man I turned out to be, huh?"

"Benji has taken his role as your understudy seriously. We'll make do. Sure you don't want to tell her sooner?"

"I'm not leaving before the wedding if that's what you're suggesting." I do have some standards. Plus, Mom would strangle me. "And I can't tell her what I have to tell her over the phone. I need her to see me when I say it."

"Let's hear it." He makes a "come on" motion to me.

I tense. "Why?"

"Because you need to make sure what's in your head and your heart comes out of your mouth the way you want it to. You have one last shot with this girl. Don't you want to make the most of it?"

Why does he always make such good points?

He waits. I stare down at the flask in my hands, trying to sort my thoughts. "I'll start with 'I love you.'"

My brother waits silently for me to continue. I shift on the bench, my gaze on the roses at the altar. "I love you," I repeat.

"I don't want to live without you. Give me one more chance to prove to you that you are ready for a lifelong love. Let me show you how it can be me." I scratch my cheek, embarrassed. "I don't know. Something like that. Or maybe I'll beg."

"I like a man who isn't too proud to beg," I hear behind me. Not Vivian this time. Nate smiles stupidly at the someone over my shoulder. Unless I'm hallucinating, or far more drunk on a few sips of bourbon than I should be, that voice belongs to the woman who belongs on my arm.

I twist my neck to look behind me. Talia is dressed in blue, standing a few feet away. I rise from my seat, blinking dumbly as my brain accepts her surprise appearance.

I tear my attention from Talia to find my other brother and other soon-to-be sister-in-law grinning proudly. "Sorry we're late," Benji says.

"Good job, you two," Nate tells them as he stands from the bench.

"You knew about this?" I ask him.

"Someone had to do something." He thumps me on the back and then goes to Talia and whispers into her ear. My brothers and Cris wander off, leaving Talia and I alone in the garden.

"This is a pretty venue for a wedding." She's visibly nervous, knotting and unknotting her fingers.

"How much did you hear?"

"All of it." Her smile is tight. Revealing nothing.

"Saved me a flight." My heart is racing, eager. I weld my feet to the grass and wait for her to say something. To say anything. I hope it's what I want to hear.

"I texted Cris a few days ago to ask if I'd be well-received if I showed up. She offered to pick me up at the airport herself."

"I'm glad you're here." My chest feels heavy and light at the same time. It's a good sign that Talia wanted to come here, right?

"Me too."

"Listen, I'll never know what it was like for you to lose your mom, or live with the guilt of not being able to say goodbye. But I sympathize as well as someone who has two living parents can."

"Archer, you don't have to do this."

Panicked that she might be telling me no after all, I blurt out, "Want me to move to Miami?"

She blinks, her eyebrows shooting up. She looks stunned. I'm stunned. I didn't expect to make that offer. With her in front of me, and my window of opportunity quickly narrowing, let's just say my priorities are suddenly crystal clear. I won't lose her again.

"You'd be willing to move to Florida?"

"I'd move to the fucking moon for you, Talia Richards. I love you. I've been in love with you since you wrecked my car, and my good sense along with it. Hell, probably longer than that. Since the first time you wrote me an email that started with 'Hey Kingpin.' I'm gone for you, Wildflower. Isn't it obvious?"

She takes a step closer, then another, a smile softening her exquisite features. "I missed you."

It's not an I love you, but I'll take it.

"God, I missed you." I wrap her in my arms, juggling the flask I still have in my hand for some reason. When we separate, I hold it between us. "Nate's version of coercing my speech out of me."

"If there's bourbon in that flask, I'm going to have to ask you to marry me," she says. Then she takes it from me, twists off the top, and tips it back. Her long hair is pinned up on one side, the rest in long, loose curls falling down her back. She's beautiful and amazing and perfect for me. How can she not see that? She hands the flask back to me and licks her lips. "Well?"

"Well what?" I ask, tucking the flask into my tuxedo pocket.

"It's bourbon. So I'm asking."

I laugh, a little confused. Hell, a lot confused.

She doesn't so much as crack a smile.

"I pushed you away when I should have been pulling you closer. I'm not good at this, Archer."

"Me neither, honey," I admit, touching her forehead to move a stray strand of hair away from her face. "We'll get there."

"You can't tell anyone I proposed on Vivian's wedding day. She'll throttle me." Talia squeezes both my hands in hers. "I love you too, by the way. Are you going to answer me or what?"

I open my mouth. Close it. Shake my head in disbelief. "You're really proposing to me?"

"I'm really proposing to you. Why don't we work out geography later and plan on seeing as much of each other as possible for the time being? I'm miserable without you."

"Good," I tell her, letting out the breath I've been choking on since I laid eyes on her today. Before she can argue, I catch the back of her head and press her mouth to mine for a long, drawn-out kiss that is our best to date. She tastes like longing and love and forever. When we part, I rest my forehead on hers.

"Is that a yes?" she whispers.

"It's technically a hell yes." A grin pulls my cheeks.

"I'm sorry I'm so bad at this."

"You're doing great. Better than great," I tell her, overwhelmed by having everything I wanted here in my arms.

"Did you change the name of the spa?" She actually looks worried.

"Why? Did you change your mind?"

"I changed my heart."

Ah, hell, that's sweet. So I tell her. "You're sweet. No wonder I fell in love with you."

We're in the middle of full-on making out again, nudging into inappropriate territory for public snogging when Benji interrupts with a deliberate cough.

"Sorry to intrude, but you're up, man." With a smile, he adds, "I can take your place if you're unable to perform your best man duties."

He's still after my title. The dick.

"Nice try, but I have this." Talia's hand in mine, I guide her to a chair next to Mom. Mom pats Talia's hand and gives me a regal nod of approval. I'm certain my expression is love-drunk and dopey as I take the spot between my brothers at the right side of the arch. I can't help myself. I've never been proposed to before. It's exciting.

The music begins to play. Vivian's friend, Marnie, and Cris precede the bride down the aisle.

Vivian meets Nate at the front, and Benji and I turn to face the officiant. During the vows, I steal a peek at Talia to see if she's still here, or if she was a mirage. She's here. She's crying happy tears, her watery smile filling my heart to the brim and beyond.

I have a ton to be thankful for. For my brothers, who know when to meddle, and for the woman I met over a year ago who just proposed to me.

Life knocks you for loops most of the time. Very rarely, on days like today, it kicks some serious ass.

EPILOGUE

Talia

A rcher promised to buy Papa a boat. I warned him not to attempt to buy my father's love, but like Papa, Archer doesn't listen to me.

Papa is overjoyed at the idea. Not only because he never thought he'd own a yacht, but because his oldest daughter is wearing a wedding ring and is finally, *finally* settled.

Archer and I were married on the water a few hours ago. The yacht we rented for the day is massive. With three shining decks and a staff. I have reminded my father twice that this boat is too big for him and he has to choose a smaller model. He hasn't stopped bothering the captain for details about the vessel.

We didn't wait long to tie the knot after Nate's and Vivian's wedding, but they didn't mind. Neither did Cris or Benji. I was adamant about finding out their wedding date so I wouldn't inadvertently race them into marriage. Cris assured me she has a lot of planning to do, and she's not rushing. She said something about her mother being married eight times, and how she's only doing it once so she has to do it right. Eight times is a lot. I have yet to wrap my head around that number.

So, today, October second, at noon in the sparkling ocean waters off the coast of Miami, I married Archer Owen on a rented yacht. Mango's catered the wedding, with Calista overseeing the menu. Julio insisted on being present to make sure everything went smoothly, and Archer agreed him being here was a great idea. I'm suspicious of Julio's motives. Mainly because I pulled a similar heist with Archer. I went to that Heart-to-Teen fundraiser for the sole purpose of convincing him to work with me. I suspect Julio has equally selfish motives for spending his Saturday here, but I'm not sure what they are.

My husband—that still sounds so strange to my ears—is standing on the upper deck with his father and mine, Nate and Benji. And oh, look at that, Julio has joined their man gaggle.

"He's hot," Vivian says, her head craned to take in the men on the top of the ship. She's wearing a sarong and bikini top, having changed from her dress around the same time I ditched mine. My bikini top is white, and my matching sarong has a train. Cris's idea.

"Are you talking about your husband or mine?" I ask.

"I'm talking about the dark-haired guy wearing the aviators."

"Julio Ramirez," I tell her. "Calista's boss and nemesis."

"Boss? I thought he was waitstaff," Vivian asks with a laugh. "He's very involved."

"He owns Mango's. He told Archer he has a vested

interest in assuring no one gets food poisoning today and ruins his reputation. Do you think he's up to something?"

Julio and Archer throw their dark heads back and laugh as William Owen passes out cigars.

"Oh, definitely," she concurs.

Cris bops into our circle with Calista in tow. They're both wearing their bridesmaid's dresses, refusing to change into bikini tops despite mine and Vivian's urging. What a couple of chickens.

"He came to torture me," Lis announces after taking a sip of her red frozen drink in a stemmed glass. "What's he doing up there? He better not be making friends. He's not welcome at any other Owen affairs."

"Nate is gesturing in that way he does when he's talking business, so you might be out of luck," Vivian tells my sister. Lis makes a sour face. "Nate personally chooses many of the restaurants for his live-work facilities. Is Julio franchised yet?"

"No." Lis's frown intensifies.

Viv shrugs apologetically, but she doesn't look all that sorry. "You never know. We might see a Mango's in Clear Ridge."

"Well, if he moves to Ohio and away from me, good riddance." My sister snorts.

"I talked to him earlier over by the seafood buffet," Cris chimes in. "He seems nice."

"So did Ted Bundy at first," Lis quips.

"With an ass like that, he can't be all bad," Vivian puts in, clearly not done poking the bear.

"His only redeeming quality," my sister grumbles.

As if Julio senses us talking about him, he looks down, a

cigar between his teeth. I can't tell because of the sunglasses, but I bet he's looking directly at Calista. She makes an excuse to go elsewhere. His head turns and follows her retreat.

"You're right. Your sister *is* pretty when she lies," Cris says to me. Vivian and I laugh.

By the time the reception winds up, the sun has dipped low in the sky. The boat is making its way to port slowly but steadily. Archer is behind me, his chin on my shoulder, his arms wrapped around my middle. My hands are clasped over his, my finger touching the band of gold on his left hand.

"You'd better not buy Papa a yacht this size. He'll need an entire crew to take it out."

"I'll buy him one he can drive solo. This one is ridiculous."

"Agree." I spin in his arms and hug his neck. "What do you say we kick our guests off and make love on every surface from stern to bow?"

"Kinky." He smiles, his teeth white behind his dark beard. He changed clothes after the ceremony too, into linen pants and a loose button-down shirt. I've been admiring him unabashedly for too many hours to count. I need some time alone with him. Some *naked* time alone.

"Julio invited everyone back to Mango's. He says he'll block off the private patio, treat everyone to champagne."

"I question his motives. He appeared to be wooing Nate."

"I thought Nate was wooing him. Also, did you catch the way he circled your sister?" He tips his head toward Lis, who is asleep on a reclining chair, a straw hat covering her face. "She didn't look at the guy she brought home that night I was in your apartment that way."

"Webber."

"Yeah. What happened to him?"

"Nothing. She never mentions him. Julio, on the other hand..." But I don't seriously think those two will do anything apart from snipe at each other. The saying "too many chefs in the kitchen" exists for a reason.

"Back to sex on the boat," my husband says. "I doubt we'll be missed if we stay behind. However, we have a staff on board that might disrupt our flow. How about we go home instead?"

"Which one?" He bought a beach house close to Mango's and Papa's house as a wedding gift to me. It's large and beautiful and cost way too much, but the gesture blew me away. When we were finalizing our plans to hire Mango's for catering, he drove me to "look" at a house for sale nearby. On the front porch, he handed me a key and told me I could be close to my family whenever I wanted.

I love this man.

"Miami, Clear Ridge," he says. "Doesn't matter as long as you're there."

"What would have happened," I ask, pressing my body to his as the sea air sticks to my skin, "if I *had* been drinking bourbon at the fundraiser that night?"

"I would have had to propose," he answers with a shrug. "I'm guessing you would have thought I was insane and laughed me out of the bar."

"Likely. And then you never would have punched my ex-boyfriend in the nose."

"I did enjoy that," he says, studying the sky as if relishing the memory. "And you never would have had to freeze your fine ass off in Ohio while helping me build the first-ever Owen night spa."

"Two more in the next year," I remind him of our future endeavors. "I also never would have wrecked your car."

"And I never would have known how much I could love someone." His tone turns serious. "Thanks, Wildflower."

"For what?" I ask, my eyes glistening with unspent tears.

"For giving us a second chance. For proposing. For promising, in front of our friends and family, to love me for life."

"Billionaire ever after," I tease.

His smile is unstoppable. "Sounds good to me."

"Me too, Kingpin. Me too."

TURN THE PAGE FOR A PREVIEW OF
ONCE UPON A BILLIONAIRE

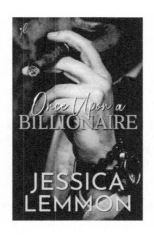

CHAPTER ONE

Vivian

Vivian Vandemark isn't my real name.

It sounds fancy, though, doesn't it? That alliteration of both Vs is to die for and reminds me of a classy label on clothing. Vandemark could have been the next Gucci. Maybe in another life.

I changed my name because my actual last name has been tainted by the man who gave it to me. My father is a criminal. Was. *Was* a criminal. It's hard to get used to the idea that he's no longer living. One would think since he was in prison for the last several years he'd be easy to forget, but that's only because I haven't told you who he is yet.

Walter Steele.

Yes, *that* Walter Steele.

The man who robbed his investors of millions and

millions of dollars to line his own pockets. That man is my father.

Was. Damn. That really is hard to wrap my head around.

The trial was bananas. It lasted one hundred days, and during that time my mother, brother, and I were harassed nonstop by the press. That was six years ago. Since then I've fallen off the radar.

My mother quite literally fell off the radar when she swallowed a lot of pain relievers and chased them with a lot of vodka. That was the day my father was sentenced. By then I was twenty-three and out of the house. My younger brother, Walt, was twenty. He's been trying to finish what booze my mother didn't since then. He'd been an addict most of his young life. I've never enjoyed escapism as a hobby.

Until now, I suppose.

Chicago is a far cry from Clear Ridge, Ohio. Clear Ridge has an unassuming Midwest vibe. The town is mostly shopping malls and chain restaurants, tall maple trees, and fences surrounding green, grassy yards. The live-work site currently being built is unique to this area. It's impressive, even if the company building it is the bane of my boss's existence.

I'm employed in a government office in this aspiring city. The building I walk into each day is half the size of my father's former summer home. *Half.*

I used to be a high-powered executive. All my faith, trust, time, and savings were wrapped up in our family's company. And then it all turned out to be a sham. On my watch, everything fell apart. Steele Investments toppled like a house of cards, taking my position with it. My father went down with the ship, the rest of my family "spared," if you could say that.

I've never felt more powerless. Watching my life crumble

reminded me of TV footage of the World Trade Center vanishing in a plume of smoke on 9/11. When I left that life behind, I swore *never again*.

I'll never again stand by, unwittingly, while someone steals (steal/Steele—how about that for irony?) people's life savings and retirement funds. I thought I was living the good life, but it was blood money.

Now, I buy my clothes at department stores or Target— they have some really nice clothes, by the way. I also cook at home a lot—not well, but I'm learning. And I endure the office coffee even though I pass a drool-worthy Starbucks each and every morning on my way to work.

I'm paying penance for a life I never chose. *Thanks, Dad.*

The second I set foot in the office, I'm met with raised voices. The loudest of the two is Gary, an otherwise mild-mannered inspector at our bureau. I don't think I've ever heard him raise his voice. My boss, Daniel, however, has a well-known temper. His blood pressure often runs high—you can tell by his reddened face.

Gary and Daniel are in Daniel's office, and while I can't make out what they're saying, it's obvious they're having a disagreement.

"Amber." I lean into my coworker's cubicle. "What's going on?"

She looks over her shoulder and gives me a smile that is half amused, half surprised. "Gary is fit to be tied."

"Yeah, I hear that. What's it about?"

"Who do you think?" She raises one prim, blond eyebrow.

"Nathaniel Owen," I answer. The billionaire in charge of

the live-work project has been mentioned about a *billion* times since I started working here, and never favorably.

"The one and only." Amber, still smiling, stands and leans a shoulder on the cubicle wall. We're both facing Daniel's closed door where the "conversation" is going strong. Nathaniel Owen's name is used like a curse word in this place. I've never interacted with him personally, but I'm familiar with the type.

Rich. Entitled. The kind of man who believes he's above the law.

The door swings open and Gary steps out, his mouth a firm line of disapproval. He huffs past Amber's cubicle and we brace ourselves for Daniel's wrath when he looks at us. No, wait.

Looks at *me*.

"Vandemark. Get in here." He vanishes into his office.

Daniel is in charge of my paycheck, a paycheck I need very badly, since I refuse to touch the money in an account I set up after Dad's trial. That money is for my brother's rehabilitation. Those places aren't cheap, and I'll drain every dime out of it if it makes him better. I failed him once—I won't fail him again. He's the only family I have left.

Anyway, my paycheck. It's all that stands between me and homelessness, so I tend to be more gracious to my boss than he deserves.

Amber whispers "good luck" as I leave her side and enter the lion's den, aka Daniel's office.

"Good morning." I try to sound breezy.

"Not even close." He's pacing the floor, hands on his hips, frown marring his receding hairline. "Nathaniel Owen is a burr in my ass."

That should be the motto of the Clear Ridge Bureau of Inspection.

"I need you to go to the Grand Marin site," he tells me. "Owen's crew is there today, and I have it on good authority he has a meeting with the mayor which means he'll likely be onsite. I don't care if the mayor is in Owen's pocket. We are not. At least we aren't any longer." He mutters that last part while looking out the window facing the alley.

"Not Gary?" I can't imagine a scenario where Gary would do anything short of aboveboard.

"Owen paid off Gary. He had to have." Daniel's face turns beet red. "That electrical inspection paperwork flew in here on wings for my approval. It was way too fast. Gary was bribed. Mark my words."

I'm not a conspiracy theorist, but in this case Daniel makes a great point. Nothing happens fast in our little government bureau, and it's particularly suspicious that Owen seems to make things happen at lightning speed compared to everyone else.

"Did Gary quit?"

"I fired him." Daniel puffs up his chest, proud.

"Seriously?"

"No one at CRBI accepts bribes and remains on my payroll." He ices me with a glare. "You'll do well to remember that since you're heading over there."

My blood heats. I'd never accept a bribe. Especially one from a stubborn billionaire.

"We have a narrow window to teach Owen a lesson. You're just the woman to do it."

"I hope you understand that I will not falsify paperwork

in order to shut him down, either. I respect your mission, Daniel, but I'm not going to stoop to Owen's level."

My boss's grin is a tad creepy, but approving. "I know you won't. All you have to do is ask Owen for proof of a passed electrical inspection. He won't be able to show you one because he doesn't *have* one—not legally, anyway. I never signed off on it. Therefore, you can shut him down."

"Wouldn't you be a better candidate?" I don't do site visits. In my six months as chief desk jockey, I haven't been to a single construction site. It's part of my plan to lay low. If I'm not in charge of anything I can't fuck it up. Not to mention I'd have no idea what to do once I got there. "We both know how much you'd enjoy nailing his ass to the wall."

"More than you can imagine, but my schedule is full. Since Gary was fired, the next inspector in line handles their shit-show. Our other inspectors are busy, and frankly, I don't want to wait another second. So, you get a raise. Congratulations. This project is a nightmare."

Did he say raise? My ears perk. Despite wanting to lay low, an increase in my income would be nice. Given that I refuse to touch my brother's and my nest egg, I have to keep the lights on at home somehow.

"If Owen isn't there when you get there, let the site manager know you mean business."

Nathaniel Owen has a reputation for completing projects on time, which is a rare and coveted quality in a builder. He also sidesteps rules and does things his way rather than follow the letter of the law. The city of Clear Ridge doesn't take kindly to rule-benders, and Daniel hates them. Look at that, my boss and I have something in common.

"No problem," I assure Daniel.

Maybe delivering justice will be cathartic. I can't go back in time and keep my father in line, or recoup the money of the people who trusted him, but I can prevent Nathaniel Owen from lining his pockets with even more money. The Owen name is stamped on nearly every new build within a thousand miles. How much more can the guy possibly need?

That's the thing about greed. It knows no bounds.

"I have a meeting in five minutes and they'll probably keep me for the afternoon." Daniel swipes his sweaty brow. He's a good seventy pounds overweight and even on his tall frame, it's too much girth. "Can I count on you not to fuck this up?"

I force a smile. His wasn't the most wholehearted vote of confidence, but I'll take it. "Of course."

"He's cocky, strong-willed and needs a knot tied in his tail," Daniel says, not quite finished with his tirade. "You're strong. Smart. The perfect candidate to take him on, Viv." His voice gentles, and I feel an odd catch in my chest at the compliment.

The last man who praised me was my father. When I learned I couldn't trust him at the end, I wondered if every ounce of praise he gave me before was a lie. There are two versions of him in my head. The man who encouraged me to believe in myself and never give up, and the man who told me those things while stealing money from innocent people.

Disgusting.

"Shut him down," my boss repeats. "Let's teach him a lesson."

I draw my chin up at those words. Owen needs taught that you can't do what you want and give the rules the finger.

"Grab a hardhat from the back. Don't want you busting that pretty noggin of yours and then suing me."

Aaaand...moment over.

"Sure thing," I reply blithely.

I grab a hardhat from the back and walk outside to my 2014 Hyundai the car salesman assured me was "reliable." I don't even miss the sleek black Audi RS I used to own. Okay, I do *a little*. But a car is a car. This gem will deliver me to Grand Marin just as well as that Audi.

Grand Marin is a soon-to-be massive live-work community. An open-air style shopping, dining, and retail area interspersed with offices for professionals as well as apartments for young, vibrant tenants who want to live in the middle of—or above—the action.

Live-works have been growing in popularity, and whenever there's a trend, I've noticed the Owen family has their mitts all over it. I've never had any personal dealings with Owen, but I know rich people. They're not that great.

As a former rich person, I speak from experience.

I also know that Gary, the city's former mild-mannered inspector, came into the office with his bottom lip dragging the ground each and every time he had to deal with this site. Gary was a softie, and we all liked him. He was rocking a five-foot-three frame and had a shy way of watching his shoes when he talked. Then he blows up at Daniel? I wouldn't have guessed he'd raised his voice a day in his life before today.

People can surprise you, though, and for me that should come as no surprise.

Gary's despondence, and the possibility that he took a bribe, proves what a bulldog this Owen guy can be.

Bring it on, buddy. I've already been through the wringer.

Daniel's grumping about the mayor isn't totally inaccurate. Rumor has it the Owens grease palms. Mayor Dick Dolans might well be their pet.

I come to a stop the moment I merge onto the highway. So much for taking a shortcut. I-70 is a parking lot, and the heat index on the car's thermometer reads 97° F.

Worse, I'm wearing a synthetic-but-made-to-look-like-real-silk shirt and it's sticking to me like a second skin. Waves of heat waft off the road as if the cars are in the process of being melted down into one big metal glob. The month of June is going out like it has a score to settle.

Again: *relate*.

I crank the A/C down and rest a hand on the steering wheel. I refuse to panic. I'll get to Grand Marin when I get there. I wish I would have dug up some much-needed intel about the site before Daniel rushed me out of there. I know next to nothing about it.

At least I'm wearing my nicest, most slimming pencil skirt and high heels. Not the best getup for tromping around a construction site, but it's a good look when wanting to bust some billionaire balls. I smile to myself, straightening my shoulders.

I'm out for a win for the good guys. A win for justice. I picture myself as Wonder Woman and lift my chin. If she did it in a bustier and panties, I can do it in a pencil skirt and knockoff silk.

Ready or not, Nathaniel Owen, here I come.

ABOUT THE AUTHOR

A former job-hopper, Jessica Lemmon resides in Ohio with her husband and rescue dog. She holds a degree in graphic design currently gathering dust in an impressive frame. When she's not writing super-sexy heroes, she can be found cooking, drawing, drinking coffee (okay, wine), or eating potato chips. She firmly believes God gifts us with talents for a purpose, and with His help, you can create a life you love.

Jessica Lemmon's romance novels have been praised as "purely delicious fun" and "lavish, indulgence-fueled romance" by Publisher's Weekly, as well as "wonderfully entertaining" and "a whole lot of fun!" by RT Book Reviews.

She is the bestselling author of over thirty books that have been translated into a dozen languages and sold in over 30 different countries worldwide, with her debut novel releasing in January of 2013.

Her work has been honored with awards such as a Library Journal starred review, an RT Top Pick!, iBooks Best Book of the Month, and Amazon Best Book of the Month. She has been recommended by USA Today and NPR.com, and has achieved the rank of #1 bestseller on Nook as well as earned a seal of excellence nomination from RT Book Reviews.

Through witty banter and fun, realistic situations and characters you'll want to "sit down and have a drink with," Jessica tackles tough relationship issues and complicated human emotions while delivering a deep, satisfying experience for readers.

Her motto is "read for fun" and she believes we should all do more of what makes us happy.

ALSO BY JESSICA LEMMON

Blue Collar Billionaires series

Once Upon a Billionaire

Charmed by the Billionaire

Billionaire Ever After

Billionaire Bad Boys series

The Billionaire Bachelor

The Billionaire Next Door

The Bastard Billionaire

A Crane Family Christmas

Real Love series

Eye Candy

Arm Candy

Man Candy

Rumor Has It

America's Sweetheart

Visit jessicalemmon.com for a complete book list.

Made in the USA
Las Vegas, NV
26 January 2024

84932730R00173